Unsanctioned Protocol

T. James LeDoux

Published by Alpha Group 3 LLC

Paperback book edition created 2017

ISBN 9780985226664

BISAC Classification: Fiction/Thrillers/Espionage - FIC006000

Cover picture: Operation Tin Cup Folder with Shuyesheh Research Facility mission documents inside and Maxim 9 U.S. military pistol with built in silencer on top of the folder.

Dedications

To my beautiful wife, Marilyn, whose patience, attention to detail and advice did much to help make this book a reality.

The Mission

The U.S., Russia and China have been in an arms race for new technology with the pinnacle of that technology being the laser weapon. As each country scrambled to get the upper hand in this new technology, leaders of each country knew that whoever had the lead in laser weaponry owned the battlefield. Any one country gaining a significant advantage in the technology could shift the power structure worldwide and bring in chaos where there was stability.

On July 18, 2015, U.S. intelligence indicated that a Russian lab in Iran was nearing completion of an advanced 500 kilowatt laser weapon that had the capability of removing aircraft and missiles from the sky at long distances and the potential of making air combat obsolete. In response, the U.S. Navy devised a mission as part of a bigger operation, called 'Tin Cup', to go into Iran to delay or stop Russia's ability to create such a weapon. For seven days, the success of the mission rested on a small group of people accidently thrown together through a series of unexpected events. This is the story of that mission.

CHAPTER 1 -- July 25, 2015, 1:20 PM - Persian Gulf Time

"Captain, they've locked on us!" shouted the sailor through the intercom system while looking at a monitor in the Combat Direction Center (CDC) on board the aircraft carrier U.S.S. Theodore Roosevelt. It was early afternoon in the Persian Gulf at the Strait of Hormuz. The display showed a red, cone-shaped symbol coming from the area on the screen that was Iranian territory facing the Strait of Hormuz directed toward the carrier. Then, as one cone disappeared, a second cone would show up with the source being from another area within Iran.

This was the third time in three days that some action was directed against the carrier from the same area in Iran. However, this time it was different. The other times were naval activities by small boats coming out to challenge the carrier and its destroyer escorts. This time the Iranians locked onto the carrier from suspected Iranian missile sites. The Captain walked slowly on the bridge as he contemplated his options.

"Mr. Casper, sound General Quarters then get me the CAG," he shouted to his XO. The CAG, Commander of The Air Group, stepped onto the bridge from Primary Flight Control Deck that was one level above the bridge.

"Reporting, Sir, I know why you called me," the CAG answered in response to the order then continued. "According to Petty Officer Lawson, they may be targeting us but they don't have any missiles to fire. They're just trying to spook us."

The Captain looked once more at his screen of the display being transmitted from CDC to the bridge as the call to General

Quarters was being announced throughout the ship and people were scrambling to their stations. "I know Lawson may be right about his observations but I would like two of your covering aircraft moved closer to the Iranian border to respond in case they've surprised us by adding additional assets. Keep the third covering aircraft to the west in case this is a diversion to draw our attention from some other action and tell McHenry to put the Phalanx guns on standby as I don't want any accidents. Lawson was right about them setting up the missile sites and he warned us that they may try to harass us by using electronic targeting but I would like to err on the side of caution."

"Aye, Sir," the CAG acknowledged as he got on the phone. Once he finished fulfilling the Captain's requests, the CAG turned back to the Captain to see why the Captain was motioning the CAG to come to him.

"I also want you to tell Petty Officer Lawson to get his gear together for the next air transport to Al Dhafr Air Base," the Captain spoke in a low voice to the CAG so that others around him could not hear. "He's got orders to report to Washington, D.C. in two days, high priority flight. The mail plane arrives at 14:45 hours. Let him know he has to be ready to go by 14:00 hours so I can talk to him before he goes. Also let the mail plane pilot know he has to wait until Lawson is on board his aircraft before taking off. According to the Commander of the Fifth Fleet, this is ultra-high priority. So, before Lawson leaves, I want him here on the bridge for some last words. Since you are Commander of all of the air resources for this battle group, you are the only one to know the nature of this order for the mail plane."

"Aye, Sir. We also have two more fighters ready for launch if needed to meet the threat. We'll need to clear one of them to allow for the mail plane to land," the CAG responded as he left to find Lawson's Division Officer. It was unusual for the CAG to do messenger duty but the need to keep the number of people knowing Lawson's departure to a minimum made it necessary.

A half-hour later, Petty Officer Jim Lawson was on the bridge, waiting to talk to the Captain of the carrier. He had been on the bridge many times but this time seemed different. There was always a lot of activity, but unlike other times, this activity had an element of panic in it with people scrambling around, orders being shouted and reports coming in to the bridge. Setting his seabag down on the deck, he watched the activity and knew it had something to do with the Iranians and the recent discovery of missile sites being set up by them. Lawson had discovered the missile sites while going over satellite photos of the area, information that was relayed to the Captain several days ago.

"Petty Officer Lawson," the Captain called out above the noise going on about the bridge, "here are your orders." Lawson took the sealed manila envelope containing his orders from the Captain while looking confused by the sudden change in direction. He had done a good job on the carrier so why was he being transferred?

"What's the reason for shipping me out, Sir?" Lawson asked.

"You've got an extraordinary skill the Navy needs. Remember when you broke into my cabin to leave me a birthday cake from the crew."

"I remember, Sir. I got a Captain's Mast and twenty hours of extra duty for that."

"You could have been court martialed. I considered the magnitude of your actions but I also considered your intent which is why I was lenient."

"That is true, Sir," Lawson acknowledged while observing his Division Officer entering the bridge.

"Your Division Officer explained how you were able to enter into my cabin and how you were able to enter the key code into my access panel."

"I see you're revisiting old memories," Lawson's Division Officer commented as he joined the conversation. "You don't mind, Captain, if I lay out the reason for his selection for his change in venue."

"Of course not. You may continue."

"Well, Petty Officer Lawson," the Division Officer began, "I recommended you for this change due to the needs of the Navy. Now before you say anything, I explained to the Captain after your Captain's Mast how you wiped down his access keypad then used ultraviolet light to see the keys that were touched the next time he went into his cabin. I also explained how you determined the timeframe as to when the access code would be changed on a weekly basis. Then how you would try only one combination between the times the Captain would key in so that he would have two more tries in case he entered the access number wrong the first time, thereby not exceeding the maximum allowed three attempts. You were able to hit the right code on your fourth try, which was impressive. All of these little details were beyond what a normal person would consider. That is the reason I recommended you to the Captain and why he recommended you up the chain of command. The only reason we knew it was you with the cake was that there was a camera picking up your activities in the captain's cabin." He was caught by the camera. He filed that observation into his memory.

"So where am I being shipped off to?" Lawson asked while wondering if he had brought this on himself because of the cake fiasco.

"You've been ordered to Washington, D.C. as an urgent request by the Chairman of the Joint Chiefs of Staff," the Captain instructed while looking around to ensure no one else was picking up on the conversation. "I would normally have asked for the order to take its natural cycle by waiting for your replacement to arrive before you leave but we don't have that luxury. You've done a great job here and we are prepared to take defensive action thanks to your observations and information. We're not being caught by surprise. Now, you've got a plane waiting for you. I hope to have you on my team again. Take care of yourself." The Captain reached out to shake Lawson's hand which surprised Lawson as he had never experienced the commander of such a large organization shaking the hand of an enlisted man unless it was during an award of a medal or commendation.

"One point before I go, Sir," Lawson stated as he stood facing the Captain.

"Another history lesson? I always like your historical examples. I'm listening," The Captain responded.

"Yes Sir, another history lesson. You got what looks like three missile sites targeting you at different times," Lawson continued. "They are each turning on at different times. It's not to confuse you but, rather, to analyze you."

"You see something we're not picking up?" the Captain questioned as he began to wonder what he was missing. Was he too close to the action to not see the intentions of the Iranians?

Lawson looked out the one of the windows of the bridge at the Iranian shoreline in the distance then continued. "In 1879, the British were in the grips of a major battle at Rorke's Drift mission station in Natal, Africa. The mission station had one-hundred fifty British defenders against around four thousand Zulu warriors. During the start of the battle, wave after wave of Zulu warriors were being wiped out by the British volleys of gunfire. Lieutenant Bromhead, commander of the British troops, asked a local Dutch farmer, whose name I don't remember, that had sought refuge at the mission station why the Zulus seemingly attacked without consideration of their losses? The Dutch farmer responded that the men on the hill in the distance were counting the number of guns the British had and were determining how the British were set up to defend themselves. The Zulu leadership was expending lives to analyze the mission station's weaknesses."

"So you think that's what the Iranians are doing here?" the Captain questioned. "They're looking to see how we respond to their threats?"

"Exactly," Lawson returned.

The Captain turned to the man in communications with the flight deck launch team, "Tell the launch team to hold launching the other fighter plane still on the flight deck. I'll explain to the CAG when he gets back." Looking back to Lawson, the Captain remarked, "That should keep them guessing until a real face-off develops. By the way, since you'll be working in the intel group you'll find this out. Because of your discovery of the missile sites here in the Strait and our expectation that they'll have missiles at those sites in about two months, at the beginning of October, the 'Roosevelt' will be leaving the Persian Gulf and no other carrier groups will be assigned to the Gulf until we set up a strategy to defend against the missiles. You feel OK with that?"

Lawson nodded that he agreed, smiled, picked up his seabag and headed out the hatch to go down to the flight deck to the waiting plane.

CHAPTER 2 -- July 28, 2015, 9:30 AM - Washington, DC Time

"Hurry up and wait, hurry up and wait," was all Jim Lawson was thinking to himself while standing in line. The Marine at the desk was slow in getting to each person. Lawson could see the guy second in line from the front failed to clear his weapon. When Lawson was out in the portico of the building putting his holster and weapon on while getting ready to come into the facility, he remembered the sign outside the door to the facility that said, 'New personnel. All weapons must be cleared before entering this facility unless instructed otherwise by your Commander'. Lawson moved his hand down to the 9 mm pistol in its holster on his belt. His hand felt for the handgrip and the magazine well at the bottom of the pistol. "The clip is out of the weapon," he thought while watching the Marine at the desk checking weapons. "No reason for him to gig me for having a loaded weapon," Lawson thought as he adjusted the manila envelope under his left arm. His mind was floating to other thoughts.

He looked around the entryway going up to the desk. The walls were a cream color with recessed lights in the ceiling on rows about twelve feet above his head. There was a sign just before the front desk that instructed those in line to 'Form a line here.' Four black camera domes were spread throughout the ceiling area. An armed security officer was seated about twenty feet to his left. He was dressed in the standard blue uniform and badge of a federal police officer with a sidearm and an M4 short-barrel rifle slung across his chest. The officer was watching intently as the line moved forward. People were coming in to a checkpoint to the right, swiping their ID cards then handing their cards to the security people for verification, bag checks and that each person had their weapon on them. Once completed, they went through security gates that opened up, walked past the gates and through several doorways.

The loud voice of the Marine shook Lawson out of his stupor. "You have a problem with following instructions, Lad?" came the Marine's Irish-accented question. Lawson saw the Marine remove the clip from the offending sailor's weapon, then ignored the rest of the Marine's conversation. Holding his hat under his left arm, Lawson pulled the paperwork from his manila envelope then glanced at the top of the first page. The page instructed him to report to the Kennedy Irregular Warfare Center in Washington, D.C. no later than 0900 hours on July 28, 2015. It was now 0930 hours and he was still in line. "Hurry up and wait," Lawson thought to himself.

Jim Lawson was five foot, eight inches tall with an athletic build, a tropical tan and light brown hair. As a Naval Petty Officer, he wore a crisp white uniform with dress white flap on the back and the black, rolled neckerchief around his neck, hanging in front in standard naval tradition. On his upper sleeve was a rating patch showing he was Intelligence Specialist 2 (IS2) along with a surface warfare badge above his service ribbons on the left side of his chest. Instructed to report to his new command without delay, his job was to analyze maps and data on enemies and potential enemies.

As a teenager, he had led his football team to second place in the State football finals as a quarterback while a senior in high school. However, his height limited his offers for a college football scholarship, so he paid his own way to Carnegie-Mellon University, majoring in Electrical Engineering. Due to limited funds, he had to drop out of the university in his senior year.

He was a quiet man, normally keeping his opinions mostly to himself except when asked. It was obvious to anyone that would be watching him that he was keenly observant to everything going on around him, something the federal police officer sitting to the left of him was taking careful notice.

The line slowly moved ahead until it was Lawson's turn to present his paperwork.

"Weapon," came the Irish voice as the Marine extended his hand to receive Lawson's weapon.

Lawson pulled the weapon from the holster, pointed the barrel toward the ceiling, pulled back the receiver to the open position, locked it in that arrangement and handed it to the Marine. While the Marine was examining the weapon, Lawson noted the name tag on the Marine's uniform, 'Glendenning'. He also noted the rank of the Marine, 'Master Gunnery Sergeant' from the patch on his sleeve. The Marine was well built with a somewhat rugged face and a very strong persona. His six foot frame was sharply highlighted by the perfectly pressed uniform. The typical stereotype of a Marine Lawson thought. He smelled of gun grease and cleaner and his hands had some residue from cleaning weapons which, to Lawson's irritation, left black marks on the barrel of his weapon.

"Here's your weapon, Lad. Keep the slide locked back and return it to your holster."

The Marine reached out his hand again. "ID," came the request. Lawson pulled his ID out of his pocket and handed it to the Marine. The Marine looked at the ID then held it up to Lawson's face. "Looks like you, you need a shave. Next time you come in use a razor first," he said then handed the ID back to Lawson. Lawson rubbed his face for a moment then realized he hadn't shaved that morning.

"Orders," came the next request from the Marine. Lawson handed him his manila envelope which the Marine took and removed the paperwork. 'Click-click' went the stamp as the

Marine timestamped the orders and handed them back to Lawson. Lawson took the orders and winced. More black marks on his orders. The Marine just smiled. Lawson wondered how the Marine's uniform was so pristine while it seemed that everything he touched was getting gun grease on it.

"You be goin' into the left entryway and down to the third door on the left," the Marine said in his Irish lilt while pointing toward the door. "They be wait'n for you." Lawson took his paperwork and proceeded to step forward.

"Thanks, Sarge," he said as he moved.

"Stop there, Lad," came the Marine's reply. "I am not Sarge! You may call me Gunny or Glendenning but don't you ever call me Sarge!" Lawson stood stunned for a moment then nodded his head and proceeded forward.

"OK, Gunny," he said while walking to the door to the hall.

"Stupid Squid," came the reply.

Lawson opened the door to the hallway and proceeded down toward the third door all the while thinking the Marine must have missed his breakfast this morning. The color of the hallway wasn't what he expected in a naval facility. On the aircraft carrier, the passageways were off-white color except where the area might be exposed to the outside. Then the passageways were a mix of gray and dark gray to ensure the ship was less likely to be seen at night. This hallway was gold with blue trim. The lights in the hallway made the whole scene give a glare that made it hard to see without wincing.

"Blue and gold, navy colors," Lawson thought as he walked down the corridor. Lawson noted the cameras mounted into their black domes in the ceiling. He counted five by the time he reached the third door which was painted a dark, navy blue and appeared to be a massive vault door. "Why so many cameras?" he thought as he turned to look back down the hallway. There were pictures along one wall. They were pictures of different ships from different times in naval history. Several he recognized. There was the carrier Enterprise from World War II, the John Paul Jones' ship Bon Homme Richard in a battle scene and the battleship USS Nevada.

As Lawson turned to open the third door he could see the label next to the door. It had two silver stars above it and just below the stars was the name 'E. Roedl, RADM'. Below the name of the person was the name 'Special Operations'.

Lawson pulled open the vault door to find a Marine inside a small space sitting behind a desk residing to the side of the entrance. The Marine was in a sharply-pressed dress uniform with his hat on the desk. He had a sidearm and an attitude that exhibited a lack of humor. The room was cream-colored and void of any pictures and had a camera mounted to the ceiling pointed toward the desk.

"ID," came the request from the Marine. Lawson handed him his ID, and in the process, knocked the Marine's hat on the floor. "Careful with my cover," the Marine snapped as he picked up the hat from the floor. Looking at the ID the Marine exclaimed, "It's about time you showed up. The Admiral doesn't like to be kept waiting!" Lawson took back his ID.

"Admiral?" Lawson said while looking at his ID card. "What am I doing reporting to an Admiral?" The Marine smiled from behind the desk at Lawson's confusion. He pushed a button under the desk which caused the vault door to the hallway to close and latch and, once closed, a second door past the desk opened. Lawson could tell the Marine was enjoying this moment of consternation he was experiencing.

Lawson stepped into the next room and saw a couple of chairs in front of another desk that was facing toward him. Behind this desk was another door. The room was again cream-colored and void of any pictures, though there was a small potted plant on the counter in front of the desk. Lawson noted that this room had two cameras, one pointed toward each door. The person at the desk was dressed in a female enlisted dress blue uniform.

"Good morning, Petty Office Lawson," came the voice from the rather attractive woman standing behind the desk. She had brunette hair with a disarming smile and appeared to Lawson to be about five foot six inches tall. Her rating patch indicated she was a Yeoman Second Class and her nametag showed her last name as 'Norman'.

"Good morning," he replied back as he gave her his ID card and smiled. She looked at him then at the card, handed the card back to him and picked up the phone.

"Petty Officer Lawson is here, Sir." Setting down the phone, she motioned for Lawson to follow her.

They stepped into the next room and Lawson watched as she left the room and closed the door behind him. He looked around the room and immediately suspected that this was a room occupied by a person that was all navy. There was a desk in the center of the room that was heavy oak and very organized. There was the obligatory phone, desk pad, a set of rubber stamps on a stand used for stamping documents and a nameplate reading 'E. Roedl, RADM' with a pen holder on one side with a gold pen in it. A computer monitor sat on his desk to the right side with the keyboard just in front of it. Behind the desk was a picture of a sea battle, obviously something out of World War II. To his left was a wall with certificates, awards and trophies with a door at the end of the wall. One award that caught his attention was a commendation for the work he did as commander of the Fifth Fleet's intelligence operations in the Mediterranean. On the right, another wall exhibited pictures of a guy that liked to play golf, go fishing and liked football. Below the pictures were a set of cabinets running the length of the wall. Behind him, above the door he just entered and to the sides of the door was a clock, a calendar (the typical three-month government calendar with last month at the top, the present month in the center and next month at the bottom). He also noted there were no cameras in the room.

Lawson heard muffled voices from the direction of the side door in the left wall. He stood there wondering how long he would have to stand. As he was considering the timeframe he would have to wait, the side door opened up and a man came through the door, dressed in the rank of Rear Admiral, Upper half, two stars on each of his shoulder epaulettes. He was a tall man, about six feet, two inches by Lawson's estimation. His uniform was crisp and perfectly detailed. He had a white web belt around his waist with a sidearm in a white holster hanging from the web belt. It was also obvious to Lawson that the Admiral hadn't slept in a while.

The Admiral stood looking at Lawson for a moment, then said, "I'm Admiral Roedl. Why don't you be seated." Lawson turned to the leather armchair nearest to him and sat down, putting his white hat in his lap while facing the Admiral and the desk. The Admiral looked Lawson over a second time. Lawson pulled out his ID to hand to the Admiral. "I know who you are. Put it away." He returned his ID to his pocket and waited for the Admiral to speak.

He felt the tension in the room. His discomfort was somewhat alleviated when Admiral Roedl began to speak. "You'll be reporting to Captain Michaels after we meet here. The Captain will give you five days of liberty to get your things together and be ready to function on his analysis team. During those five days you will be providing a service for me." Lawson nodded his head and Roedl continued. "We called you up quickly because you are one of the few people I feel can pull off this mission."

Lawson began to fidget. "What mission are we talking about, Sir?" Lawson asked while feeling that a surprise was about to be unloaded on him.

Roedl smiled for a moment then said, "Instead of calling you Petty Officer Lawson all the time, I'm going to call you Jim. By the way, all personnel in this facility are armed for security reasons. Everyone responds to the intruder alert alarm. No exceptions. Take out your weapon, slam the receiver forward then put the clip back in your weapon."

Lawson nodded an acknowledgement, did as he was told and reholstered his weapon then asked, "What is your first name, Sir?" Roedl smiled, glanced around the room for a moment then said, "My first name is Admiral." They both looked at each other then laughed. Any tension still present was gone.

The Admiral stared at Lawson for a moment then said, "I'm going to give you a little test to see if your observation skills are what I was told." Lawson nodded his head and the Admiral continued, "While facing me, tell me what is on the wall behind you."

Lawson thought for a moment then responded, "There is a three-month calendar with the three months set in their proper positions, a clock that has not been dusted in a while and is three minutes later than the real time, a loose frame at the top of the door and a chipped ceiling tile just above the door."

Admiral Roedl looked at the items Lawson was mentioning, walked over to the door behind Lawson, wiped his hand across the top of the clock and saw the dust on his hand indicating the clock hadn't been dusted in months. He was impressed by Lawson's observations. "Well, they did say you were observant and I can see that I am not disappointed," the Admiral said while wiping the dust from his hand with a tissue. Roedl then told

Lawson to follow him into the next room, the same room the Admiral came out from.

In the room was a long, highly-polished wooden oak conference table with a number of comfortable looking leather armchairs. At the far end of the room was a large oak cabinet that extended the full length of the wall with an equally large flat screen monitor at the center of the cabinet. The part of the cabinet that was lower than the monitor had three drawers on each side and underneath the monitor. There were cupboard doors at the same level as the monitor but to the left and right of it. The wall on the right had a couple of pictures and a door just before getting to the cabinet. The wall on the left had three pictures and a fire extinguisher hanging against a red painted rectangle on the wall near the cabinet. The rest of the room was painted off-white. A three-dimensional layout of some type of facility was sitting on the far end of the table. Lawson walked over to look at the three-dimensional layout while the Admiral followed.

"Take a close look at this facility," the Admiral instructed as Lawson picked up the facility model. Each room in the layout, including the hallways of the facility, was identified with labels. Lawson saw that there were security doors in several places throughout the facility. There was a lab area that extended almost the whole length of the facility to the right behind a security door and security area located at the back of the facility. On the left side of the facility, offices took up a portion of the back end of the facility behind another security door and security area. The two security doors were positioned across a hall, opposite each other. A Commander's office and administrative office was in the same hallway as the two security doors, though closer to the front of the facility. There was also a galley for preparing and serving food, an armory, a maintenance room, berthing areas, a communications center, a security center and prisoner cells. The main security door at the entrance to the facility appeared to be one large door that allowed people and equipment to enter and exit the facility. It struck Lawson that there was only one entrance to the facility which he felt was poor design if a fire broke out in the facility. As Lawson was looking at the layout Roedl instructed him to memorize every detail of the facility.

"Where is this facility?" Lawson asked.

"You'll be told later," was Roedl's response.

"OK," Lawson continued, "What am I supposed to get or do in this facility, how am I to get in and how am I to get out?"

The Admiral folded his arms for a moment then said, "You understand this is strictly voluntary. We have a plan to get you in. You must figure how to get out." Lawson looked over the layout again.

"How do we know this layout is accurate?" Roedl was beginning to like this guy. He was asking all the right questions.

"It is accurate because we have an inside man in the facility that has been providing us with the information at great risk to himself."

Lawson was perplexed. Why me? Roedl could see that there was some question in Lawson's mind. The question seemed obvious.

"You were picked because your Division Commander on board the carrier indicated that you tended to solve problems on the fly and you're very good at picking up details. We don't have time to train a person because time is of the essence. We also picked you because you are an unknown to the people tracking our agents. You'd never get into the facility if you were being tracked by our adversaries. The only other person they don't know is my top female agent and she wouldn't fit into the culture I'm sending you into."

Lawson sat down in one of the chairs and proceeded to ask question after question on the facility, its construction, the personnel inside, the purpose of the facility and the timing. After over an hour of conversation Lawson posed the question, "What am I supposed to do?"

"First," Roedl said, "you have to get information from an office that's controlled by one of the Russian scientists, the fourth door inside the Russian office security area on the layout toward the back of the facility. The scientist's name is Doctor Isaak Polevsky. Second, you have to get that information by the morning of July 31st before it gets sent to Moscow."

"So, I'm going to Russia," Lawson supposed.

Roedl sat down next to Lawson, put his hand on Lawson's shoulder and said, "You will be nowhere near Russia, and if you are in Russia, you've failed."

Lawson thought over Roedl's comment then asked, "What is the composition of the walls in the facility?"

Roedl opened the file in his hand and replied, "It's concrete block, 3 feet wide by two feet high for each block, each block mortared in."

Lawson looked at the layout again. "Is it reinforced with steel?"

Roedl looked again at the file. "Except for the lab and scientists' office area walls, I don't think so."

"Come with me," Roedl motioned as he moved back toward his office. As Lawson came into the office, Roedl had opened the door to one of the cabinets and was spinning the dial on a safe. Seconds later he opened the safe door and pulled out a file folder that had a red diagonal stripe on it and the words 'Top Secret' across the middle. Roedl opened the folder and handed it to Lawson. Lawson looked at the first page in the folder. It was a picture of a man in a uniform that Lawson recognized as being that of an Iranian Colonel. The face was square-formed with a rugged look to it. He had black hair and a determined face.

"That is Colonel Askan Rouhani," Roedl spoke while pointing to the picture. "He is the Commander in charge of the facility complex except for the labs. He also determines the outcomes and charges of any prisoners that are arrested for failure to do their jobs, anyone caught spying and anyone not reporting at the proper times. He is also responsible for all of the facility security and maintenance, again, except for the labs and the scientists' offices. He speaks Farsi."

Lawson took a long look at the face and the uniform. He then flipped to the next page, another photo, this time of an Iranian Captain. The face was interesting. The man had blond hair, blue eyes, a mustache and goatee. Lawson thought this was quite unusual for an Iranian. Roedl figured the hair color and eyes were a question as he broke Lawson's thought process.

"That is Captain Hamid Behzadi. He is the child of a Russian father and an Iranian mother. That's the reason for the hair and eye color." Roedl looked at Lawson for a response then continued, "Behzadi is responsible for the security of the labs and Russian offices, the security of prisoners in the cells and carrying out executions, when ordered by the Commander. He also does the security checks for all Russian personnel. He speaks English, Farsi and Russian. He had to be validated by the Russians as being trustworthy to handle their security. He was approved by the Russian Duma to provide the Russians with security in their areas even though he is an Iranian officer. The Russians wanted someone to act as liaison between the Iranians and the Russians. The Iranians wanted to have one of their own people to provide that role or else they would not allow the Russians to use the facility." Lawson thought it interesting that

Behzadi had an Iranian last name yet his father was Russian. Although he thought it curious, he didn't pose the question to the Admiral.

Roedl then handed Lawson a small piece of paper. Lawson looked it over for a moment. It was obviously some short Farsi inscription. Roedl looked at Lawson's face for any indication of understanding. He then explained to Lawson, "That is Commander Rouhani's signature. Learn to write it flawlessly. You may need it to help you get out of the facility." Lawson put the slip of paper in his pocket and proceeded back to the room with the layout of the facility.

Roedl made a statement almost as an afterthought, "On your way out of the research facility, you must get the recording disks for nine different cameras. The recorders are located in the facility communications center. They will contain images of you and they are the only place that should have them. By the way, there is no rank in the field for our operations. Whoever has the assignment for the operation commands the operation. So it's possible for an enlisted person to give orders to an officer. However, you can transfer the command to someone else if you figure that person has more experience than you do for a specific scenario. You can also take back command whenever you think it's appropriate. In your case, since you are a single asset going into a mission, I don't think you'll have that problem."

Lawson sat staring at the layout for over a minute then said, "When do I leave? I'll need a few items."

The Admiral smiled, shook his hand and said, "Glad you could join us. You leave this afternoon. Give your list of what you need to Petty Officer Norman at my front desk. Now go report to Captain Michaels and be back here at 13:00 hours."

Lawson always had trouble thinking in military time. "Yes Sir, 1:00 PM" came Lawson's reply followed by a smart salute to the Admiral.

"We don't salute inside this facility," Roedl said then realized that Lawson was not acting out of habit but was showing him real respect with the salute.

"Evan," the Admiral said to Lawson.

"What?" inquired Lawson over the one-word comment.

"Evan", the Admiral repeated. "My first name is Evan."

Lawson grinned then exited the Admiral's office.

Ten minutes after Lawson left, Captain Michaels entered Admiral Roedl's office. As he stood in front of Roedl's desk, he opened the report folder and waited for Roedl to finish reading the daily reports. Roedl looked up from his desk at the captain.

"What do we have, Bill?" Roedl asked.

"I have the training reports for last week, sir," Michaels answered. "I also have a question and a concern."

"Put the reports on my desk and let's go for a walk," Roedl said. He picked up his hat, checked that his weapon was in its holster, walked out the door and through the security room with Michaels in tow. After going down the 'golden' hall and out of the facility, Roedl and Michaels went to the courtyard outside of the front of the facility. They watched for a moment as personnel coming into the building were stopping in the portico to take their weapons out of their briefcases or purses and strapping them onto their bodies. Roedl watched without noticing their actions as numerous thoughts passed through his mind.

"I know what you're going to discuss," Roedl started.

"Even so, sir, why did we have to come outside to discuss it?" Michaels queried.

"Because, Bill, it's possible we are being bugged or have a mole in our organization," Roedl responded. "Too much information is getting out to our adversaries too quickly. It maybe just coincidence, but I don't want to take any chances with an operation of this significance. Now, I figure you want to talk about Lawson."

"Yes, sir," Michaels began. "You see Sir, Lawson has no training in foreign operations and acquiring information. He can't speak Farsi, has no familiarity with the region he's going into and hasn't exhibited any experience in working in an environment where we can't support him. Why didn't we send an experienced agent into this operation? After all, you know how important this operation is and how significant the outcome is if we fail." They both looked around to see if anyone was in listening distance. Once assured they couldn't be heard, they continued their conversation.

"Your concerns have been noted," Roedl answered. "First, Lawson's Division Commander on the carrier said that Lawson was not only the best person for this job but also the most likely to succeed at completing this operation. Second, outside of one female agent we have, everyone else is known, in some form, by our adversaries. I doubt we could even get into the research facility much less operate within the facility with those we could send and sending a female into the environment would not match the culture or the need. Follow me so far?"

"Yes, Sir, but…," Michaels started when Roedl went on with his explanation.

"Bill, the most important factor in sending Lawson in is that he won't be going by any book so he will be unpredictable. The people managing the research facility are highly trained in looking for patterns of behavior signifying a person is an agent because they know what to look for. Most likely, our agents will go by the book from their training and that will show a pattern that will give them away. You're right. This is probably one of the most significant operations we have had in the past five years. We fail at this and we've opened the door to the potential of a widespread Middle East war if not a world-wide engagement."

"I understand, sir," was Michaels' reply. "I just feel uneasy about sending an amateur into such an important operation."

"Understood," Roedl said while looking around once more for anyone or vehicles that might indicate someone was listening in.

"Michaels shuffled his feet as he rested his hand on his sidearm. "So what is this operation designated as?"

"Operation Tin Cup," Roedl answered. "We are piggy-backing this effort within the Tin Cup operation that was set up to limit the amount of weapons and materials going from Iran to Gaza."

"I know about Tin Cup but who knows about this part of the operation to infiltrate the Iranian research facility?" Michaels questioned while he started looking around at anyone who might be within listening distance of their conversation.

Roedl looked around as well as he explained, "The only people that know are our internal office, the Chairman of the Joint Chiefs of Staff and the leading committee member of the House Joint Intelligence Committee."

"What about the President?" a perplexed Michaels asked.

"The White House is leaking information like a sieve," Roedl explained. "We have our own issues of a possible mole and I don't want the Iranians to know of this operation because of information coming out of the White House. That's too much to manage. I'll inform the President about the mission at the proper time. Let's go back in."

They both turned and headed back toward the entrance to the Kennedy Irregular Warfare Center.

CHAPTER 3 -- July 28, 2015, 5:50 AM – Iran Time

Near Shuyesheh, Iran, was the Shuyesheh Research Facility that Lawson was tasked to enter to get a document. The facility was on the edge of the Kurdish-controlled region in the northwest part of Iran. The Kurds were self-governing in an area called Kurdistan, an area that covered the northwestern part of Iran, eastern Iraq, northern Syria and eastern Turkey. The Kurds were primarily Sunni Muslims while Iran's majority population was Shiite Muslims. The Kurds were very tribal in structure and very protective of their families. As a result of these differences, there were times that the Kurds and the Iranian military clashed. This was more likely to happen when Iran attempted to enforce some Iranian regulation or rule on the Kurds.

The research facility was located inside a small hill east of the mountain range that defined the Iraq/Iran border. The area was a mix of trees, bushes, grassy areas and areas of dry soil. There were numerous ravines coming down from the mountain ranges in the west into a long valley area just east of the mountains and west of the research facility. The mountain regions were occupied by the Kurds while the area where the research facility was built was occupied by Iranian nationals and the Iranian military. The military had a significant presence defined by a large army base that was approximately fifteen miles east of the research facility. Although the Iranian military would fly helicopters over the Kurdish mountain areas, they stayed away from the mountain areas on the ground.

Inside the Shuyesheh Research Facility was a laboratory and set of offices that only the Russians and several Iranian women workers were allowed into. The rest of the facility was run and controlled by the Iranian military.

Doctor Isaak Polevsky, a Russian scientist, was in the lab checking out the results of a laser test that was performed the day before. An older man with a graying beard and a slight frame, he was as close to genius as a person could get. His background as a scientist was in wave energy sciences and was well known for his theories on high-powered, focused-energy generation such as those uses found in laser weaponry.

As he wrote notes on the results of his most recent laser weapon testing, he realized that they were near the completion point where the laser weapon could be produced in large quantities.

"So, from my observations from yesterday, we have this proof the laser works," Doctor Polevsky said to an aide while looking at his notes and speaking into a hand recorder. "We fired the laser for one-tenth of a second at a 7 mm thick target twenty-five kilometers away and cut a clean hole six centimeters in diameter approximately a millimeter from where we were targeting. It works." As Polevsky looked at his notes once more, a sense of anxiety came over him. He realized that he needed to finish off his report and prepare it for his superiors in Moscow. It was a dilemma for him. Putting this capability in the hands of a people that were known for their aggression into other countries was of great concern to him. Russia had recently gone into the Ukraine and had taken the Crimean peninsula. He was not only concerned about Russia's use of the weapon but was also concerned about Iran's ability to get enough information to duplicate the weapon. He had already been writing documentation on the progress of the weapon development but had not provided any of the information yet to Moscow. The Russian leadership agreed that holding off on sending any information to Moscow until the project was complete would reduce the capability of someone else acquiring the information or learning of its existence.

Polevsky went back to his office across the main hall from the lab. Passing through the security vault and security room, he unlocked the door to his office and entered. Once inside his office, he went to the white board and wrote the last of the equations on the board. After he completed that task, he went to his computer, entered the equations in a document and printed out a copy. Pulling the copy from the printer, he sat down at his desk and proceeded to read each page. As he did so, the anxiety within him increased. "What am I doing?" he thought as he comprehended the reality of what he had just created. For almost three years, he worked at a furious pace to create the weapon that he had just finished. This was the first time he really took the time to consider the consequences of a working model. He had passing thoughts about its use throughout the project but, now that it was real, the impact of its use hit home.

He went back to the computer and proceeded to look through the document page by page on the monitor. As he did so, he started changing formulas to bring the results on the last page to a different conclusion. Satisfied that the changes would be difficult to reverse-engineer, he printed out a second, modified copy of the document.

Going to the white board, he erased portions of the formulas on the board and changed them to match what he had modified with his second copy of the report. Once he was satisfied that the changes matched the second copy, he went back to his computer and deleted the document from his computer.

Next, he inserted a jump drive into the computer's USB port. He was able to bring the jump drive into the facility due to a flaw in the facility security procedures. The security team would do a thorough check of everything he had on him when he left the facility but only did a cursory check of his belongings when he came into the facility. No one checked him for the jump drive when he came in.

He clicked on an application on the jump drive that allowed for him to modify the sector map for the disk drive on his computer. Making sure the sector map no longer pointed to his deleted document, he ran a disk defragmentation program which would make it more difficult to follow the trail of what he did on his computer.

Satisfied that he had removed the ability to pull up his document or previous versions of it, he took one of the documents he printed, put the pages in a courier pouch and zipped it closed. He put a wire with a lead seal (as in the metal element Pb) on the courier pouch and crimped the lead seal with a tool he had taken from his desk.

The seal was set up in such a way that the pouch was protected by a wire that was looped through the zipper handle opening and a metal eyelet at the end of the pouch. The wire was fed into a round lead piece where one end of the wire was soldered into the lead from one side and a hole through the side of the lead allowed for the other end of the wire to be fed into the lead piece. At this point, the lead piece was crimped with a sealing tool that locked down the other end of the wire and left an impression of a logo of the controlling party. The zipper and eyelet were next to each other which made opening the pouch difficult without cutting the wire.

Satisfied that everything was in order, he took the courier pouch and the jump drive he used to clean the document from the computer, put them into the filing cabinet in his office and locked the cabinet. Taking the other copy of the document, he read back through the writing and formulas. He took that document and went back to the lab.

Upon entering the lab, Polevsky found Captain Behzadi and the senior Russian enlisted man, Senior Sergeant Salnikov, waiting for him. With Captain Behzadi present to observe the results, he proceeded with a test to show the cutting capability of the laser and the ability of the mirrors' servo motors to direct the beam by cutting a clean line through a piece of aluminum hanging on the other side of the lab. In a split second, the laser cut a three foot length slot, a quarter-inch wide through the quarter-inch thick aluminum plate. Behzadi watched the demonstration, read the results of the previous day's testing and motioned to Doctor Polevsky to bring over the approval paperwork.

Behzadi looked over the final document and signed off on the approval of the project's completion. Behzadi handed the papers to Salnikov who looked over the contents, put the papers into an unsealed courier pouch and handed them back to Behzadi. Then Salnikov signed off on the line on the approval document showing he had verified the existence of the document. The pouch would be taken to another location on July 31st by an Iranian Colonel that had been vetted by the Russians, with the pouch to be handed off to a Russian Colonel once the terms of the transfer were met. Polevsky knew that a math genius would not be able to tell whether the pages the Russian was receiving were real or fake. His document shell game began.

Polevsky went back into his office and took his notebook out of his pocket. Tearing off the first page, he lit it with his cigarette lighter, dropped it in his ashtray and watched it burn. While the page was burning, he tore off another page and dropped it into the fire. He continued the process through each page of his notebook until all of the pages were destroyed. Once the task was completed, he took the ashes of the pages and rubbed them into a fine powder, dumping the resulting debris into his wastebasket.

Polevsky smiled to himself as he left the lab. Almost three years of intense effort in Iran and the only proof that the laser worked against aircraft at long distances in any type of weather resided in one of the two copies of the document. Only he knew which one it was. He closed up his office, walked out through the security vault and through a series of hallways to the Central

Security Office. There at the Central Security Office, he would have to strip completely down while the security personnel scanned him and his clothing for any possible pieces of information Polevsky might be carrying or have on his person. Once the inspection was completed, he put on his clothes and left out of the facility through the main door.

CHAPTER 4 -- July 28, 2015, 1:00 PM – Washington, DC Time

At the Kennedy Irregular Warfare Center in metro Washington, D.C., IS2 Jim Lawson met with Admiral Roedl. After meeting with Roedl, Lawson proceeded to the vehicle that would take him to the airbase. He was given a change of clothes and told to change in the vehicle. The clothing consisted of a pair of old jeans, work boots, a gray sweatshirt and a gray light-weight jacket with the name of a company contracted to build cement security barriers in Iraq. The driver of the vehicle took his uniform, shoes, hat, ID, wallet and weapon and put them in a box.

"These will be waiting for you when you get back," the driver said while taping the top of the box and marking it with letters and a number. "Be sure you wash that clothing just issued to you when you finish your mission and before you return the clothes back to me."

Arriving at the airbase, Lawson was given no time to catch his breath. He was immediately rushed into a C-17 aircraft. Upon entering the aircraft he noticed that there were pallets of materials in the middle and toward the rear of the aircraft, but it was too dark to tell what they were as his eyes had not yet adjusted from the bright sunlight. There were also several other persons sitting on the netting benches on either side of the craft. It was also too dark to tell who they were.

"About time ye made it," came the voice across from him. The voice was distinctly recognizable. It was Gunny

Glendenning. Lawson looked toward him and began to recognize his features as his eyes adjusted.

"What are you doing here, Gunny?" Lawson inquired as he looked around at the other occupants then sat down on the netting that was made into seats along the forward section of the fuselage wall.

"I'm supposed to get you to your drop off point then take the other guys to another operation," came Gunny's response. "By the way, here are the items you requested," Gunny said while handing Lawson a gray canvas bag. Lawson looked over the contents of the bag and sat the bag next to him.

Gunny extended his hand toward Lawson with items held by his fingertips. "This is your worker ID badge to get entry into the facility and a journalist ID to use for your cover inside the facility. Get rid of the worker ID at the earliest possible time." Lawson thought it odd that Gunny would give him these instructions with the other people around. Lawson figured they must all be cleared or in some way part of the operation so he didn't give it much thought.

Next, Gunny handed Lawson a rolled up bundle of clothing. "Once you're at the location of your mission, you'll wear these with the worker badge clipped to the outside. Once you get rid of the worker ID, use your journalist ID from then on." Lawson took the clothing and laid the bundle next to the canvas bag.

The pilot came back to the area where everyone was sitting and closed the door to the aircraft. He then turned to those sitting and said, "This is a high-priority flight. Do not go near or touch any of the crates at the back of the plane. It will take us 22 hours to get to our destination. It is now 13:55 hours Eastern Daylight Time. We will be arriving approximately 19:00 hours tomorrow, July 29th, Baghdad time. We will be aerial refueling at the halfway point. We take off in about 15 minutes. I suggest that sometime early in the flight you guys find a place to lie down and get some sleep."

While the pilot was talking he had laid his clipboard down on the web seat next to Lawson. Lawson looked at the clipboard to see a cover sheet that had the words 'Tin Cup' in large letters. Underneath the cover sheet was a thick stack of paperwork. Lawson wondered if 'Tin Cup' was the name for this flight, his operation or something far bigger.

Lawson laid his head back. It seemed like millions of thoughts were racing through his mind as he began to wonder how he ever got himself into this mess. As he looked at the crates in the middle of the aircraft, he recognized the markings on one of the crates. He had seen the same markings on equipment delivered to the aviation techs to assemble on the aircraft carrier. They were components to build a drone or series of drones. These were not the type of drones used to attack targets. The attack drones looked more like airplanes. These drones were more like helicopters and, unlike the attack drones, these drones could hover, which allowed them to set down vertically. They were cargo drones, used to carry materials and messages to friendlies inside enemy territory. They had enough lift power to carry up to one-hundred twenty pounds and go up to an altitude of nine-thousand feet. They also had a flying range of approximately two-hundred miles, round trip with a full load. Better distances with lighter loads.

As he was lying in the netting, Lawson saw the man next to him. Sitting up, he turned his head and introduced himself. The man shook Lawson's hand, "I'm Nick Myers, ET2 just off the carrier ..." Myers stopped as Gunny waved his hands toward him. Lawson saw the motion and wondered what was so secret about what aircraft carrier Myers came off of.

Nick Myers was medium height, Lawson guessed about five foot nine inches, and a thin build. It struck Lawson that Myers looked much older than what a person in the Navy would be for a Second Class Petty Officer. He figured that Myers had to be around thirty or thirty-one years old. He could also tell that Myers had a strong Bostonian accent.

"Anyway," Myers continued, "I'm with this guy." Myers pointed to another man sitting next to him.

Just then, the man reached out his hand to Lawson while showing a disarming smile. "I'm Staff Sergeant Mike Taylor. And you are?" Lawson reached for his hand. "I'm Intelligence Specialist Jim Lawson." They shook hands while both of them looked at Gunny Glendenning. He seemed to show no interest so both men smiled and sat down.

Mike Taylor was a tall man at six foot one inch with a heavy build. Lawson could tell the man worked out a lot as the weight of the man was all muscle. Taylor spoke with a slight New York accent. Lawson figured it was most likely the Bronx. Taylor had a disarming smile and a relaxed persona that gave him an appearance of charisma. Lawson thought that he would make a good politician or spokesman for a company.

As the engines began to start up, the Loadmaster for the aircraft came forward and gave each of the passengers ear protectors and box lunches. Lawson was grateful as the level of noise from the engines was deafening without the ear covers. Lawson ate a sandwich from the boxed lunch, drank some water and laid down for the flight. He quickly fell asleep.

When he woke up, he checked his watch. They had been flying for about eight hours. The level of noise prohibited any chance of conversation. His mind was filled with thinking over and over again about the layout of the facility. There were many ways the whole operation could go wrong and every time he thought through the sequence another possibility popped up.

"Thirty minutes till we land," came Gunny's voice as he shook Lawson on the shoulder. Lawson realized he had fallen back asleep for the rest of the flight.

"That was a long flight," Lawson thought as he gathered his items. He opened the canvas bag and checked its contents again. Everything he requested was there. He then unraveled the clothing to find a pair of old woolen pants, a course woolen shirt, old worn-out shoes, some type of head cover and a long, draping, colorful robe with no front opening. He figured he'd have to put it on by pulling it over his head.

"Don't put any of that on til we get to your drop off point," shouted Gunny. Lawson rolled the clothes back up.

As soon as the plane taxied to its stopping point the pilot opened the door and told everyone to leave immediately. As soon as they got out of the plane, they were directed to a nearby waiting helicopter that was already up and running, ready for takeoff. The sun was low in the sky as it was apparent evening was approaching. Gunny was motioning everyone to hurry. Lawson looked around as he ran to the helicopter. It was obvious they were in Baghdad, Iraq.

"Move your MIT butt," Gunny shouted to Myers as Myers stopped to tie his shoe. Lawson checked to make sure he had everything as he boarded the helicopter. Moments later, the helicopter took off and proceeded east. Everyone put on headphones that allowed for them to communicate internally inside the helicopter.

"We had to leave as quickly as possible," Gunny said while the helo was moving toward the next stop. "There are spies everywhere in Baghdad and they try to photograph anyone getting off planes. We were close enough to the helo that it's a good bet no one got any pictures."

Once at their destination, the helicopter landed and everyone, except the pilot, got off. The helicopter pilot shut down his engines as they moved away from the aircraft. It was getting toward twilight but it was still easy to see the area and colors. It appeared to be a desolate area with one yellow pickup truck sitting in the landing area. The area was dusty with a light breeze blowing and mountains all around. There was grass growing but the heat of summer had turned most of it brown. There was a smell of moisture as though it had recently rained but the ground showed no indication of any wetness except for some tufts of green grass mixed among the brown grass. The skies were mostly cloud free. As Lawson looked back, the pilot started his engines back up, lifted off and headed back west.

"In case you are wondering," Gunny shouted, "We are east of a town called Halabja in Iraq about two miles from the Iranian border. We will wait until it's totally dark to leave and cross the border into Iran. By the way, Halabja was a town that was the target of a chemical weapons attack in the Iraq/Iran war in the early 1980s. The border between Iraq and Iran moved back and forth during the fighting. During one of the battles in which Halabja was in Iranian hands, under orders from Saddam Hussein, a chemical attack was launched against the occupants of Halabja. A lot of people died in that attack. This is one reason we knew that Saddam Hussein had chemical weapons before we invaded Iraq."

"Great," Lawson thought, "We now have a tour guide providing us the history of the place."

Gunny walked over to Lawson while smiling. "Ye don't like a little history?"

Lawson looked at Gunny for a moment. "How do you do that?" Lawson replied. "How is it you get what I'm thinking when I'm not sure what I'm thinking? After all, I'm just a stupid squid."

Gunny looked Lawson eye to eye as he began his reply. "One thing, you're not is stupid, me Lad. If I can figure out what you're thinking, then I know you well enough to trust ye."

Lawson smiled then said, "OK, What am I thinking about now?"

"An elephant," came the reply.

"Damn, you're good," Lawson said while trying to figure out how Gunny knew that.

"Works every time," Gunny thought. "They always think of an elephant."

As darkness approached, they all got into the truck and Gunny drove forward with no headlights or brake lights. Lawson checked his watch which he had set to local time while the plane taxied in Baghdad. It was 9:05 PM, July 29th. Gunny and Taylor were in the cab of the truck while Lawson and Myers sat in the truck bed.

For almost five hours it was a game of stop and go across both rough terrain and smoother roads as Gunny tried to time the border crossing to avoid being detected by any border guards or patrols. The moon was rising above the horizon and almost full. It was truly a cat and mouse game as it didn't take much light to see things moving. Gunny stayed as much to the mountain shadows as possible, while swearing about the fact they gave him a yellow truck that appears white in the moonlight instead of something darker. There were some points in the trail that made staying in the shadows impossible. So they moved slowly. While they were traveling through the mountainous area, Lawson struck up a conversation with Myers.

"Did I hear correctly that you're an MIT graduate?" Lawson asked.

Myers thought for a moment, wondering how Lawson found that out, then replied, "I got my Masters in Electrical Engineering at MIT. I joined the Navy shortly after graduating."

Lawson was perplexed. "Why are you an enlisted man rather than being an officer?"

Myers smiled and proceeded to explain, "If I became an officer, all I'd be doing is paperwork. They pressed me to be an officer but I refused. You see, I like working on the latest new inventions. Stuff that even the public doesn't know exists. As an enlisted guy, I can work on equipment worth billions of dollars on someone else's dime. And I don't have to spend months requesting grants and money for research."

Lawson began to understand Myers motivation. "Sounds like you've got your priorities in the right place but why are you still an ET2? From what I gauge from your age you should at least be a Chief Petty Officer."

"I have been offered promotion several times," Myers responded, "and I refused because, if I had accepted the promotions, I would be doing paperwork rather than working on the latest equipment. I found that I wasn't pressed to be promoted because I always made sure I was a couple of courses short of what was needed to take the Electronic Tech First Class Petty Officer Test. As for my age, you must also remember that I have a Masters so, because of the time it takes to get a Bachelors and Masters, I didn't get into the Navy until I was twenty-six. What's your background?" Lawson took a drink of water from his water bottle then proceeded to answer Myers' question.

"I went to electrical engineering school at Carnegie-Mellon University. I finished all but my last semester and ran out of money. I joined the Navy just after that and was sent to intelligence analysis school. After school, I was ordered to the aircraft carrier Teddy Roosevelt. There, I was involved in the beginning of the ISIS crisis and provided intelligence reports to senior officers on the progress ISIS was making in the northern part of Syria, Lebanon and Iraq. I was also responsible for determining Iran's intentions in the Strait of Hormuz. I got called up for this mission four days ago."

"Sounds like you're the right guy for the stuff we're doing in Iran," Myers replied while wondering what Lawson's operation involved. "I saw the Gunny giving you badges for access into a facility. I guess you're not free to tell me what's going on." Lawson nodded his head 'no'.

"So why do they have a guy with your expertise and training on a mission in Iran?" Lawson queried. Myers leaned back against the back of the truck cab.

"What we have to do I can't tell you," Myers responded. "However, they needed someone with experience in electronics to carry my mission to completion. We don't know what's available when we get to where we're going so I'm going to have to improvise. Taylor knows Farsi but doesn't have a lick of knowledge concerning electronics, so I got nominated. Taylor is good at weapons and insertion efforts. He seems like an OK guy but it's hard to tell where he's coming from. It always seems like he is trying to manipulate people."

Lawson wondered what mission would require Myers' level of experience. Was there another facility in the area? He also thought more about his first impression about Taylor. Politicians and salesmen are good manipulators. Maybe that's why he thought that Taylor would make a good politician or spokesman, that sense of charisma. Myers and Lawson laid back against the truck cab and watched the passing landscape.

The moon made everything seem like a scifi-eerie scene with the areas exposed to the moonlight showing small bushes and trees littering the landscape. The mountains all around made the picture appear desolate with little to give the impression that there was life going on here. Yet, it was obvious there were areas of rich, green growth as Lawson could tell more by smell than by sight. Once in a while, Gunny would stop the vehicle, turn off the engine and listen for any sounds that would indicate a patrol was in the area. On occasion, the sound of a helicopter could be heard but it was far off in the distance. Finally, around 2:00 AM on July 30th, they came out of the mountains to a valley area. Gunny stopped the vehicle and motioned for all to get out. Everyone exited the truck and stretched.

Lawson looked around at his surroundings. Down the road, to what Lawson thought was to the east, were some lights that he assumed was a town. To the left of the road was a dirt road going off into the darkness. Lawson guessed that the dirt road went to the north. The air smelled of a sweet aroma coming off of the trees and bushes in the area. The air was cool and a hint of moisture was in the air. Lawson figured that they were nearing dew point and dew was forming on the plants in the area which was creating the fragrance. Leaning down, Lawson brushed his hand over the top of the grass and felt the moisture collecting on the grass. It was quiet except for the faint sound in the distance of an aircraft, probably a helicopter.

Gunny broke Lawson's thought process. "We're near Shuyesheh, Iran. That road we were on was actually Road 46 in Iran. Our first drop-off point, where we let Lawson go, is about five miles north of here. Then I will take the rest of you to your drop-off point for your mission. Lawson, I will pick you up at 02:00 hours at this location forty-eight hours from now. You'll have to walk the five miles from your target to get here so plan for that in your escape. You'll have to hide during the day after you complete your mission as we can't travel during daylight hours. Too much of a risk of being stopped to check our papers and, if you are successful with your mission, we all may need to do some serious hiding until nightfall."

"OK," was Lawson's reply.

They got back in the truck and headed north, traveling on the dirt road swinging in different directions as the road turned to go around low hills. The ruts in the road didn't make the ride any easier. It wasn't long until the truck came to a stop.

"Lawson," came Gunny's voice. "This is where you get off."

Lawson grabbed his stuff and got out of the back of the truck. His rear was sore from the constant bouncing. He staggered a little as he got out and went to the driver-side window.

Gunny looked at him and his items. "Got everything?" Gunny asked while checking Lawson out.

"Everything," Lawson confirmed.

"Give me your watch. You get captured with that and they'll probably figure you're an American. Why they didn't take that from you with your other stuff when you turned in your gear is a good question. Good luck me Lad. You're going to need it," Gunny said while shaking Lawson's hand and taking the watch. Lawson just shook his head as the truck moved forward.

As Lawson watched the form of the truck move out of sight, he had a sudden sense of feeling very lonely and afraid. The success or failure of this mission was solely on his shoulders and the possibility of failure meant the end for him. He shook off the feeling and looked up at the sky. The turns in the road had caused him to lose his sense of direction. The stars were brilliant, much more brilliant than he ever remembered seeing them since his time on the carrier even with an almost full moon at its peak. He looked for the big dipper and then followed the stars of the big dipper's bucket to the North Star. From that point he knew where east was and walked in that direction.

About twenty minutes into his walk, he saw light farther east. Rather than a definitive point of light, it was more of a lighter area he was seeing with the darkness around it. As he continued to walk forward the light became brighter. Coming to the top of a small ridge, he looked down to see large spotlights and a small mountain with a large opening. The opening appeared to have a large door that was closed with two guards outside, one on either side of the entrance. This appeared to be the research facility.

Lawson sat down on the side of the ridge opposite from the facility. He took off his clothes and put on the clothing and shoes Gunny had given him. There were light brown, loose-fitting pants with a rope for a belt, a shirt that was made of a coarse weave and apparently gray in color and a head wrap was already formed to fit on his head. Lawson realized that he would need this to cover his head so that none of his hair could be seen. Having light-brown hair would probably give away the fact that he wasn't from this area. His face was tanned enough from spending a lot of time in the sun that he figured he could pass a cursory look without raising questions. There was the robe that was to be worn as outer cover. In the moonlight, it appeared as gray and light brown with the highlights of each color interwoven within the robe. It was pulled over the head much like a poncho and had no sleeves. There was a woolen cord of the same colors as the robe sewn in a couple of spots around the midsection. He'd figure out how that was tied later once he could see how other people in the area wore their clothing.

With the clothing was a bandage and some instructions along with a second card with instructions. There was some dried solution on the bandage that looked gray in the moonlight. He couldn't read the instructions in the dark so he put the items in the loose pocket of the pants he had just put on.

He buried his original clothing all the while complaining to himself that Gunny hadn't provided him with a shovel. The ground was soft but had lots of rocks in it. He began to wonder how the guy who issued this clothing to him will feel when Lawson comes back without the ability to return the clothes. Lawson figured he will probably have to fill out DD Form 200 to explain how the clothes were lost.

After burying his clothes, he pulled out a sandwich, a bottle of water and waited. It was colder than he thought it was going to be so he wrapped himself tighter in the robe. There were helicopters flying around to the southeast of him but they were far away. Figuring that sleeping on the ridge would not attract attention, he fell asleep.

Lawson awoke to the sound of peoples' voices and the sun shining down on his face. He had no idea of the time but realized that it was mid-morning based upon where the sun was. It was already getting hot and the wind would pick up at times, blowing dust around that made the eyes sting.

As he looked to the west, he could see the mountains they had crossed the night before. To the north was a continuation of the small ridge he was hiding behind. There was a large valley filled with trees, bushes and areas of grass on his side of the ridge. To the south was another valley area with a town in it in the far distance. He figured that was the town of Shuyesheh. To the east, he could see the mountain with the facility and helicopters flying around along the horizon to the southeast. To the northeast was a village that was on the same road as the research facility. A dirt road went from the facility, past the village and proceeded to the north beyond his sight. There were trees and bushes everywhere with the sound of leaves rustling each time a puff of wind came through. Looking out across the valley to the west and northwest, he could see some plots of land that had been cultivated and were growing crops. There also ravines scattered about but all sharing one common characteristic. They were running mostly from west to east, from the mountains into the valley and the ravines had more trees and bushes along them than areas away from the ravines. Having spent some time on a farm, he could tell that this was good land for growing crops. In some places, crops were being cultivated but a majority of the land was still fallow.

Taking inventory of what he had, he picked up the bandage and instructions along with the card. The instructions stated, "Put the bandage on your throat. The card that is with these instructions says in Farsi that you have a wound and can't speak. This should keep you from having to answer any questions."

Lawson put the bandage on his throat and the card in his pocket. While doing so, he felt a couple more cards in in his pocket. One had a clip. These were the cards Gunny had given him. One identified him as a journalist working for the London Chronicle. The other was a picture of him with some Farsi writing. A sticky note attached to it said 'for entry into the facility'. He put them back in his pocket.

Lawson laid and waited for the events of the day to unravel themselves. The day was getting hotter as dust blew around and the waiting seemed to go on forever.

CHAPTER 5 -- July 30, 2015, 1:35 PM – Iran Time

It was early afternoon when things started to happen. Lawson could hear voices of people off in the far distance on the other side of the ridge. The heat was almost unbearable. "How can people live in these clothes when it's this hot?" Lawson said to himself while climbing to the top of the ridge to get a look at what was going on. Lying down so as not to be seen by the guards at the facility but still being able to see the area on the other side of the ridge, he took inventory of the activity to the east.

At the village about two miles northeast of where he was, people were walking down the road from the village going toward the facility. Off in the distance, he could see a column of dust rising and determined that it was from a vehicle and not from the wind. It was about twelve to fourteen miles away and heading toward the facility.

Lawson went back down to the bottom of the ridge and began to walk to the north. After traveling about half a mile, he walked to the top of the ridge and saw that the people walking from the village were just passing by his location. He adjusted the head wrap to match how the people below wore theirs and tied the loose waistband on the robe to mimic how they were wearing the outer clothing. Waiting until the last person was past his position, he proceeded over the ridge and down to the road. He got to the road just as the truck was passing on its way to the facility. Lawson began a quick walk to catch up to the others but remained behind the last person so as not to raise questions. As he neared the facility, he pulled out the badge with the Farsi words and his picture, clipping it to his robe, checked the bandage around his throat and pulled the note that was with the bandage from his pocket. He also checked the canvas bag with the items Gunny had given him that were under his robe to make sure it was secure and not visible from the outside.

As he approached the entrance to the facility, he could see a guard just inside the entrance. The entrance was much larger than he thought. The entrance was around forty feet high and fifty yards wide which made the truck look small compared to the entrance. Not much could be determined of what was inside while he approached the truck as the space beyond the entrance was dark compared to the outside.

Men were taking cases of food from the truck and walking toward the entrance. He froze in his steps. As each man was getting to the guard at the entrance, the guard was checking each badge against a list on a clipboard. Lawson felt a sense of panic. Was this expected and prepared for. He knew if his name was not on the list it would be a short mission but he was already committed. If he turned and left now there would be no question as to his capture.

Walking up to the truck, he grabbed a case of lettuce from the back of the truck, lifted the case up to his shoulder and started toward the guard. Looking across the front of the truck he could see that a guard on the other side of the entrance was checking each ID badge against a list for those coming back out of the facility to get another load.

The man ahead of Lawson was showing his badge when the guard grabbed the badge and yelled something in Farsi to others inside the facility. Two uniformed Iranian soldiers with rifles came out and grabbed the man in question. He screamed something in Farsi as they dragged him inside. Lawson expected the same thing would happen to him.

Lawson walked up to the guard and showed him his badge. The guard said something to him at which point Lawson pulled out the card that came with the bandage and showed it to the guard. Lawson then pointed to the bandage on his throat. The guard nodded his head, looked at the bandage on Lawson's throat then looked for Lawson's worker ID badge name on the list. Lawson waited. The time seemed to tick away very slowly. While Lawson waited he could hear the sound of gunfire from inside the facility. He figured that the guy taken by the soldiers was just shot.

"What's taking so long?" he thought. The guard put a check mark on the sheet and waved him on. Lawson felt like his knees were rubber as he carried the box of produce into the facility. He passed another guard in the main entrance area then opened a door into a hallway. The hallway had two mounted cameras, one just above his head pointed toward the other end of the hallway and the other camera at the other end of the hallway pointing toward the entrance to a doorway that opened to the right side. The hallway was painted gray with dim lighting.

At the end of the hallway, a third guard was motioning him to come forward. Lawson walked to the end of the hallway and made a right turn into the doorway that the camera was pointed toward which led him into a kitchen area.

"This is the galley," he thought to himself. To his left, at the other end of the galley, was a stack of crates like the one he was carrying. He walked over to the stack and put the crate on top of the others. Looking at the wall to his left where pots and pans were stacked on racks, he made a mental note of where the racks were in relationship to the entry door. He turned and walked back out of the door, past the guard and back down the hallway.

Just before he reached the exit door into the main security area he looked back at the guard at the galley entrance. The guard was looking into the galley so, while facing the guard,

Lawson made a left turn into another hallway instead of going back through the doorway to the entrance area. He knew the camera closest to him in the hallway would not pick up his change in direction since it was pointing away from him.

The hallway he turned into led to the entrance of the prisoner cells. To his right, there was a long hallway followed by an entryway into an area where rows of cells could be seen to each side of the main walkway. Lawson moved into the entrance of the cell area. The passageway through the cell block was dark. Lawson could make out the figure of a guard sitting at a table reading a newspaper and smoking a cigarette at the other end of the passageway. The area smelled of cigarette smoke and urine. The passageway had one light at the end where the guard was sitting.

Lawson slowly moved down the right side of the passageway. There were five cells on each side of the passageway with all but three of the doors closed. Two doors on the right side were open and one door was open on the left side of the passageway next to the guard's table. Lawson moved down to the farthest open cell on the right side careful not to draw the attention of the guard. It was cell 131. He moved into the cell and quickly scanned the cell for its layout. It was constructed of three foot wide by two foot high cement blocks with mortar joints just as mentioned by Admiral Roedl. The room was the gray color of the cement blocks. In the far corner to the right, there was one rack with a dark blanket on it but no mattress. There were also no cameras. A bucket sat in the corner opposite the rack against the far wall, most likely used for toilet needs. The walls had no windows and the door was steel, painted light blue with a small observation window that had a small door closed over it that was a darker blue. There was one dim light bulb that appeared to be on all the time.

Lawson began to wonder about the cell when it was closed. "About enough oxygen in here for about five hours," he thought while looking around. He spotted a vent at the top of the right wall that was perpendicular to the entrance to the cell. He put his hand up to feel the air flow.

"Air coming in," he thought while looking around for another vent. "There has to be an exhaust vent." He finally found the vent in an upper corner of the wall opposite the previous vent. He held his hand up to it and could feel air being drawn out of the cell. "Air going out."

He pulled the canvas bag he received from Gunny out from under his robe and put the bag under the bed at the farthest corner from the door where it could not be seen by anyone unless they moved the rack or looked under it. He then exited the cell, moved slowly down the right side of the passageway, stopping at intervals that corresponded to when the guard shifted his position. After having to stop several times, he exited without the guard seeing him.

Lawson went into the hall and back to the hallway where the galley guard was standing at the other end. Lawson watched the galley guard and when the guard changed his attention to something in the galley, Lawson stepped into the hallway, toward the galley guard about four steps and opened a door to the right side of the hallway that took him into another hallway. This hallway was painted yellow with bright lighting and no cameras. The hall was long with one door at the far end on the left. There was a trashcan about halfway down the hallway.

As he walked down the hallway, he pulled off the worker ID badge and dropped it into the trashcan. Going down the hallway to the end where a door on the left opened to a longer hallway, he entered the hallway that led to the labs and the Commander's office. The hallway was painted white and well lighted. There were two cameras. One was halfway down the hallway, pointing to the door he had just opened. The other camera was toward the end of the hallway and pointed to two partially opened heavy-looking vault doors on either side of the hallway at the other end. He moved slowly down the hallway, noting that there were three doors on the left ahead of him, two of the doors were open. He passed the first open door and could see a couple of people dressed in white clothing at tables. He figured this to be the dining area and the people were workers from the galley area. Passing the first door without being seen, he reached the next door which, from the symbols on the door, indicated that it was a restroom. He moved forward slowly toward the third door.

He was halfway between the second and third doors when alarms went off. He could see the vault doors close and heard latches and bars locking the facility down. Seconds later, the hallway was filled with guards. Lawson lifted his hands in the air and surrendered.

The closest guard grabbed Lawson's arm and slammed him against the wall while a second guard kicked his legs out from under him. Lawson sat on the ground with an instant headache and one leg throbbing in pain. The guards were yelling something to him in Farsi so he thought it best to stay still.

Finally, a voice spoke in English to him. Lawson recognized the face as Captain Hamid Behzadi.

"It appears that you have some explaining to do," Behzadi said while he threw Lawson's worker badge to him. "You have a problem with keeping your working badge on?"

Lawson picked up the badge, realizing they somehow saw him throw it in the trashcan. "Stupid of me," Lawson thought, "ordered to remove any pictures and video of me when I leave but forgot to keep the worker ID with my picture on it." He began to wonder when they had started watching.

"We caught you going through the door to the admin area instead of going out the door to pick up another load. Who are you?" Lawson reached down to lift up the robe. The guards moved forward in unison with their weapons pointed at him. One guard chambered a round as he moved forward. Lawson stopped and froze in position.

"I'm just getting my credentials out of my pocket," Lawson said as he motioned with his hands. Behzadi nodded his head in affirmation and the guards backed off.

Lawson hid the worker ID in the palm of his hand and placed the worker ID in his pants pocket as he pulled the journalist ID card from his pocket and handed it to Behzadi. Behzadi had failed to notice that Lawson had put the worker ID in his pocket.

Behzadi looked over the journalist ID then asked, "So what's your name." Lawson glanced around. "It's on the card. My name is Jason Kendrick and I work for the London Chronicle," he said while feeling the bump on his head.

"How and why did you get in here?" Behzadi questioned.

"I got in here through the main entrance," Lawson responded. "I was living with some village people up north the past two days and heard about this facility. I thought it would be a good story to tell about how the Iranians are doing their research and how well organized they are."

"I thought I knew everyone in the Shahidar village but I don't remember you and then there are issues with how you entered. We shall also see about your claims of being a journalist," Behzadi said while motioning to the guards. He said something in Farsi to them at which point a guard on either side grabbed Lawson by the arms and lifted him up. They frisked him for any weapons.

"Oh," Behzadi grinned and grabbed at Lawson's throat. "It appears you can speak. You won't need this anymore," he said as he ripped the bandage off of Lawson's throat. Lawson had totally forgotten that the bandage was there. The guards pulled him along half dragging, half walking through the third door into an office that was obviously the Captain's.

There were two desks in the office perpendicular to each other. Each desk had numerous files on them, a phone, a pencil holder full of pens and a name plate. The other desk belonged to Colonel A. Rouhani, the facility Commander. Lawson thought it strange that the nameplates were written in Farsi, Russian and English. Lawson noted that there were no cameras and two doors in the room. One door was the one they used to drag him in from the hallway and the other door in the adjacent wall appeared to go to an administrative office. It matched what he had remembered from the layout in Admiral Roedl's office which increased his confidence that the inside person feeding the information to Roedl was accurate in his description on where things were at in the research facility.

The room was painted a light green with dark green trim around the doors. The only place that was not green was the red rectangle on the wall where the fire extinguisher hung. It struck Lawson funny that the Iranians would use the same color codes for emergency equipment as the Americans did.

Lawson sat in a chair in front of Captain Behzadi's desk with his back against the wall while a guard across the room watched Lawson's every move. Before he knew it, the clock on the wall indicated that he had been sitting in the office for over two hours. It was 5:25 PM. Lawson pulled a pen out of the pencil holder and started to examine it. The guard shifted nervously.

Suddenly, an officer that Lawson recognized as Colonel Rouhani stepped through the door from the admin area and handed a folder to the guard. They exchanged some words in Farsi and the guard put the folder on Captain Behzadi's desk. The guard then went back to his position. Lawson glanced at the folder on the desk. When the guard had dropped the folder on the desk, Lawson's journalist card had partially slipped out from the folder. Lawson knew he needed to see the contents of the folder. Moments later, Behzadi walked in and motioned to the guard to come to him. For the moment, both men had their backs to Lawson. Lawson figured it was so he couldn't hear them talking in case he could understand Farsi.

Lawson watched them as he quickly picked up the folder on the desk and laid it in his lap low enough so they couldn't see it. He opened the folder. There on the top was his journalist ID card. There were a number of pages behind the first page. The first page was a form consisting of a full page written in Farsi.

What caught Lawson's attention was the number '132' in the upper right hand corner. He found it curious that the number was written in Western Arabic Numerals and not Farsi. Lawson figured this had to be a cell number. He immediately crossed it out and wrote '131' above the crossed-out number. He looked up to see the two men still talking. He looked back down and wrote the Commander's signature next to the number. He then closed the folder and watched for both men to be facing away from him.

As he sat back, he saw the guard looking toward him. After a moment, the guard turned back toward the admin office while saying something to Behzadi, who was also facing toward the admin office. At that moment, Lawson put the folder back in its original position on the desk.

"I'm sure glad the Admiral had me practice that signature. This was a use of it I wasn't expecting," Lawson thought while he quietly slipped the pen back into the pencil holder.

The two men talked for about three more minutes before Captain Behzadi turned and walked to his desk.

"You should know that we called the London Chronicle." Behzadi stated while looking at Lawson. "They confirmed that you are a journalist there. Your reasons for being here raises a more significant question." Behzadi then picked up the folder. Opening it, he frowned briefly then proceeded to tell Lawson his future.

"I see here that you were originally assigned to cell 132. However the Commander has decided to change that to cell 131, which is too bad for you." Behzadi looked at Lawson to see his reaction.

"You see Mr. Kendrick," Behzadi continued, "You were originally assigned for transfer to Tehran but the orders have been changed to have you executed." Lawson gave Behzadi a startled look.

Behzadi went on, "It's like this. The even cell numbers are for those being transferred or being held for a specified time. The odd cell numbers are for those being executed. You will be executed with several others tomorrow at noon."

Lawson thought, "Well, that was a stupid decision to change the sheet," then realized there was no other choice.

A moment later, Colonel Rouhani stepped through the door from the admin office and handed Behzadi a pack of American cigarettes and a box of strike-anywhere matches. They exchanged a few words in Farsi, then Behzadi turned around and handed Lawson the cigarettes and box of matches.

"The Commander feels that you should have cigarettes to enjoy while you sit in the cell." Lawson thought the cigarette exchange was very curious. He knew enough in his experience from serving in the Persian Gulf that the Iranians highly valued American cigarettes. Why would they be giving him a new pack of cigarettes? It didn't make sense.

Benzadi nodded to the Guard. The guard motioned for Lawson to stand up, then escorted Lawson over to cell 131.

CHAPTER 6 -- July 30, 2015, 5:44 PM – Iran Time

Lawson entered cell 131 and sat down. He opened the pack of cigarettes while the guard was watching. Lawson struck a match, lit up a cigarette then offered one to the guard. The guard looked around the passageway for a moment, smiled and accepted the cigarette. Once Lawson lit the cigarette for the guard, the guard closed and locked the cell door and the observation door in the cell door.

Lawson smoked his cigarette while watching the smoke being pushed by the airflow. He estimated that it took about 10 minutes for the air to clear. Lawson threw the cigarette on the floor and crushed it with his foot. Looking in at the cigarette pack before closing it, he saw a piece of paper in the pack. Pulling the paper out, he read the note written on it.

The note said, "Whatever you are planning, be careful. I'm trusting you'll be smart enough to recognize you have inside help."

He pulled out a match and burned the note then crushed the ashes on the floor of the cell.

Listening for any movement outside, he crawled under the rack and pulled out the canvas bag. Sitting on the bed with the canvas bag against his leg opposite the door in case there was a surprise visit, he reached in the bag and felt around for a watch. Pulling the watch out of the bag, he checked the time. The watch was set to local time, 5:55 PM. He slipped the watch into his pocket and proceeded with the inventory of the bag.

One U.S. Maxim 9 mm pistol with a built-in silencer and one extra clip. Lawson pulled out the weapon and checked the clip in the weapon. There were 10 rounds and one in the chamber. During the time he was examining the bag contents, he was listening for any sign of movement outside the cell.

Next, he pulled out a 16 oz. bottle of muriatic acid, a face mask with an acid fume protection cartridge, a small bottle of water, two 12 inch thin metal rods with teeth bent down at the end of the rods and a 12 inch steel rod shaped in the form of a thin wedge throughout the full length of the rod. Lawson put all of the items except for the watch back in the bag and returned the bag to its original location.

Shortly after that, Lawson could hear the clanging sound of metal against metal. It was quiet for a moment then he heard it again, even louder. Finally, the observation door to his cell opened and the guard looked in as Lawson sat on the rack. The door closed with a clang and everything went quiet again. Lawson pulled the watch from his pocket and checked the time, 5:59 PM.

Putting the watch back in his pocket, he shifted the blanket on the rack and laid down. Just as he did so, the observation door opened again and the voice of Captain Behzadi came forth. "Are you comfortable, Mr. Kendrick?"

Lawson nodded his head affirmative then responded, "I thought Iranian jails had nothing but a floor. What's with the racks?"

Behzadi smiled for a moment, looked at the rack and quipped, "Would you like it removed?" Without waiting for an answer he continued, "The only reason we have these racks is that the Russians wanted the prisoners to sleep on something other than the floor. So we accommodated them." Lawson nodded again but remained silent.

"Get some rest," Behzadi said, "We don't give the condemned prisoner any last meal or water. Why waste it on someone who's going to die. Your time is 12 noon tomorrow. That gives you, ah, 18 hours to make your peace."

Behzadi closed the observation door and left. Lawson figured that would be the last time Behzadi would visit until execution time so he laid back down on the rack.

Lawson was deep in thought when he heard the distant clanging sound again. It got louder then finally his observation door was opened and the guard looked in. He looked at Lawson then closed the door. Lawson waited a moment then pulled the watch from his pocket. It was 6:52 PM.

"So it appears they check the cells about once each hour," Lawson thought as he started to move back under the bed. He stopped then realized that it was still too early to start the next part of his operation. He figured that it would be safe by the time 9:00 PM came around. Behzadi could still throw another surprise visit and the guard appeared too awake to take a chance. Lawson laid back on the rack, lit up a cigarette and waited.

The next time the guard came around was at 7:40 PM. Lawson figured he came early because a change in the guard probably was scheduled to happen at 7:45 PM. Lawson assumed that the Iranians were following the western military traditions of changing the sentries every four hours at fifteen minutes before the top of the hour. His suspicions were solidified by the next guard check being at 8:55 PM. Even when 9:00 PM came around, he felt that it was still too early to move forward with his plan. There appeared to be too much activity outside in the passageway as there were footsteps going back and forth while some sort of conversation was going on. The conversation was followed by a loud clang sound of the door of the cell next to him being closed. The muffled conversation continued for the next five minutes then all went quiet.

The waiting was beginning to wear on Lawson. He knew time was growing short if his plan was to have any hope of success, yet he also knew that if he moved too soon and was discovered, nothing could save him. "Hurry up and wait," he thought to himself.

It was 9:30 PM when Lawson made sure the blanket covered all of the rack so the items underneath couldn't be seen if someone looked in. He then went under the rack and pulled out the bottle of muriatic acid. Lying under the rack, he removed the small cap from the top of the squirt bottle holding the acid and started squeezing a small stream of acid on the mortar around the lowest cement block in the wall at the head of the rack. It was one of the cement blocks that was part of a wall for his cell with the opposite side of the block being part of the wall for the galley. Once he covered all of the mortar around one block, he put the cap back on the bottle, set the bottle next to the bag in the far corner of the rack and moved out from under the rack. He could hear the fizzling sound of the acid eating into the mortar. He could also smell the fumes which exhibited a strong sulphur smell that was filling the room.

"If the guard hears the sound of the mortar and acid interaction or smells the sulpher, I'm finished," Lawson thought while trying to check his options. He looked at the watch. It was 9:51 PM. "That all took twenty minutes," he thought. "Way too long!"

He heard the clanging sound of an observation door being closed. Looking around for a solution to his problem of the smell of the fumes, he focused on the cigarettes and matches. Grabbing the cigarettes, he put one in his mouth and fumbled to open the box of matches. The observation door of the cell next to him slammed shut. Lawson struck a match and proceeded to hold it to the cigarette. Just then the observation door to his cell opened. The guard looked in the cell for a moment, watched Lawson shake his hand up and down to extinguish the match then motioned to Lawson for a cigarette. Lawson handed him a cigarette through the observation window and lit the cigarette. The guard took a puff on the cigarette, nodded to Lawson then closed the observation door. Lawson sat on the rack for about five minutes until he was sure there were no further interruptions. He looked at his watch, 9:57 PM.

Lawson went back under the rack and pulled the acid protection mask from his bag. Putting it on, he grabbed the steel wedged rod and proceeded to scrape away at the mortar. It came out rather easily. He had gone all around the cement block, going about halfway through the mortar with the first use of the acid. He now had to do the whole process again to get completely through.

He remembered that he had to get all of the mortar off the bottom of the block before taking the mortar off the top of the block. If he didn't do that in the proper sequence, the weight of the block would be too much for him to get all of the mortar off the bottom of the block. He'd be stuck. He had to remember too that he had to make a small hole in the mortar to the other side before scraping out the rest of the mortar to make sure the lights in the galley were out.

Lawson put more acid on the mortar surrounding the block, capped the acid bottle and took off the protective mask. Pulling the spare clip from the bag, he ejected a round from the clip and pushed the round under the cement block so that if the mortar became too soft, the block wouldn't shift down before he could clear the mortar from the bottom of the block. Finishing that task, he placed the other items near the canvas bag under the rack and proceeded to sit on the rack again. The fumes continued to create a minor problem with breathing.

It was 10:42 PM when Lawson was able to confirm the galley was deserted and proceeded to remove the rest of the mortar from the bottom of the block and the round he had placed under the block. The block dropped with a 'thump'. He halted and listened for any sound of movement. Once he was sure that no one heard the block drop, he continued to remove the rest of the mortar from the top and sides. After finishing the removal of the mortar, he removed the 9 mm round from under the cement block then took the two metal rods with hooks at the end and inserted them to the left and right top side of the block. He made sure the hooks were grabbing onto the other side of the block and proceeded to pull on the rods. As he pulled on the rods, the block started moving toward him. He pulled a little harder, first with one rod then the other, wiggling the block slightly back and forth with each wiggle bringing the block closer to him. Finally, the block was completely out. Lawson moved the block to the place where the bag had been.

Even though it took a greater effort to pull the block toward him, it was much riskier to push the block into the galley. He had no idea what was in the galley and the block hitting something in the galley would undoubtedly make noise that would result in an investigation.

He looked at the time. "10:55 PM! Beyond the time check period for the guard!" He shoved the items he was working with next to the block he had pulled, got out from under the rack, brushed himself off and grabbed a cigarette. Sitting on the rack he waited for the sound of the clanging of the doors. Nothing happened.

At 11:15 PM, the guard finally went down the line checking the cells. When he got to Lawson's cell and looked in, Lawson could tell the guy had been sleeping. If the guard had been caught sleeping on duty, he probably would have been shot.

"Lucky guy," Lawson thought while thinking through his plan for the next steps. Getting into the galley is the first step.

As he was thinking, the guard was still standing at the door and motioned for another cigarette. Lawson got up, handed him a cigarette then proceeded to light it. While doing so, he could hear an argument going on in the next cell, then the sound of a very distinctive, very Irish voice.

"Gunny", Lawson thought, "then that means the other guys I was with are the ones facing the firing squad tomorrow!" The guard started to turn toward the other cell to see what was going on just as things were quieting down. He stopped, turned back and closed the observation door to Lawson's cell. Lawson had to work fast. He waited until he could hear the guard's steps going toward the table the guard normally sat at.

Climbing back under the rack, Lawson grabbed the acid bottle and squirted acid around a cement block that was also under the rack but was part of the wall of the cell next to him. He put the acid on the mortar binding and sat down on the rack. He figured that 11:45 PM was the next changing of the guard.

As he expected, the guard went down the line of cells and checked each one at 11:40 PM, time for changing of the guards. Lawson was lying back in the rack with the blanket over him when the guard checked. Once the observation door closed and the guard left the area Lawson proceeded to put on the acid mask and carved away at the mortar at the bottom of the cement block. After removing as much mortar as he could, Lawson squirted more acid on the mortar, put the 9 mm round under the block and set the bottle aside. He laid back on the rack and covered himself with the blanket. Time to wait for the acid to work.

It was 12:05 AM when Lawson got back under the rack and removed the last of the mortar from the bottom of the cement block. He could hear some conversation going on followed by a finger moving along the other side of the block.

Lawson whispered, "Don't touch that, it's acid. Get Gunny." The next thing he heard was Gunny's voice. "Quiet down," Lawson instructed then proceeded. "We need to talk in low voices. I'm about to remove the rest of the mortar from this block. It'll take five minutes. Once I do that I need for you to push the block my direction. Understood?"

"Aye," came the whispered response.

Lawson removed the round then the rest of the mortar, sweeping the residue back to the far corner of the rack. "Now push," he whispered. The block moved smoothly toward Lawson. When it was clear of the opening, Lawson pushed it to the side. A face appeared in the opening.

"Never thought anyone would be comin' to our rescue," Gunny stated while pulling himself through the opening. He barely fit but was able to make it through with Lawson's help. Once Gunny was in Lawson's cell, Lawson put his hand on Gunny's shoulder to stop him for a moment. Lawson reached into the bag and pulled out the Maxim 9 pistol with the silencer. He handed it to Gunny.

"Hold onto this until we all get into the next room," Lawson stated. He pointed at the opening to the galley to Gunny. Gunny nodded and Lawson continued, "While you're going into the galley, quietly pass back some of the cooking pans on the shelves in the galley. We need to put them under the blankets to make bulges to make it look like we're still in the room."

Everyone went to work moving the pans, putting them under the blankets then moving from the cell into the galley. Taylor had trouble getting through the opening because of his large size. Lawson and Myers moved the rack to the other side then both men pulled Taylor through the opening. It took a couple of minutes but they finally got him through. Myers put the last pans and blanket in front of the opening in their cell wall to cover the escape opening should the sentry look into the cell the others just came through. Lawson moved the rack back into position and made sure the blanket covered the rack to hide the openings. He wiped off the round he put under the cement blocks and put it back in the spare clip. Once these tasks were completed, Lawson pulled his way into the galley.

The galley was dark except for one overhead light. A large cooking island was in the middle of the galley. The center cooking island had a large griddle and a vent over the cooking area with pots, pans and utensils hanging on hooks that were attached to a bar on the ceiling. Against the wall they came through, Lawson could see large cooking pots on one end of the galley, stoves next to them then the pots and pans on rolling racks that they had moved to clear the opening Lawson had made to get into the galley.

The opposite side of the galley had stainless steel serving stations where food was served to the crew. On the far end of the galley were floor to ceiling cupboards extending half the length of the wall with the other half of the wall showing locked doors to three built-in freezers. On the wall opposite the wall with the cupboards and freezers was a door that exited to the dining area and another door leading to the hallway. On that wall there were seven white boards with a 3 inch wide magnetic strip running the full length of the seven white boards, each board holding what appeared to be menus for the galley for each of the next seven days. Lawson also noted what appeared to be a working schedule. He couldn't make out the Farsi scribbling but the times were numeric, which he finally figured that it was probably due to the fact that the Russians couldn't read Farsi numbers and the Iranians couldn't read Russian numbers so they settled on Western Arabic Numbers, with which everyone was familiar. He saw that the first schedule started out at 03:30. "We've got till 3:30 AM before anyone notices the damage to the wall," he thought to himself. He checked his watch. It was 12:20.

Once everyone was in the Galley, Lawson told them to hide using the center cooking island as cover. Motioning to everyone to sit down close to him, he proceeded to explain.

"I have to get copies of a document being sent to Moscow this morning. The document is in a secure area. It is critical that I get them. It appears that whatever these papers are, they could start or stop a war."

Lawson remembered seeing a vault door close and heard the bars slam shut at the time he was captured. "It's within a secure area behind a vault door."

Petty Officer Myers spoke up, "You say a vault door. Did it appear to automatically close and could you see bars in the sides of the door of the vault?" Lawson nodded affirmative. Myers continued, "While I was on the carrier, there were times I had to repair sensors on the vault doors going into the crypto area and the secure communications center. It's probably a double secure system where the vault door has to close before the inside door can open."

Lawson suddenly had a great interest in Myer's knowledge. "Is the inside door a vault door as well?" Lawson asked while looking at Myers.

Myers thought for a moment then replied, "No. The inside door is typically some type of steel pocket door that slides open when the guard, in the secure area, pushes a button. The inside door won't open until the vault door completely closes. It functions much the same as the entry area to Admiral Roedl's office."

There was some noise in the hallway just outside the galley so Lawson motioned for everyone to stay behind the center cooking island.

CHAPTER 7 -- July 31, 2015, 12:25 AM – Iran Time

Lawson went to the door that opened from the galley to the hallway. As he opened the door and looked out, a uniformed man was exiting one of the rooms. Lawson ducked back inside the galley. "Rover coming," was Lawson's statement as he motioned everyone back behind the center island once more.

He suddenly realized that if the man comes in here the first thing he will see is the hole in the wall where they came through. Moments later, the guard opened the door to the galley and walked in. His hand reached for his mike as a 'phfut' sound was heard. The guard dropped to the floor with a small stream of blood coming from his head. Lawson turned to see Gunny with the Maxim 9 pistol in his hand.

"One more second and he be callin' his lads," Gunny said while handing the weapon to Lawson. Lawson agreed and took a survey of their condition.

The first thing that struck Lawson was that the guard was coming out the armory when Lawson saw him. That meant that his keys or badge opened the armory. Second was the fact that the radio he was carrying would be very useful to keep up on what was going on.

"I remember that someone here speaks Farsi," Lawson stated as Taylor raised his hand. Taylor could listen to the radio and translate for them. Before Lawson could tell the others what to take off of the guard, Gunny had already gathered up the items.

Lawson opened cupboard doors to see what was on the shelves. There was bread, some large rolls of cheese and jars of peanut butter. He also noted there were many sixteen ounce bottles of water on the cupboard shelves next to the cupboards where the food was located. He closed the cupboard doors, taking a mental note of where everything was.

He explained to the others, "We need to get arms and ammunition out of the armory. We also need binoculars and some grenades." Lawson checked the keys and the badge. Looking down the hallway at the armory door, he saw the security pad that the badge would need to swipe to open the armory door.

Gunny spoke up, "That is probably a key and badge system. You must first put the key in the door, swipe the badge against the pad then turn the key within five seconds."

Lawson looked down at the keys. Which key opened the armory door? He went from key to key until one caught his eye. All the other keys were the typical brass color but one key was red. He held the key up. "This one," he said. Everyone nodded agreement.

Once he entered the hallway, he looked to where the ceiling cameras were at. Lawson went to the armory door, inserted the key, swiped the card and turned the key. The door opened. Once the door was opened, everyone else went down the hall to the armory one by one until everyone was in.

"Don't close the door," Gunny said as Lawson was getting ready to push the door closed. "You need the key to get back out." Lawson reached to the outside of the door and pulled the key out of the lock. "If you had left the key in the door, we would have never have been able to get out," Gunny explained while picking up an AK-47. Lawson pushed the door closed and proceeded to examine the contents of the armory. He first noted that there were no cameras in the armory.

There was a weapons rack with AK-47 rifles sitting upright in individual slots in the rack. Next to the rack were cases of ammo for the AK-47s. Toward the back end of the armory were RPG rounds and launchers. Next to them were 9 mm pistols and ammo for the pistols. In the far corner to the right were several wood boxes containing explosives and another cardboard box with detonators. In the middle of the floor was a table that contained binoculars, radios, spare parts, web belts and ammo pouches. Against the wall next to the door were hand grenades, empty rifle and pistol clips and rolls of trip wire. A desk sat at the front of the armory by the door.

Gunny handed an AK-47 to each person after checking each weapon to ensure each rifle had a firing pin. He gathered several other AK-47s as backup. Next, Gunny handed six clips of ammo to each person in ammo pouches attached to web belts.

While Gunny was handing the ammo out, Lawson found some binoculars and took a pair of the smallest but most powerful. Myers was collecting trip wire, detonators and plastic explosives. The explosives appeared to be C-4. Lawson told Myers that they needed approximately 20 pounds of the explosives and threw a canvas bag to Myers.

Meanwhile, Gunny had turned his attention to the pistols. He examined two of them, put one in his belt and two clips in his ammo pouches. He gave Lawson the other pistol and clips. Heavily armed, the men exited the armory and went next door to the maintenance room. The maintenance room had no card pad to swipe, only a lock. They tried several keys until one worked.

Once inside the maintenance room, Gunny found a backpack and started putting tools into it. Both heavy-duty and small screwdrivers, a hammer, a knife, two different sizes of crescent wrenches, a socket set, a pair of pliers, wire cutters and several rolls of duct tape were selected. He handed the backpack to Taylor. Once they were finished, they went back to the galley.

Gunny brought extra web belts with grenade pouches and several grenades. They stopped to catch their breath. Lawson checked his watch. It was 12:45 AM. He was curious why no alarm had been raised yet. The security people surely would be missing the roving guard by now and the guard at the prison cells should have noticed something wrong, if he's awake. Lawson also wondered why no one raised the alarm as someone should be watching the cameras.

Myers moved next to Lawson. "If those vaults are as you described," Myers started, "the sensors are most likely magnetic with the magnets in the door to match up with the sensors around the frame of the vault door."

His comment caught Lawson by surprise. "This means we have to go back to the maintenance room and find some magnets," Lawson asserted. Myers shook his head "No" then pointed to the seven white boards in the galley. Lawson suddenly realized that Myers was pointing at the magnetic strip holding the menus in place on the whiteboards. Almost in unison, Lawson and Myers jumped up, pulled the magnetic strip from the white boards and started rolling it up. They were almost finished when the alarms went off.

Taylor, holding the earpiece in his ear, spoke up. "They've announced the sentry has not reported in and discovered we're not in our cells! We need to get out of here! I'm thinking there is one place they wouldn't look for us, the Commander's office." Lawson realized that everything will be locked down. He looked around at the galley then at the ceiling.

The ceiling was a false ceiling typical of commercial buildings. There were large squares of ceiling tiles held in place by metal frames. The metal frames would be held by wires fixed to the real ceiling.

Lawson grabbed one of the racks the pots and pans were on, rolled it to the edge of the wall closest to the hallway and climbed up to the ceiling. The walls of the hallways were wood frame and stud construction with drywall sheets making up the surface of the walls. Pushing up the ceiling tile closest to the wall, he moved it out of the way and climbed up to stand on the wall support. He had each man pass their weapons and materials up to him as each man came up, then handed the weapons and materials back to each one as they got to the top of the wall support.

Lawson could hear the wall support creak as the last man got up and it was obvious that this was not a load-bearing wall which, to Lawson's observation, would not hold their weight for long. He instructed them to spread out on the wall support to reduce the stress and not step on the metal frames holding the ceiling tiles as the frames would not support them. He also told them not to rely on the wires holding the ceiling tiles to support their full weight. He could hear guards running all over the place while the alarms were continuing their racket. Lawson pushed the rack away from the wall and put the ceiling tile back in its place.

It was dark above the false ceiling. There were little dots of light where the ceiling tiles had small holes that were part of the tile texture. Enough light was present to make out the wall support they were standing on. Lawson could also see the wall support for the wall across the hallway from where they were standing. He knew it was a long jump but by using the false ceiling support wires as a balancing tool, he could get to the other wall support. He knew each of the men had to make the jump and if one of them lost their balance, the person doing so would probably go crashing through the false ceiling and end the whole effort.

Lawson motioned the others to follow him. He handed his weapons and belt to Gunny, grabbed one of the ceiling support wires for balance and jumped across the area above the hallway to the other wall support. He caught himself at the edge of the wall support and repositioned himself. He reached out to Gunny and grabbed his weapons and belt. One by one, each person did the same until everyone was standing on the other wall support but was spread out to reduce the pressure on the wall. Taylor provided a moment of panic as he started to fall backward when he landed on the wall support. Both Myers and Gunny caught him by the shirt and pulled him to the upright position on the support. Everyone stopped for a moment to catch their breath and to slow down their racing hearts.

Walking along the wall support while using the wire supports to help him keep his balance, Lawson struggled moving while carrying several rifles and the added weight of the ammo in the pouches on his web belt. He had to move slowly to ensure the rifles wouldn't swing against each other which would result in making enough noise to give away their position. He saw another wall support that was perpendicular to the support he was on going to the left and followed it. The alarms had stopped but there were a lot of people running around. The other men followed Lawson, careful not to step off the wall support. Gunny followed up the rear with the backpack of tools on his back, his AK-47, ammo pouches around his waist and the twenty-pound bag of explosives and grenades.

After several steps, Lawson saw another wall support perpendicular going to the right of one he was on. That would be the Commander's office. He stopped at that point and motioned the others to stop. Lawson moved down the adjoining support to what he calculated was the center point of the Commander's office. Lawson listened for a moment then whispered, "This is the Commander's office." Everyone nodded and followed Lawson while still spread out along the walls.

Lawson handed the rifles to Myers, slowly pulled up the ceiling tile closest to the wall of the Commander's office and looked down. He was right above the Commander's desk with the Captain's desk to the right, next to the adjoining wall. He was just getting ready to move the tile out of the way when he could hear keys going into the lock. Immediately, he put the ceiling tile back into position, hoping that none of the particles falling from the tile could be seen by the person coming in.

The person spoke in Farsi but Lawson could tell it was Captain Behzadi. The door to the office closed and desk drawers started opening. "Strange," Lawson thought, "It sounds like Behzadi is in Commander Rouhani's desk."

Moments later, the door opened again and an angry exchange took place. Lawson found a small hole in the tile where he could partially see what was going on. There was a soldier holding Behzadi's right arm and it appeared someone was also holding his left arm. Suddenly Rouhani came into view as he was motioning for the Captain to be escorted out. They all left the room except for Rouhani and another guard. Rouhani said something to the guard, at which point, the guard stepped out of the room and closed the door. Taylor moved around Myers and toward Lawson and whispered in his ear, "The Commander has placed Behzadi under arrest. The Commander told the guard he wasn't to be disturbed under any condition."

CHAPTER 8 -- July 31, 2015, 1:10 AM – Iran Time

Lawson pulled out the Maxim 9 pistol from his waist. He quickly lifted the ceiling tile as Rouhani looked up to see what was causing the noise. Lawson immediately pointed his weapon at Rouhani. Taylor whispered to him in Farsi not to move as Taylor pointed his AK-47 at Rouhani while Lawson climbed down into the room. Then one by one, each person climbed down from above, quietly passing all the weapons down. Lawson put his pistol in his belt and told Taylor to find out what he could from Rouhani. "Keep it in low whispers," was Lawson's instructions. Taylor would question Rouhani, then repeat in whispers what Rouhani said. During the interrogation, a muffled sound of gunfire was heard.

"Ask Rouhani what that was," Lawson queried. Taylor said something in Farsi to Rouhani and after Rouhani answered, Taylor said, "They're just checking their weapons."

After about ten minutes of questioning, Myers motioned to Lawson to move with him. Lawson walked over to a corner of the office to see what Myers wanted.

"We'll have to find a way to get them off of the alert," Lawson stated.

Myers shook his head in agreement then whispered, "That's not what I wanted to talk to you about." Lawson stood waiting for Myers to continue. "Taylor's not telling the truth in what Rouhani is saying," Myers stated. Lawson squinted at Myers' comment.

"How do you know what is being said?" Lawson asked.

"I can speak and write Farsi but I don't want anyone else knowing that," Myers explained. "Half of what Rouhani has said is changed by Taylor. Rouhani said that the gunfire was Behzadi being executed while Taylor said they were checking their weapons."

Lawson began to see a pattern that was disconcerting. He had doubts about Taylor but now they were becoming clearer. He also began to wonder about Myers. Was Gunny waving his hands on board the plane to stop Myers from telling Lawson where he came from indicative of Myers being more than just an electronic tech, maybe instead being an agent of one of the three-letter alphabet intelligence agencies? Lawson took the Maxim 9 pistol from his belt, walked over to Rouhani and pointed the weapon at Rouhani's head.

"Wait," Rouhani whispered in English, "you don't want to do that! I can help you."

Lawson swung the weapon around to Taylor as Taylor's hand moved toward the mike on the radio. Lawson pulled the trigger, followed instantly by a 'Phfut' sound as the bullet struck Taylor in the forehead. Gunny caught Taylor's falling body before it hit the floor as Gunny gave Lawson a questioning look.

The guard outside the door began to move. Lawson grabbed the stapler on the desk and slammed it down hard as though he was stapling a stack of paper. He rustled some more paper and hit the stapler again. He stopped and waited. The guard had apparently bought the sound as that of a stapler. They could hear the butt of the guard's rifle hit the ground indicating he had gone back to his normal guarding position.

"What did you do that for?" Gunny exclaimed in a whispering voice. "Why did you shoot Taylor?" Lawson stood for a moment gathering his thoughts.

"Taylor had the radio and the mike was next to his mouth," Lawson quietly explained. "It's obvious that Taylor is working from a different agenda. I couldn't risk giving Taylor time to key the mike because that's all he would need to do to bring the whole house down on us. We'd be captured before we even started."

Lawson looked at Rouhani.

"You're the inside man," Lawson said while looking Rouhani up and down. Rouhani then spoke, "Yes, I'm the inside man. And if we don't get moving, you're not going to finish your mission. It's already 01:25 hours. We've got to get to the vault."

Rouhani picked up the phone and said something in Farsi. Lawson looked at Myers. "The alert is over," Myers said. "He's ordered everyone back to their stations." As Myers was speaking, Rouhani opened the top drawer to his desk and turned on a flat screen monitor.

"This is tied to the camera in the Security Center," Rouhani said while watching the monitor. "The soldiers in the security center are watching everyone go back to their stations. In about five minutes, the soldiers in the center will go back to playing their card game and the monitors in the center will be ignored for the most part. This is their practice every night after about midnight."

Those in the Commander's office could hear the guard outside of Rouhani's office move from the door back to his station. Just then the phone rang. Rouhani answered the phone, had a brief conversation then hung up the phone.

"They wanted to know what to do with the dead soldier in the galley," Rouhani explained. "I told them to take his body to the Training Area and lay his body next to Behzadi's."

They waited approximately five minutes then proceeded to the door of the office. As everyone was leaving the office, Rouhani reached into his desk and pulled out a cellphone and a jump drive. He took one last look at the monitor in his desk drawer to see that the security people in the Security Center had gone back to their card game. Lawson went to Behzadi's desk, rifled through a bunch of files until he found the file he was looking for. Once he found it, he tucked it under his robe.

"The vault is down at the end of the hall to the left once we go out the door," Rouhani motioned. "Give me the gun with the silencer," Everyone looked at Lawson. Lawson seemed unsure about fulfilling the request but, after looking at Myers and seeing his response that it was OK, he handed Rouhani the weapon.

Lawson checked his watch. It was 1:35 AM. They walked down the hallway toward the vault and saw that the vault door was partially open. Rouhani stepped into the vault, a couple of words were exchanged then the 'phfut' sound of the weapon firing. Lawson stepped into the vault.

"Help me keep this man on the chair," Rouhani whispered. "If he leaves the chair, alarms will go off!"

Lawson jumped forward to help Rouhani hold the man in place. The dead soldier was in a Senior Sergeant Russian uniform. Rouhani was looking across the hallway at the other vault door to see if there was any movement. The vault door was almost completely closed. No movement from the other side.

"Give me the duct tape," Lawson called out to the others in a loud whisper. A moment later, a roll of duct tape was handed to

Lawson. Lawson wrapped the duct tape around the Russian soldier and the chair while Rouhani held him in place.

Lawson looked over the security room. There was a desk to the side where the Russian soldier was sitting and taped into his chair. The room was painted in white with a gray linoleum tile floor. The vault door was a heavy bank-type rectangular door with two steel rods built into each of the four sides of the door that would slide into holes in the door frame once the door closed. The other end of the security room had a metal door that was closed. According to Myers, the metal door would open when the vault closed. The security room was small, six feet wide and twelve feet long.

Once they finished strapping in the Russian soldier, they motioned to Myers to move forward. Myers came to the security room carrying the backpack with the mechanic's stuff inside. He quietly sat the bag down and examined the frame of the vault. "It's like all the other ones," he whispered.

Myers pulled out the rolled-up magnetic strip and proceeded to lay it around the frame of the vault. "The metal frame will hold the strip," Myers whispered. "The areas where the sensors are located have no metal above them but the rest of the frame is steel which should hold the magnetic strip in place. This strip should activate all of the sensors since the sensors need a magnetic field to switch them on. The electronics then senses that the door is closed."

After Myers put the magnetic strip around the door, he pressed down on a small piece of metal extending just below one of the vault's hinges and put the duct tape over it.

"That's the hinge switch that tells the electronics that the door is completely closed," Myers stated as though he was teaching a class. Myers continued, "The hinge switch still allows for the second door to open even if one of the sensors fail. A failing

sensor will turn on an indicator light on the control panel in a
security monitoring area. Since we should have no failing
sensors, there will be no warning given to the security people. If
we didn't press the hinge switch, the second door would not
open. The door's electronic logic should not care about the
sequence of the button being pushed and then the sensors being
tripped followed by the hinge switch being activated like some
bank doors do. This manufacturer is French and I happen to
know that they just check the switches and sensors to be
activated but they don't care in what order. They just care that all
of the necessary switches and sensors have been activated. Now,
there should be a button underneath the guard's desk. It'll be
close to the edge where the guard can easily reach it." Lawson
looked under the desk and found the button. He looked to Myers
at which Myers nodded his head 'Yes'. Lawson pushed the
button and the second door opened.

Lawson watched the vault door in case there were other
switches. At the same instance the second door started opening,
the vault door didn't move but the locking bars moved out from
the door with a 'clang'. Everyone turned to look toward the other
vault door at the other side of the hallway. Nothing moved.

Gunny was the first person inside the office area beyond the
vault security area. There were six doors. Lawson looked down
the hall at the doors. "We want the fourth door," he said while
wondering how they would be able to get the office door open.

It had a standard keyed lock. Lawson recognized the lock
maker was an American one, causing him to smile for a moment
at the observation. He noted a name was on the door written in
Russian but was sure he had the right room. The lock was still an
issue.

Gunny, knowing what was disturbing Lawson, smiled, then
stated, "Lift me up." Lawson and Myers both looked up at what
he was looking at. Inside the vault was a false ceiling. By lifting

Gunny up, he could remove a ceiling tile from the hallway and another from the inside of the office and climb into the office. Lawson didn't fancy lifting a man of Gunny's size up and over the wall into the office. After a couple of words, Rouhani and Lawson lifted him up. Gunny removed the ceiling tile, made some motions on the other side of the wall and disappeared. Seconds later, the door was opened.

Lawson stepped in and looked around. There was one wooden desk on the left side of the room situated near a white board that covered the full length of the wall. The white board was covered with diagrams, formulas and comments. Against the wall opposite the door was a filing cabinet. There were three computers of different types on a table next to the filing cabinet all in the process of running programs. There was no camera in the room. The room was painted white with fluorescent lights built into the ceiling. The room smelled of old tobacco smoke.

Lawson grabbed a small slot screwdriver out of the backpack and went to the right hand desk drawer. As he was getting ready to force the lock on the drawer Myers tapped him on the shoulder and pointed to wires coming out of the back leg of the desk and going into the floor.

"The desk is wired, probably with explosives," Myers stated while examining the wires. Lawson moved to the back of the desk.

"What if we take the back off?" he said while motioning with the screwdriver. Myers looked closely at the back then shifted his gaze to Lawson.

"Good idea," Myers answered. "But do it slowly and let me see if anything looks like it's attached." Lawson agreed and proceeded to slowly remove the back of the desk.

"Save the nails," Lawson ordered while he removed the back. "We want to put everything back as it was before we got here if we can and don't touch the filing cabinet until we finish here."

Rouhani moved toward the vault door. He disappeared for approximately a minute then came back in pulling a body with him. "It's the roving sentry," Rouhani said. "Help me get him in here."

Myers and Rouhani pulled the sentry into the vault security area where the other dead guard was strapped to the chair. Rouhani got on his phone and after a couple of moments gave some instructions over the phone.

"I've informed the security people that the roving sentry was reporting to me until everything settles down. We should have no trouble with more surprises," Rouhani said while walking back to the scientists' office area. Lawson looked back to Myers. Myers nodded his head 'yes' and everyone proceeded with the efforts in the office.

With the back off of the desk, Lawson gingerly felt around the top drawer. He pulled out a pack of Russian cigarettes and a lighter from the main space inside the drawer, both which he placed on the desk. Feeling around the top drawer further, his fingers came upon a couple of trays and some metal pieces that could only be keys. Noting where he got the keys from, he pulled them out and examined them.

One of the keys was obviously for the file cabinet. Myers was busy examining the outside of the cabinet as Lawson threw the keys to Rouhani. Something made Lawson stop.

"Wait, before using the key," Lawson declared. He walked over to the cabinet and began to feel around.

"What's wrong?" Myers asked. Everyone else stopped to see what was bothering Lawson.

"Think about this," Lawson replied. "Here is the most important information in the whole facility. Whatever they're doing in the lab, the results are stored here. Is one little key all that separates that information from someone that has access?" Gunny and Myers both looked at each other.

"He's right," Gunny concluded. Myers took a closer look at the cabinet. He felt around the edges and the handles. The top drawer handle had a release strip on the back of the handle. He didn't press it.

"We have a problem," Myers declared. "This handle has a switch on it. My guess is that it has to be pressed and the key turned within about five seconds or the switch has to be pressed for more than five seconds before the key can be turned." Myers looked around for the predicament to sink in. "We have a 50/50 chance of doing the right thing."

"If we are wrong," Gunny asked, "what happens?"

"We'll all know what heaven looks like while we pet sheep and tune harps," Myers replied.

After the quiet laughter subsided, Lawson told everyone to leave the vault. "This is my mission and I'll take the risk," he said while motioning for the cabinet keys from Rouhani. Everyone else except Myers stepped outside of the vault while Lawson analyzed the situation.

"It seems to me," Lawson stated, "that the natural motion for a person to do is to grab onto the handle while turning the key in order to pull open the drawer as soon as the cabinet is unlocked."

Myers broke into Lawson's thought, "If what you are saying is true, you must have a delay required before opening the cabinet. You have to figure that five seconds is only a guess. It could be ten or fifteen seconds." Lawson saw the logic in Myers argument.

"If there is a window of time," Lawson continued, "it would create more danger for the person opening the cabinet if they had to do it within a set period of time because most people don't have a real sense of the passage of time. My guess is that the longest a person can count accurately on the amount of time is approximately 10 seconds. I don't think there would be an end time to the wait, only a delay until you turn the key after hitting the switch in the handle. However, it seems to me that the key needs to be turned first before the switch in the handle is pressed. The reason is that if a person were to grab the cabinet handle first and then realize they've got to put the key in, they could accidently bypass the security delay and get in even though they are not authorized. However, a delay after putting the key in and turning it then pressing the handle it is less likely to be bypassed." Myers agreed then left the room.

Lawson spoke a short prayer, put the key in the lock, turning it to unlock the cabinet. He counted until he was past 20 then pressed the switch in the handle. He heard two clicks and the drawer opened. His next thought was about what they will need to do to close and lock the cabinet. A problem for later.

Lawson walked out of the room to the entrance of the vault and motioned everyone back in. Once they were all back in the room, Rouhani walked over to the cabinet, looked in the top file drawer then pulled open the second drawer. He was about to close the top drawer when Myers grabbed his hand.

"If the top drawer has a switch," Myers observed, "it would behoove us not to close the drawer all the way." Rouhani agreed and reached into the second drawer.

He withdrew a courier pouch from the drawer and as he pulled his hand out, Lawson responded "That's it!" The pouch had been sealed with a wire and lead seal. The question was how to open the courier pouch without damaging the wire or the seal.

Myers came up with a solution to the pouch seal problem. He grabbed the lighter off of the desk and motioned to everyone to listen. "We can use the lighter to melt the solder around one of the ends of the wire seal," he started. "We can't heat the wire that's part of the seal because that will discolor the wire and they will know someone has been tampering with it. I propose that we take a small piece of trip wire, heat it up to melt the lead at the side where the wire goes in and pull out one of the ends of the wire embedded in the seal." It seemed like a reasonable solution. Lawson looked at his watch. It was 2:15 AM.

Myers took a pair of pliers out of the backpack, tore a small piece of cloth from his t-shirt and, using wire cutters from the backpack, cut a short piece of trip wire. Next he took the pliers, placed the cloth in the plier's teeth and put the trip wire in between the layers of cloth in the pliers.

"Using the cloth in the pliers will allow for the trip wire to get hot without the heat being drained off by the metal of the pliers," He instructed as he grabbed the lighter and proceeded to heat the trip wire while holding the trip wire against the entry point of the wire seal. The opening melted quickly. A small drip of molten lead fell from the seal which Myers quickly caught in the drawer.

The wire separated from the seal. The pouch could be opened. Myers pulled the wire and seal from the pouch and inspected the lead seal. The logo was intact with no damage done to the roundness of the seal. He sat it aside and opened the pouch.

Lawson reached into the pouch and pulled out a document. It was 18 pages with lots of diagrams, formulas and comments. Lawson looked up at the whiteboard. Some of the material in the document was the same as on the whiteboard but he also noted that some of the formulas didn't match. Although it seemed that they may have the wrong information, something told him that the information in the sheets of paper was important enough to keep even if they weren't the real formulas. Myers looked over the differences between what was in the papers and what was on the whiteboard and agreed. "Anyone can see the formulas on the whiteboard but only the person controlling the file cabinet would be able to see the information on the papers. It's likely the scientist forgot to update the information on the white board or didn't need to."

Rouhani handed Lawson the cellphone. Lawson passed the cellphone to Myers and told him to take pictures of each page, ensuring that each page was legible in each photo. He also instructed him to use the external memory on the cellphone and not the cellphone memory for the photos. Then Lawson grabbed an eraser and wiped the whiteboard clean.

Lawson looked at his watch again. It was 2:30 AM. Time was running out. He knew that people would start moving around in about an hour.

While Myers was taking the pictures, Lawson talked to Rouhani and Gunny. "We have about an hour before we need to get out of the facility. It'll take us ten minutes to get everything back in order. What can we do to get out of the facility?" Lawson left Rouhani and Gunny to talk it out.

Myers was just finishing taking photos of the pages, courier pouch and seal. He handed the phone to Lawson and proceeded to put the document back in the pouch and reseal the wire and lead piece. He used the lead that had dripped out to finish the seal so that a person couldn't tell the seal had ever been broken. Myers then closed and locked the cabinet.

Lawson finished looking over each of the photos and verified that the photos were on the external memory. He took the memory chip out of the phone, put the chip in his pocket and handed the phone back to Myers. It was at that moment Lawson noticed the cabinet was closed.

"How did you figure out what to do for the sequence to close the cabinet?" Lawson asked.

Myers smiled then answered. "I figured that no one was concerned about a person closing the cabinet only opening it. I just closed the drawers and turned the lock, here's the keys. By the way, you wanted to leave the room exactly as we found it so why did you erase the whiteboard?" Lawson looked at the whiteboard and realized that he hadn't thought of all of the possibilities. He realized that it was an amateur mistake and something he was not prone to do.

Lawson took the keys, lighter and cigarettes, placing them back in the top drawer of the desk where he found them. Then, Lawson and Myers put the back of the desk on and nailed it in place. Next, they replaced the ceiling tiles, picked up all of their materials and did one last check before locking and closing the door to the office.

They stepped out into the vault security area where Myers pushed the button under the dead soldier's desk to close the inner security door. The bars in the door slammed back into the vault door with a bang. Everyone stopped and looked at the other vault door across the hall. There was no movement. Once the inner security door was closed, Myers removed the duct tape holding the vault door switch and the magnetic strip around the vault door frame. As he removed the tape from the door hinge switch, Myers checked to make sure there was no duct tape residue on the switch. No need to give anyone suspicions that they had made it through the inner security door.

CHAPTER 9 -- July 31, 2015, 2:40 AM – Iran Time

Rouhani stepped out of the vault and into the vault on the other side of the hallway. Another 'Phfut' sound caught Lawson running into the vault Rouhani had just entered. Myers was right behind Lawson with the duct tape which Rouhani and Lawson used to tape the Russian soldier in the chair. Once they finished securing the soldier, Lawson turned to Rouhani.

"What are you doing? Are we just going to run around killing everyone in sight?" Lawson angrily queried. Rouhani smiled while Gunny grinned.

"You asked us to have a plan to get out," Rouhani explained. "It's dark outside. Myers has natural camouflage, he's black with black hair. The rest of us have light skin and blond or light brown hair. There's a full moon tonight. We'll look like a beacon against the night. Plus, how are you going to get past the guards at the main entrance without a major confrontation?" Lawson began to see the problem but he still didn't see how killing the guard in lab vault security would solve the problem.

Gunny continued the explanation, "We need something dark to cover us. According to the Colonel, the berthing area at the back of the lab is where four Iranian women sleep. Just outside the sleeping area is where they hang their chadors and scarves."

Lawson listened for a moment then asked, "What's a chador?"

"It's a loose-fitting piece of outer clothing that drapes a woman like a tent," Rouhani explained. "With that and the scarf around the nose and mouth, called a niqab, they cover themselves in public. The clothing here is usually black. We can dress up in the clothing to keep from being seen in the dark. It will appear to the guards that I'm escorting the women out for some fresh air, which will be you guys. It will also allow us to hide the weapons and materials under the chadors when we leave. We just have to make sure the weapons don't bang against each other and that the outer clothing covers the weapons well enough to not be discovered." Lawson nodded agreement while Myers was putting the magnetic strip on the door and the duct tape over the door switch. Once more the bars in the vault door extended with a clang sound when he pushed the button under the guard's desk.

Lawson watched while the inner security door to the lab opened. He stepped inside to see a single overhead light on. The far end of the lab was dark with just enough light to see a large metal plate hanging from the ceiling, its reflection making its presence known as it slowly swung: the swinging a result of the air conditioning system blowing air against the metal plate. The lab area was a long room that Lawson estimated to be fifty or more yards in length and approximately twenty-five yards wide. Under the light, there were numerous tables set up with small square mirrors, plates of metal with burn marks in them and a unit the size of a small refrigerator with a long rod and lenses protruding from the outside of the unit pointing toward the first set of mirrors that were highly reflective and had a strange, prismatic effect to them. It was obvious to Lawson that this was the laser system. He also noted there were servos attached to the mirrors. The servos were small motors that moved in very small steps. These servos were set to such fine settings that they could move in microns of an inch of movement. Lawson made a quick calculation of the servo capabilities and a mental note that the laser could be set to hit a target the size of an airplane at forty-five miles away. Definitely something far in advance of anything the U.S. had. He also noted that there was a frequency generator next to the laser system. Lawson turned on the frequency generator and made notes on the twenty preset settings of the frequencies on the generator. Myers was looking over the laser system and noted the frequency generator as well. They both wondered why it was hooked up to the laser system. Myers observed that the preset frequencies may have some relationship to the type of atmosphere the laser beam had to pass through as the frequencies matched up to different frequencies in the light spectrum. They also noted that the laser system was built in such a way as to make it mobile, probably to do outside testing.

As Lawson continued to look at the setup of the laser system, he noted that there were metal tubes running to the laser setup. Following the tubes back to their source, he found that there was a complex arrangement of valves that were connected to two large thermal containers standing eight feet high and approximately five feet in diameter. The symbols on labels on the containers indicated that they were filled with liquid nitrogen. From Lawson's assessment he determined that they had serious heat problems with the lasers and the liquid nitrogen was used to cool down the internal system.

He saw a cabinet sitting against the same wall as the entrance, about 10 feet from the door. Pointing to the space on the opposite side of the cabinet away from the door, he instructed Myers, "Put the 20 pounds of C-4 here and wire it however you can so that opening the door will set off the charge." Myers nodded and proceeded to get the explosives out of the bag he was carrying.

"Why destroy this room?" Rouhani inquired.

"If we leave this room intact," Lawson explained, "the Russians will have no problem reproducing the tests. They will have the document with the formulas redone within a week so destroying the lab means that they have to start from scratch. Now I've got to clear the way for our exit. I'll be back shortly," Lawson said while moving toward the lab exit.

While the Myers was in the process of setting up the charges and Gunny went to get the clothing needed for the escape, Lawson took the Maxim 9 pistol from Rouhani and proceeded out of the vault and down the hall. He turned right into the yellow hallway then left into the hall going to the main entry area.

Watching for the guards at the entrance, Lawson arrived at the door that should be the Communications Center. Taking out the badge and the keys he had taken off the first guard that Gunny had shot in the galley, he took one key, put it in the lock of the door and slowly put pressure on the key to turn it. Nothing moved. He took the next key and put it in the lock and tried the same thing. The key moved slightly.

Lawson stopped the pressure on the key and swiped the badged against the pad by the door. He immediately turned the key. The door unlocked. Lawson pushed the door open. A quick glance around the room brought him to recognize the red button on the wall: The emergency alert button. Lawson pointed the weapon to the head of the man closest to the button and fired. The man fell forward onto the communications control console. Two other men were sitting at communication's units with headphones on as he fired at each one of them. Lawson noted both were sitting back with no conversation going on and the shots were terminal.

The room was dark with small lights over the transmitters and receivers. Lawson pulled out his watch. '6.75 Mhz' was inscribed on the back of the watch. Lawson moved over to a transmitter that was obviously used for short wave communications and dialed the frequency into the unit.

"Coffee Rabbit Fifty this is Tango Bulldog, do you copy?" Lawson said while pressing the transmit button. He waited about ten seconds and tried again. "Coffee Rabbit Fifty this is Tango Bulldog, do you copy?" Lawson realized he was running out of time. He looked at the watch. 'It's 3:00 AM," he thought to himself. Too much left to do.

He was about to set the headset down when he heard, "Tango Bulldog this is Coffee Rabbit Fifty."

Lawson responded, "Coffee Rabbit Fifty code word."

There was silence for a moment then the response came back, "Code word two-three-zero Sirloin."

With the code word verified Lawson responded, "Code word Red Dawn two-three." Again silence for a moment.

The voice at the other end continued, "Did you get the gift?"

"Affirmative," Lawson answered, "Though we had one casualty."

"Was it Taylor?" came the inquiry.

"It was," Lawson confirmed. "I need a pickup point." Lawson looked around the room for a map. On the wall to his left was a large map of the area that appeared to cover approximately a twenty-five mile radius. He never knew of a communications center that didn't have a map. Lawson pulled the map from the plastic sheet that was covering it, careful not to damage the map.

Moments later the radio came alive again. They proceeded to give Lawson coordinates for pickup and a pickup time of 22:00 hours local time July 31st. That's tonight. Lawson marked the coordinates and confirmed the location and time. "That's 10:00 PM, 19 hours from now," he thought while he switched off the radio and switched the frequency back to its original setting.

Lawson went to some cabinets on the same wall as the door. Opening the cabinets, he looked at the front displays of nine video recorders. Each recorder showed approximately three hours left of recording time. Pressing the menu button, he selected the total time recording and saw that it was approximately twenty-one hours of recording already done. That would put the time they started recording at 6:00 AM yesterday. That means that these were the only DVD's with his or the other team members pictures. He pressed buttons on each of nine video recorders and pulled out the DVD's in each unit. He pulled the folder from his belt and put the DVD's in the folder he had taken from Captain Behzadi's desk. Next, he folded up the map and put it in the folder and slipped the folder inside his waist band. The folder was getting bulky so he tightened his rope belt even tighter to keep the folder from slipping.

Lawson opened the door to the Communications Center just enough to look out and see where the entrance guards were located. Neither guard was in sight. Lawson stepped out of the Communications Center, closed the door and moved to the next door toward the entrance. This would be the Security Control Center.

Watching for the entrance guards, Lawson slipped one of the keys in the door lock and put some slight pressure on it. It started to turn. He took the badge once more and swiped the badge then turned the key. The door opened. Holding the Maxim 9 pistol in his hand, he stepped into the room and closed the door. The guards were sitting at a table with cards in their hands. One guard started to lunge toward the red button on the wall when Lawson shot him twice. He fired in quick succession at each of the men at the table, hitting the last man as the man was pulling his weapon from his holster.

Looking at his weapon, Lawson saw that the receiver on his weapon was locked to the open position. Lawson pulled the clip from the weapon. It was empty. He had forgotten to keep a count of the rounds in the weapon. If the weapon was empty before he shot the last person, he would have been dead. "Lucky me," he thought.

He put the empty clip in his pocket, slipped the loaded clip into the pistol and slammed the receiver forward. The cartridge going into the chamber on the weapon didn't feel right. He pulled the receiver of the weapon back which seemed to pull back a lot harder than he remembered. The cartridge came out and dropped to the floor. As it did so the next bullet went smoothly into the chamber. He picked up the cartridge from the floor noting it appeared to be slightly deformed. He remembered that this was the cartridge he used to hold up the block of cement. "Stupid, me," he thought while dropping the cartridge on the floor. "I should have thought about the fact that the bullet would be damaged from the weight the cement block put on it. That's two mistakes that could have put an end to this effort." Thinking about his mistakes, Lawson walked around the room checking that each man was dead.

In the back of the room were nine monitors built into the wall. In the center of the room was a center console with controls for switching screens and controlling the movement of the cameras. To the left of the room was a large map on the wall of the facility with the camera numbers labeled on it. Next to the map was the red emergency alert button. To the right of the room was the table where the four men were playing cards and at the back of the room on the right side was a doorway that Lawson remembered was where twenty security guards slept. The door appeared to open into the room so Lawson took one of the chairs and positioned the top of the chair under the doorknob and the feet of the chair forced into indentations in the floor so that the door could not be opened.

Next, he went to the two monitors that were displaying the view of the cameras showing the outside of the front entrance of the facility. Looking at the map on the wall, he found the two cables associated with the cameras to the console. He pulled the cables from the back of the console and pushed them down into holes in the floor. Next, he pulled the two monitors that had been showing the camera views of the outside cameras out from the wall. Taking the cords off the back of each monitor, he shoved the cables into openings in the wall and pushed the monitors back into position. He estimated that it would take them at least fifteen minutes to figure out that the views for the cameras were disconnected at two points.

As he was getting ready to exit the Security Control Center, he noticed a number of keys hanging on the wall. They appeared to be vehicle keys. Lawson took all of the keys and put them in his pocket. He opened the door of the Security Control Center just enough to look out and check for the entrance guards. He could see one guard walking from the right to the left across the inside of the main door so he waited for the guard to move out of view. Once assured he could get out of the room without being seen, he exited the room, going quietly back to the vault. He checked his watch. 3:10 AM.

While Lawson was gone from the vault, Myers had packed down the C-4 explosives against the lower part of the wall with a hand grenade tied to a railing in the middle of the explosives. He attached two wires to the hand grenade pin and ran the wires to the inner vault door.

The first wire was placed over the top of the cabinet and ended at the entrance to the door where the end of the door would be when the door was closed. The second wire was routed across the top of the ceiling, over the emergency light at the door entrance and hung down at the other end of the door where the door surface would be when it was open.

Myers took off his belt buckle, the standard friction type belt buckles used in the military. The cloth belt would go into the buckle smoothly but would grab at the cloth when pulled the other way. This was accomplished by a roller in the buckle that would open wider when the belt went into the buckle but would close and get tighter the more the belt was pulled the other direction.

He ran the second wire through the buckle and taped the buckle to the backside of the door using duct tape. The clearance was tight with the buckle and wire being taped about seven inches inside the leading edge of the door. This would prevent someone from being able to feel the buckle or wire if they felt around the back edge of the door. The buckle's distance from the edge of the door was farther than a person's fingers could reach.

By taping a piece of duct tape around the trip wire about eight inches before the buckle and looping the wire around the tape, he knew that if everything worked ok, the piece of tape on the wire would pass through the buckle when the door closed and would catch on the buckle when the door opened thereby pulling the pin from the grenade.

Myers tied a crescent wrench to the wire at the end opposite from the end tied to the grenade. The wrench would provide weight keeping tension on the wire while the wire went through the buckle when the door was closed and would keep the wire from moving when the door opened. This would allow for the taped part of the wire to get caught in the buckle, providing the tautness necessary to pull the pin when the inner security door opened. Myers was finished with the wiring job when Lawson came back.

As Lawson entered the vault, Myers had the inner door closed with both Rouhani and Gunny pulling on large screwdrivers to keep the inner door partially open.

"Don't force it open any farther. If you do it will set off alarms," Myers said while holding onto the end of a wire. It was the first of the two wires he ran to the inner security door. He took two pieces of duct tape and attached the wire to the end of the door. He then motioned Rouhani and Gunny to pull their screwdrivers from the door. When they did, the door slammed shut the last inch of movement. Everything was in place.

Myers explained the setup for the explosives to Lawson. "I have two sets of wires," he started. "The first wire will pull the pin as soon as the door is opened. Most likely, the wire will separate from the door before enough tension can be realized to pull the pin. This will hopefully convince the bad guys that this is the main setup for the booby trap. If the first wire works, the job is finished. If the bad guys are suspicious that the door has been wired and discover the first wire, I have a backup that will pull the pin when they think it's safe to open the door and the door goes back normally."

Lawson thought about the plan for a moment then asked, "Will it work?"

Myers grinned, "It should. The theory is good."

CHAPTER 10 -- July 31, 2015, 3:13 AM – Iran Time

Lawson looked at his watch. "It's nearing 3:15," he said while dumping out the tools from the backpack knowing that the security people seeing the tools on the floor would cause them to wonder if the team had gotten into the lab thus giving them a reason to immediately open the inner door.

"We need to go to the galley and get some items on our way out," Lawson continued. "Myers, I need for you to quietly sneak into the Security Control Center and be ready to push the entrance door button when the entrance guards ask for the door to be opened. Gunny and I will carry the weapons under our garbs. You'll need to wear the web belts with the grenades under yours. This is so that you can get into and out of the control center without making noise."

Lawson handed Myers the keys, the badge and the walkie-talkie taken from the guard killed in the Galley. "It's this key," Lawson explained as he showed Myers the key to use. "You have to turn the key within five seconds after swiping the badge. Otherwise, alarms will go off. Take your clothing with you and be ready to respond on the radio when they request to have the main door opened." Myers took the web belt with the grenade pouches from Gunny and strapped them around his waist then left.

Everyone except Myers went to the Galley. Lawson opened the cupboards and pulled out bread (it looked like pita bread) along with a roll of the cheese, a jar of peanut butter and six bottles of water. He put the food and water in the backpack then everyone put on the clothing that was taken from the lab area.

Gunny put the backpack on after lengthening the shoulder straps so that the backpack wouldn't be obvious under the chador. They hung the rifles and equipment from their shoulders and waists under the clothing, making sure they could walk slowly but normally without the weapons and equipment making noise. Everyone except for Colonel Rouhani was dressed in black as he was in his uniform.

The time for them to do or die had come as Lawson looked at his watch. It was 3:25 AM. All those that were dressed in black garb wrapped the veils around their faces to hide any possibility that they were all male. They proceeded to the entrance.

"I thought the guards had everyone strip down and submit to a search before they were allowed out of the building," Lawson remarked to Rouhani as they walked toward the doorway taking them to the entrance area.

Rouhani turned to Lawson and stated, "They do unless we're going out for some air. The outside guards watch to make sure that an Iranian officer is with anyone going outside, that nothing is dropped on the ground and that no marks are made on the pavement or dirt. They watch very carefully." Lawson nodded and proceeded forward.

"Everyone look down," Rouhani said as they entered the main entrance area. Rouhani said something in Farsi to one of the guards. The guard pressed the button on the mike and said something. A moment later, the main door opened.

Myers left the transceiver in the Security Control Center once he got the call to open the main door. He slipped out of the Security Control Center while the guards were watching the door open. No one noticed that he was black, which would have been unique though not unheard of as his impersonation of an Iranian woman. In his hand was a cellphone he had found in the Security Control Center. As they walked out of the entrance, the guard that requested the door to be opened pressed the mike button once more and said something in Farsi. Myers faced away from the guards as he pressed numbers on the cellphone while they walked to the outside. Once outside, he glanced around to see what the outside guards were doing. They were also staring at the main entrance door. The inside guard started to walk toward the Security Control Center just as the main door proceeded to start closing. He stopped, looked at the Security Control Center door for a moment then turned toward the main door as it closed.

Once the main door completely shut, Lawson pulled the Maxim 9 pistol from his belt out from under his chador and shot both outside guards.

"What are you doing?" Rouhani asked.

"First," Lawson responded, "The guards in the Control Center are dead. Second, the cameras here on the outside have been disconnected so no one inside knows what is going on out here. And, third, how are we going to be able to leave with the guards watching us?" Rouhani just turned and walked toward the ridge.

Lawson turned to Myers. "How did you get the main entrance doors to close. I thought we would have to get out with a shootout."

Myers lifted the cellphone and explained, "I figured the doors would have to be closed once we got out. I grabbed a book from the shelf, leaned it against a second cellphone I found. I set that cellphone to vibrate then positioned the setup over the button that opens and closes the main door. When I called the number, the vibration caused the book to fall, hitting the button."

Lawson was impressed. "What if it didn't work?" He questioned.

"Well," Myers replied, "I guess we would have had a shootout. By the way, don't you think we need to get out of here." They all agreed and proceeded to the ridge Lawson had stopped at the previous morning.

They got to the opposite side of the ridge, removed their weapons from under their garments, checked them to make sure they were loaded and stopped to rest. "We still have a mission to complete," Rouhani declared.

Lawson frowned and looked at Gunny and Myers. "Haven't we taken enough chances without stretching our luck," he stated while looking at the others.

"Their mission is just as essential," Rouhani explained. "There's a munitions storage dump ten miles north of here that is a temporary storage area for munitions and weapons being shipped to Gaza, ultimately to be used against Israeli cities. We have to destroy it. That's what the other team was supposed to do before they got caught." Lawson recognized the significance of the statement.

"How did you get caught?" Lawson asked, directing his question toward Gunny. Gunny settled back and quietly uttered, "They were a wait'n for us." Lawson felt a cold chill and knew it was not the night air. He posed the question to all of them, "If they knew you were coming, then what's the possibility they knew I was coming?" The question troubled them all.

Lawson asked himself about how much of this effort was a result of them being played and, if they were being played, who was doing the playing. "Was it a patrol you ran into?" Lawson queried.

"No," Gunny responded, "they were waiting there as though they knew exactly where we would be."

"Since we didn't know about these operations until two days ago and the number of people that knew about the operations were very limited, the only conclusion I can come up with is that we have a mole in the Irregular Warfare Center," Lawson remarked as the others nodded their heads in agreement.

"Well, it couldn't be Taylor," Gunny remarked. The others looked at Gunny waiting for him to continue.

"Why couldn't it be Taylor?" Lawson questioned while the others waited for Gunny's response.

Gunny looked at each of them then said, "Taylor knew about the mission but not about the timing. The soldiers that were waiting for us were there for not more than half an hour. I know this because, while they were putting wrist ties on us, they pushed me against the hood of one of the vehicles. It was still hot. They knew exactly when we were to arrive at that point so the mole has to be someone that has information that's up to date and is passing it to the Iranians and, maybe, the Russians, someone that has access inside the Kennedy Irregular Warfare Center."

Both Lawson and Myers looked at each other. Gunny's argument was the only explanation that made sense. Lawson also wondered why he heard no Irish accent in Gunny's explanation. Was he really Irish or was it just a cover and he was something else? Then Lawson wondered if he was getting paranoid about everyone. There seemed to be elements of each person's behavior that suggested that Lawson had every reason to be cautious.

No sooner had they considered the question of the other team's capture and the possibility of a mole when they could hear the sounds of a car pulling into the facility parking lot.

"That would be Dr. Polevsky," Rouhani declared. "He arrives precisely at 03:45 hours each morning. It appears he's going to have trouble getting in."

They could see Polevsky clear enough to tell that he was on his cellphone. It appeared that he had noticed the outside guards were both dead as he stopped and looked at them and was obviously talking to the people inside about his discovery. Immediately, the door opened, and as he walked in, the door closed again. As the door opened, Lawson and the others could hear the echoing sounds of alarms going off inside the facility. "I guess they've discovered the level of our destruction," Gunny said with a certain tone of accomplishment.

Lawson dug where he had buried his clothes and pulled out his work boots and jeans. He took off the shoes he was wearing and put the boots and jeans on. As he was removing the pants he had on he felt a bulge in his pocket. Reaching into his pocket he pulled out a handful of keys. "You said we've got to go ten miles to get to this munitions dump." Gunny got up to determine what got Lawson so excited. "Well," Lawson went on, "I've got the keys to all of their vehicles! Let's grab one." The impact of Lawson's statement hit everyone at the same time.

Once Lawson got dressed and put the chador and veil back on, they ran back over the ridge and down to the area where all the vehicles were parked while Lawson was running while trying to get the second boot on. Grabbing one of the military vehicles, they piled in with their weapons and the backpack. Lawson pulled a key from his hand and proceeded to try it. Gunny reached for Lawson's hand and took the keys while Lawson looked at him with some concern.

"This is the military," Gunny said calmly while handing the right key to Lawson. "The number on the vehicle matches the number on the key."

Lawson handed the key back to Gunny while saying, "You're driving." Gunny took the key and started the engine. As he was backing out, Rouhani observed, "You two act more like two married people instead of two team members." Everyone laughed as Gunny started forward down the road.

CHAPTER 11 -- July 31, 2015, 3:50 AM – Iran Time

When Dr. Polevsky entered the facility to the sound of alert horns going off, the door to the Security Control Center was open and soldiers were pulling bodies out of the room.

"We also found the guard in your office security area was shot as well as the guard for the lab security area," the entrance guard shouted to be heard above the alarms. Polevsky hurried down the hallways that got him to the security vaults. He entered the vault that went to his office. Ordering one of the soldiers to sit in the vault chair, Polevsky moved to have the access to his office area opened.

"We don't know if it's safe yet," one of the soldiers told Polevsky.

"It doesn't matter," Polevsky shouted, "Open the door!" The soldier in the chair pushed the button under the desk. The main vault door closed and the inner security door opened.

Polevsky went immediately to his office and opened the door. After a brief inspection, it appeared that nothing had been touched. At that moment, the alarms stopped. He sat down at his desk and opened the top desk drawer. There were his cigarettes, lighter and file keys in the same place. Taking the cigarettes, lighter and keys, he closed the drawer and pinched the center of his Russian-made cigarette.

Russian cigarettes are unique in that they have tobacco in one end with a long tube that, at the other end, goes into the person's mouth. Pinching the tube allows for the smoker to control the amount of smoke being drawn in when they inhale.

As he lit the cigarette and pinched the tube, he heard what sounded like a pin drop, very faint but distinctive. Getting out of his chair, he walked around the room looking for the source of the sound. On the floor, behind his desk was a small nail. Polevsky picked it up then looked at the back of his desk. Putting his fingers into the separation between the back panel and his desk, the panel came off easily, too easily.

Setting his cigarette into the ashtray, Polevsky grabbed the keys for the filing cabinet from his desk. As he did so he looked up to see that his whiteboard had been erased. Someone had definitely been in his office. Going over to the filing cabinet, he inserted the key into the cabinet lock, turned the key and counted to ten. He pressed the handle switch, opened the top drawer then the second drawer.

Pulling out the courier pouch, he examined the outside of the pouch for any tears or cuts. There were none. Next, he examined the wire and lead seal. It seemed normal. He stopped and took a closer look at the seal knowing there should be something of an opening on one side where the wire went in when the crimp was made. This seal has a melted look to the entryway to the seal. Someone had been in the pouch.

Polevsky returned the pouch to the drawer, closed the cabinet and smiled, realizing that it was most likely the Americans that got the information based upon the casualties he saw in the entrance area. Grabbing his cigarette, he walked across the hallway to the lab security vault. This concerned him. Had the intruders gotten in here? He figured they'd go after the document but why risk going into the lab as well.

The Russian soldier directing the team inside the lab vault turned to Polevsky. "Is everything OK in your office?"

"Yes," was Polevsky's response. "What are you doing here?" He inquired while watching two soldiers pry the inner security door open enough to see along the edge of the door.

"We're looking for booby traps, and it appears we have one," the Russian soldier said while gently peeling the duct tape from the end of the door without putting tension on the wire attached to it. As the two soldiers kept pressure on the screwdrivers to keep the inner door slightly open, the other Russian soldier felt around both the lower and upper areas for any other wires. He felt none.

"It appears to be safe," he said to Polevsky. "In case it isn't, why don't you stand out in the hallway away from the vault door." Polevsky moved out of the vault and stood in the hallway. The Russian soldier pushed the button under the guard's desk causing the vault door to close and the inner door to open.

Myers' rigged-slide mechanism caught the taped piece of wire and pulled the wire taunt resulting in the pin being pulled from the hand grenade. The Russian soldier stepped into the lab seeing that nothing had happened, not realizing there was a delay.

A moment later, the ensuing blast threw tables, chairs, equipment and cabinets across the room with some items propelling themselves into the opposite wall. The center of the room was cleared of any materials. The laser unit and associated equipment were destroyed, wrapped into a little ball that resembled some origami design. The two liquid nitrogen containers immediately ruptured, turning the whole room into a minus three-hundred degree chamber. The room was frozen in place.

As the charge had been set against the wall adjacent to the main hallway, the explosion also blew an eight-foot hole in the rebar-reinforced wall bordering the hallway. The blast with its associated concrete and metal debris shot out at supersonic speeds hitting Polevsky, throwing him across the hall and against the wall. He was killed instantly, dead before his body hit the floor. The man that had stepped into the lab area vanished while the others in the vault security area were killed, their bodies mangled from the compression of the explosion then frozen by the liquid nitrogen. The large metal plate that was slashed during laser testing while hanging at the far end of the lab was pushed through the wall of the Iranian women's sleeping room and into the berthing area where the off-duty security guards were sleeping followed by a freezing blast of nitrogen that froze everyone in their place. The devastation was immense and complete.

CHAPTER 12 -- July 31, 2015, 5:35 AM – Iran Time

While the events continued to take place in the research facility, Gunny had driven the vehicle about eight miles, moving slowly so as not to get surprised by any checkpoints. Lawson checked his watch. It was 5:37 AM. The sky was beginning to lighten up as sunrise was about thirty minutes away.

Lawson pulled out the folder and unfolded the map. Looking at the map, he noticed the road turned about sixty degrees about a half mile before the munitions dump. He found it curious that the munitions dump was penciled in. He mentioned the change in the road to Gunny.

"It's best if we park the vehicle somewhere before the turn and walk in," Gunny suggested. "That way we don't have to confront the gate guards until we know what we're facing."

"Take it slow," Lawson advised. "It's getting light enough to where the dust from the vehicle can be seen some distance away."

"Good point, got it," Gunny responded.

They arrived at the place to stop about fifteen minutes later. Lawson pulled the folder from his waistband and laid it on the floor of the vehicle while Gunny grabbed the binoculars. Lawson kept the map and climbed out first with the rest of the team following behind him. They walked parallel to the road about two hundred yards east of the road. The trees and bushes covered their movement from those at the gate of the munitions storage area.

After another 20 minutes, moving slowly and watching for any activity ahead, they came upon the munitions storage area. It was set up on a small hill that had been leveled resulting in a rise up to the storage area on all sides of approximately twenty-five feet with the road to the storage area sloping up to the entrance to the gate. The fence around the storage area had obviously been expected to be very temporary being that it was a chain-link fence made of components and fencing that had been used numerous times and it showed the wear.

On the inside of the fence, approximately ten yards from the corner of the fence that Lawson and his team were approaching was a makeshift shed with a window open. The shed had no power or air conditioning.

"That shed must get hot during the daytime," Lawson thought as they approached the bottom of the rise that went up to the corner of the fence. Rouhani motioned them to sit down. Beyond the shed inside the fence were large stacks of crates, boxes, spools and tubes. They removed their black clothing as the sun was just rising.

Rouhani whispered to them, "I'm going to go up to see how many are in the building. You all stay here until I get back. Lawson, give me the Maxim 9 pistol." Lawson handed him the weapon and motioned for Myers to go with him. Myers looked at Lawson for a moment with a confused look then followed Rouhani up the slope.

Lawson was still not trusting Rouhani and there were questions he was beginning to have about the whole set of circumstances at the research facility. He couldn't put his finger on it but something wasn't adding up. They sat and waited for almost twenty minutes. Once in a while, they could hear voices and the sound of someone communicating over some type of electronic gear that had a tinny-sounding speaker. The distance was too far for them to make anything out.

As the sun was rising higher above the horizon, Gunny tapped Lawson on the arm. Lawson looked at Gunny then where Gunny was pointing. Gunny had the binoculars up to his eyes and something had caught his attention. Lawson took the binoculars from Gunny and looked in the direction he was pointing. It was to the east. Lawson could see small streams of dust coming up from the ground and little black specks that were creating the dust. There was no wind so the dust was only visible because of the sun's rays passing through the dust. Lawson looked back to Gunny for an explanation.

Gunny whispered, "Most likely they're military vehicles moving very slowly. Almost like they're trying to drive someone in front of them to the west or they're moving slowly so as not to be detected." Lawson saw Gunny's logic.

"How far do you think they are?" Lawson asked while continuing to observe the movement.

"Fifteen to twenty miles and moving at about five miles an hour," was Gunny's response. Lawson thought this very strange as they appeared to be strung out in a line almost three miles wide. Lawson estimated that it was probably a battalion-strength force and was responding to a request by the security people at the research facility to find Lawson and his group.

Rouhani's and Myers' return broke Lawson's thought process. "Polevsky is dead," Rouhani whispered.

Myers then broke in, "The documents we photographed are fake. The real papers are sitting on the desk in this shed in a courier pouch. They are waiting for a Russian courier to come by chopper to pick up the papers at 09:15 hours. The chopper will be here in about three hours and ten minutes."

Lawson began to understand his feeling that things weren't right. There were two sets of documents. "There's one more thing," Rouhani stated, "The papers in the pouch in the shed is the only copy of the document." Lawson just realized his mission wasn't over.

"We have the opportunity to complete both missions at the same time," Gunny offered while continuing to scan the movement of the vehicles to the east. "We've got visitors about fifteen miles out moving very slowly this way," he added. Rouhani took the binoculars and looked where Gunny had been watching.

"It's a request for assistance move," Rouhani said while looking through the binoculars. "They're doing that in response to our escaping the research facility. They're driving forward slowly so that it makes it much more difficult for us to bypass the wall of vehicles and personnel coming toward us. My guess is that they're moving slow because they have a lot of people moving on foot and they want to keep everyone together so that they can keep the appearance of a net."

Lawson looked at Rouhani and was wondering, if this was a move to push Lawson's team in a particular direction, why was the force moving toward them at the ammo dump and not moving more to the south in the vicinity of the research center. Had someone tipped off the Iranians as to where Lawson's team would be.

Gunny asked for the Maxim 9 pistol from Rouhani to which Rouhani complied. "I'll be back shortly," was Gunny's comment as he ran at the bottom of the rise, parallel to the fence toward the far end of the munitions compound. Lawson looked at his watch. It was 6:15 AM.

Gunny passed stack after stack of munitions that covered almost one-hundred yards and at the other end of the fence, he could make out two sentries talking to each other. They stood next to racks of FAJR-5 missiles, neatly stacked four levels high.

Gunny recognized that these missiles were Iranian-built medium range missiles with the ability to do considerable damage in a populated area, the second largest missile in the Iranian inventory. Gunny waited for the security guards to move to a position where he could hit each of them in quick succession. Once they were in a position, he dispatched them with a single shot into each of them.

The team waited about fifteen minutes before Gunny came running back, careful not to make noise that could be heard in the shed.

"I took out the two sentries on the far side of the compound," Gunny said while tucking the weapon into his belt. "They had mikes on them. We need to get to the front guards before someone radios the sentries and realizes something is wrong."

As a group, they moved slowly along bottom of the rise near the fence toward the main gate. As they passed the shed they could hear two people talking in Farsi. The gate was about seventy-five yards from the corner where they had previously been. The ground sloped up to the road to the gate at a steep angle which allowed for them to get into position without being seen.

Gunny pulled the Maxim 9 pistol from his belt, lifted his head up to where he could see the gate guards. Raising the weapon, he methodically pulled the trigger twice, the quiet sound of each shot hitting each man in the head. The men fell with their rifles clattering on the ground.

Knowing the sound of the guns hitting the ground would draw some attention, Gunny jumped up and ran through the gate entrance and to the shed. He kicked the door open followed by the hushed sound of two shots. Lawson followed behind him and entered the shed.

The shed had one metal desk at the center of it with two chairs. There was one window to the back. The walls were wood with 2 by 4 lumber supports and just a simple flat wood roof. The floor was also wood with many of the floor boards warped and scored from long periods of use. The room was dusty with rays of the rising sun coming in highlighting the level of dust in the shed. There was a courier pouch on the desk along with a cell phone, an ashtray with a cigarette burning in it, two bottles of water and a half-eaten sandwich. The chair at the desk was laying on its side.

On the ground was a dead Iranian Colonel with an equally dead Russian Colonel sitting upright but motionless in the chair against the wall that was facing the front of the desk. Lawson walked over to the courier pouch and noticed there was no seal on the pouch. By this time Myers had come in and Lawson showed him the pouch.

"I forgot to tell you," Myers explained. "The pouch has no seal because the courier is supposed to inventory the pouch then put his seal on it. At least that's what I heard the Russian officer saying to the Iranian officer in Farsi. The Iranian Colonel also mentioned something to the Russian Colonel that the courier doesn't get the papers until the payment is confirmed. So from that comment, it appears that a monetary exchange must take place before the Russians get the plans. Maybe that force out there is coming to guarantee that the exchange takes place. They may be moving slow to allow the personnel on foot to keep up with the vehicles. After all, they did appear to leave early enough to make it here on foot by around 09:00 hours."

Lawson nodded his head in approval to Myers' observations as he picked up the cellphone off of the desk. "Did either one of you determine who they were speaking to on the phone?" he asked while looking at the call log on the phone. Neither Rouhani or Myers knew. Myers took the cellphone from Lawson and went through the log. It appeared that the cellphone belonged to the Russian officer as the call log was all in Russian. Since no one knew Russian, the cellphone was of little help.

Rouhani still had the binoculars. He stepped to the window and watched for the movement of the force coming their direction. He did not seem to agree with Myers' conclusion. "It's possible the unit coming toward us is tracking us from the cellphones," he observed while extending his hand. "Everyone give me your phones. I'll take them to the vehicle, drive them about five miles down the road and drop them off then bring the vehicle back here. That force out there should follow the signal of the phones." Lawson thought that might as well explain why the force was moving toward the ammo dump and not toward the research facility.

Everyone handed Rouhani their phones at which point Rouhani headed out of the door, through the gate and down the road. While Rouhani was walking down the road to the vehicle, Gunny headed for the munitions area to start setting up the explosives while Lawson and Myers walked away from the shed.

"Be sure to get about forty RPG rounds and three RPG launchers," Lawson called out to Gunny. Gunny raised his hand in acknowledgement as he headed into the storage area.

Lawson pulled the chip with the photos out of his pocket. "Now I wish I had one of the phones to look at the photos. Myers, did you get a photo of the seal impression on the pouch in Polevsky's office and do you remember what it was?" Myers nodded 'yes', reached into his pocket and pulled out a cellphone.

"You don't think I was going to leave us blind, do you?" he quipped while handing Lawson the phone. Lawson thought about the risk Myers was taking by keeping the phone. He surmised that the only number the Iranians should have is Rouhani's. Then he remembered that this was the phone Myers took out of the Command Center at the research facility. So it could be a phone the Iranians were tracking. He thought about the situation for a moment then determined that the risk of keeping this phone was small compared to the value of being able to look over the photos from the lab. Lawson took the phone, inserted the chip into the memory slot in the phone and pulled up the photos Myers had taken back at the facility.

Lawson scanned the photos until he came to the photo of the seal on the pouch. He could barely make out what looked like an American Indian standing with a bow in his right hand. Myers took a look at the picture. "I've seen this somewhere before," he said while zooming in on the seal. "Not sure where I did but it is very familiar. Something to do with MIT, but what?"

Lawson took the chip out of the phone and handed the phone back to Myers while putting the chip back in his pocket then proceeded back to the shed.

"Another thing bothers me," Lawson disclosed while walking with Myers toward the shed, "We haven't seen any helicopters around. It seems that being near the border and a large base just fifteen miles away, we should have seen choppers patrolling the area, particularly when they would be looking for us." Myers stopped at Lawson's comment.

Myers looked at Lawson then stated his concerns. "While we're talking about things that bother us, why is it that the courier pouch in Polevsky's office was sealed, yet the pouch being picked up by the Russian courier isn't being sealed until the courier gets it?" They were concerns that both men had to think about.

Myers turned his focus to Lawson's comment. Why weren't there helicopters out searching for them? That was one of many questions that rattled around in Myers' mind as he looked at the contents of the phone he had taken from the Command Center.

"Nothing unusual on this phone," he thought as he put the phone back in his pocket.

Lawson and Myers went out to help Gunny wire up the munitions dump. Gunny had already packed C-4 around the cases of rockets and missiles. There were stacks and stacks of them. Gunny was in the process of wrapping Primacord around the stacks of rockets with the C-4 explosives directly under the Primacord.

Lawson saw the reel of Primacord and remembered that the cord is made of a plastic explosive compound that detonates at a rate of 23,000 feet per second. A perfect tool for setting up disconnected charges to go off all at once.

"Where'd you get the C-4?" Lawson asked Gunny. Gunny pointed to a large stack of wooden cases, "There's close to four tons of the stuff over there. Apparently, the Iranians are getting rid of their older plastic explosives. They're handing off the old stuff to the Palestinians while the Iranians are replacing C-4 with the newer Semtex 10 explosives. By the way, these missiles are the newer ones the Iranians are making. I figure there's about three-hundred of them here. These babies can do some serious damage if they land in cities. Why would the Iranians be giving these to the Palestinians unless the plan is to do a major strike against Israel that could lead to the collapse of Israel. Just a thought."

Lawson grabbed some bricks of C-4 and a spool of primacord while he thought about Gunny's comment about the missiles. Following Gunny's lead, Lawson continued rolling out the Primacord to other areas of the dump, wrapping the cord around stacks of RPG rounds, ammunition and weapons. Each time he would wrap an item, he would put a brick of C-4 against the item to be destroyed and wrapped the Primacord over the top of the C-4.

As he was doing so he came upon some cases with NATO markings. Opening up one of the cases, he found racks of 9 mm pistols. Then it hit him. If there are 9 mm NATO pistols, there has got to be 9 mm NATO ammo. Searching around the area he finally found several crates of 9 mm ammo with NATO markings. Opening up one of the crates, he found a neatly stored set of metal boxes. Pulling out one of the metal boxes, he opened it and pulled out paper boxes holding one-hundred rounds each. He took one of the paper boxes, shoved it in his pocket and continued to string out the Primacord.

While he was doing so, Rouhani pulled up to the gate in the vehicle. Lawson handed off his work to Myers and walked over to Rouhani as Rouhani was getting out of the vehicle. "Everything OK?" Lawson asked as he passed Rouhani.

"All's completed," Rouhani stated as he walked toward the shed. "The phones are hidden alongside the road about five miles back."

Lawson continued walking toward the vehicle. He reached the vehicle and leaned down to pick up the folder that he laid on the floor of the vehicle. Lifting the folder, he realized it was thinner. Opening the folder, he could see the disks were there but some pages were missing.

Lawson set the folder back in the vehicle and headed for the shed. As he was nearing the shed, Myers came up to inform him that everything appeared to be wired. Lawson handed Myers the Maxim 9 pistol, "Just in case someone shows up we weren't expecting. Also we need a timing detonator for the whole mess. And put one of the vests with the full detonator package in the vehicle." Myers nodded affirmative as Lawson walked toward the shed.

Gunny walked up behind Myers and Lawson and cautioned, "The force moving this direction is getting close. I put them out about three miles and they seem to be moving faster." Lawson gave a quick look to the east before walking into the shed.

As Lawson entered the shed, he picked up the pouch off the desk and looked into it. He could see the document and proceeded to pull it out.

"You need to put the chip in its place," Rouhani stated, "Otherwise, they'll know you're on to them."

Lawson thought for a moment. "I'm taking both," Lawson declared as he took the documents.

Rouhani seemed agitated as he spoke, "If there are no items in the pouch, they will know that we've got the document."

Lawson scanned through the pages. "I can set up some mockups to convince them that both copies were destroyed," Lawson said while he sat the pages down and started to look in the desk drawers for sheets of paper. Lawson heard a 'click' and as he turned, he saw Rouhani with another pistol with a built-in silencer pointed at him.

"I don't think so," Rouhani replied. "I will take the chip."

Lawson began to understand the picture. "So you took the vehicle out with our phones not so that the force coming this way would follow that signal but so that you could call your handlers and let them know where the real data existed."

Rouhani nodded his head 'yes' then said, "I also took the phones so that there would be no memory chips around that you could use to make me think you were putting the real chip in the pouch when, in fact, you were using a counterfeit."

"Now for the chip," Rouhani requested once more.

"I don't get this," Lawson continued. "Why all the game playing with so many people getting killed?" Lawson was stalling but he knew that Rouhani was proud enough of his plan to rub it in Lawson's face. It was buying time. Rouhani knew it but his ego wouldn't let him finish the job without some bragging.

"It's simple," Rouhani said, "We couldn't get the document from Dr. Polevsky. The Russians controlled the labs but the Iranians controlled what went in and out of the facility. The only way to get it out so that Russia had the development ahead of everyone else without paying a ransom for it was for someone else to steal it thereby getting it out of the facility. That would make the Iranians think that some other country, meaning you and the US, were responsible for its theft and not Russia. The Russians are thinking that this delivery from the shed are the real documents but they're not. I figured that out when I realized there were two sets of plans and the set in Polevsky's office was so tightly secured. I have a deal with the Russians to ensure they get the real data. Now, for the last time, the chip."

"Why couldn't Doctor Polevsky smuggle the plans out. He's Russian?" Lawson continued.

" Anytime Doctor Polevsky left, they would do a full check of him including an internal scan. They made him completely undress and scanned his clothing as well," Rouhani explained.

"So the chip has the real development information," Lawson reiterated.

"Yes, it's the real data," exclaimed Rouhani as he pointed the pistol ever closer to Lawson's head. "No more talking, the chip," Rouhani shouted.

Lawson reached for his pants pocket for the pistol Gunny had given him at the armory. Wrapping his fingers around the butt of the pistol and moving his finger onto the trigger surface, he realized he needed extra time to pull the weapon. To buy time, he dropped down to his knees.

Rouhani looked questioningly at the move and pulled the trigger. "Phfut, Phfut" came the sound of two shots in rapid succession. Rouhani stood straight up for a moment, dropped his weapon and fell to the floor. Lawson looked at the wall behind him where Rouhani's shots should have hit. He saw only one hole. He felt around his body to see where the other round had hit. Looking up, he saw Myers in the doorway of the shed with the Maxim 9 pistol in his hand, realizing then that the second shot came from Myers.

"I remembered what the logo was on the seal on Polevsky's pouch," Myers stated. "It's a part of the seal on the Massachusetts State flag. I should have known, seeing that flag for almost six years while I was at MIT. That's why I came to the door. I knew Rouhani couldn't be the inside man and he was playing us. The doctor was giving us the message of which copy was real by using a logo that was strictly American."

Lawson stood stunned by the turn of events. "I heard enough," Myers went on, "to put the pieces in place. Dr. Polevsky was the inside man. And if Gunny is right, we're stuck in a developing war between the Russians and the Iranians, yet neither side realizes it yet."

Lawson took the papers from the courier pouch and placed them in his belt. Quickly opening a drawer in the desk, he pulled out nine sheets of paper and folded them in half. He placed the folded nine pages inside the courier pouch.

Noticing that Rouhani had kept his own cellphone, Lawson examined the cellphone. He noticed that Rouhani had taken an external memory chip from one of the other phones and put it in his.

Lawson moved his finger along the screen until the page came up that showed him the 'file' icon. Opening the icon, he selected the 'external memory chip' icon and looked to see the directory. Nothing was on it. Looking out the window of the shed, he could see the Iranian force about two miles away.

Pulling the external memory out of the phone, he placed the chip and the phone on the desk and went out the door, running for the vehicle. Once at the vehicle, he pulled out the backpack and felt around until he found the box of matches. Taking three matches out of the box, he dropped the box back into the backpack, dropped the papers he had taken from the courier pouch into the backpack and ran back to the shed. Once inside the shed, Lawson picked up the courier pouch and set it aside.

Myers looked out the window at the approaching force. "You'd better get moving with whatever it is you're doing. They're going to be on top of us in about ten minutes," Myers exclaimed with a serious sense of urgency.

Lawson proceeded to wrinkle some paper and lay it in a stack on the desk. Lighting one of the matches, he ignited the papers within the pouch, placed the pouch onto of the stack of wrinkled papers and set the wrinkled papers on fire as well. As the fires burned, the nylon courier pouch started melting and the papers inside the pouch were completely burned.

While the fire under the courier pouch was burning, Lawson took a ballpoint pen with a clip on it. Putting the memory chip he had just taken from the phone into the clip of the pen, Lawson lit a second match and held it under the memory chip while the chip melted and he could hear the IC chip inside the plastic chip pop. The IC chip was destroyed. Accomplishing this, he took the courier pouch off of the fire, removed the damaged memory chip from the pen and dropped it into the remains of the courier bag then zipped the bag to close it. After putting out the fire, he knelt down on the floor.

"What are you doing that for?" Myers asked while Lawson was pushing the remains of the pouch under Rouhani's body.

"If the Iranians find this, it should convince them that both copies of the Polevsky papers were destroyed," Lawson replied.

While he was positioning the pouch underneath Rouhani's body, Gunny stepped inside, looked at Rouhani on the floor and asked, "Do you guys realize what time it is? We've got to set the charges and get out of here. The force out there is a little over a mile out." Gunny once more looked down at the body of Rouhani. Looking at Lawson, he commented, "You do have a way of settling arguments, don't you."

"I didn't settle it, Myers did," was Lawson's retort. He pulled out his watch. It was 9:03 AM. The Russians were going to be here at 9:15 AM and the Russians were always on time.

Myers pulled his phone apart and pulled the wires going to the speaker. Next to him was a suicide vest he pulled from a stack of vests. Pulling one of the two detonators off the vest, he wrapped one of the detonator wires tightly around one of the wires previously connected to the phone speaker. "I hope no one calls this number while I'm doing this," he said while making sure the wire would have a good connection. Grabbing a piece of paper, he took one more look at the screen of the phone and wrote down the phone number. Tucking the piece of paper into his pocket, Myers continued to wrap the other wire of the detonator to the remaining wire of the phone.

Lawson went with Myers while Myers took the phone and detonator to the crates of C-4. Going to the open crate, he pushed the detonator into a C-4 block and closed the lid after Gunny pushed the end of the long run of primacord that went to the rockets, ammo and various munitions into the C-4 in the box Myers had put the detonator in.

"That's great," Lawson responded, "but we need another phone to call it."

"Where do we get another phone?" Myers inquired.

Lawson stopped for a moment then raced back to the shed where Rouhani was laying. He picked up Rouhani's cellphone sitting on the edge of the desk. He stopped for a moment and looked at Rouhani's body. "What about the missing papers?" he thought. Feeling around Rouhani's body, he felt something move under his jacket. Lawson lifted the jacket to find the papers that were taken from the folder in the vehicle. There were pictures of Gunny, Myers and himself along with information on them written in Farsi. It struck Lawson that Taylor's picture and information was not in there. As Lawson felt around, he discovered that there was also the jump drive in Rouhani's pocket that Rouhani had taken from his desk at the research facility. In Lawson's logic, if Rouhani felt it was important enough to grab it from his desk at the facility it must have something important on it. He took the pouch and shoved it back under Rouhani's jacket then rolled his body face-down on the floor.

While Lawson was in the shed, Gunny had loaded the RPG rounds, launchers, primacord and a suicide vest into the back of the vehicle. He ran back to the box of C-4 and checked the detonator and the end-point of the primacord strings to check once more that everything was ready. Looking up, he could see that the Iranian force was rapidly approaching.

CHAPTER 13 -- July 31, 2015, 9:07 AM – Iran Time

Going out of the shed, Lawson shouted for everyone to head for the vehicle as time was getting short and the Iranian force was getting close to the ammo dump. Gunny went running to the vehicle and jumped into the driver's seat while Myers got in the passenger seat. Lawson looked in the back of the vehicle to see AK-47 rifles, RPG rounds, RPG launchers, ammo, the backpack and a spool of Primacord. There was also one suicide vest. Lawson jumped in the back, landing on the assortment of items. His thoughts went to wondering how much stress these munitions could take before they started detonating from the pressure and back and forth movement he was creating as the vehicle moved.

Gunny shouted for everyone to hold on as they went down the steep incline from the gate heading west. "The force coming for us is less than a mile from the ammo dump and moving fast," Gunny shouted as he turned a sharp left to avoid a ravine. Gunny was traveling at high speed for the landscape, somewhere around fifty miles per hour while Lawson held on to keep from falling out of the back. After they traveled a distance, with one hand on the vehicle's top rail, Lawson used his other hand to pull his watch out of his pocket. It was 9:13 AM. As Lawson looked back, he could see a dark speck in the air along the horizon. He knew this was the helicopter coming for the document.

"How far are we from the ammo dump?" Lawson shouted.

Gunny looked down at the speedometer. "About four miles," came Gunny's reply. Gunny suddenly slowed down and turned toward one of the ravines. Moving slowly along the ravine, he found a spot where they could pull into the ravine without rolling the vehicle. Gunny pulled into the ravine and continued to a place where the ravine turned south. He stopped at a spot where they could see the activity at the ammo dump but be protected from anything coming from that direction.

The ravine was about five feet deep and wide enough to park two of the vehicles side-by-side. The walls of the ravine were hard dirt with rough sides and a relatively smooth bottom that was damp from the runoff of recent rains. There was a lot of green brush and grass in and around the ravine. Standing up, Lawson could see above the top edge of the ravine, over the top of the grass, with a clear view of the ammo dump.

Gunny grabbed the binoculars off of the seat of the vehicle and looked at the ammo dump. "You better be firing off that phone now, Myers," Gunny barked as Myers grabbed for the phone from Lawson. "They're inside the fence and there's three more vehicles going over the road and coming after us," Gunny continued. At the same time the Hind helicopter was circling the ammo dump getting ready to land.

Myers pulled the slip of paper from his pocket and held the phone up. "Got a signal," Myers yelled. He proceeded to dial the number. The phone rang once, then twice. "Darn, it's not working," Myers called out. Myers hung up and hit the number he just called again. He waited for connection. Suddenly, there was a brilliant flash in the distance followed by an enormous column of fire and debris shooting skyward.

The vehicles south of the ammo dump instantly disappeared in the explosion while the helo was lifted sideways and driven into the ground. This was followed by an ever expanding ball of fire. The vehicles that had crossed the road and heading their direction were caught in the fireball and disappeared from view behind the wall of fire. Lawson watched as a ripple effect seemed to be rapidly moving toward him.

He felt Gunny grab him and quickly pull him down as the ripple effect became a wave passing over their heads carrying rocks and debris at bullet speeds. Lawson looked to see that Gunny had also grabbed Myers. Moments later came a roar so loud they had trouble hearing any other noise. The fireball was still expanding on the ground and was several thousand feet high. As the sound of the roar diminished, Myers started laughing. Lawson and Gunny both looked at him thinking the poor guy had lost it.

"This is great," Myers exclaimed. "My little hookup changed the landscape here!"

Myers stopped laughing, his face changing to a grim frown while staring at Gunny while instantly changing his observation to one of remorse. "How many people do you think were killed by my set up?"

Lawson looked at Myers and saw that the change in his demeanor was real. The implications of what just happened hit Myers with a full impact. Lawson felt Gunny tug on his sleeve.

"This is real for him," Gunny whispered while he motioned for Lawson to follow him. "He was going to be a minister and he really walks the walk of following Christ. In my experience with him, I found he was closer to God than anyone else I've known. He's also the most honest person I've known. His response is real. Killing people was not what he expected he was going to have to do and seeing people die from his work, that just hit him, big time. Let him deal with this. He needs to be alone."

"Where did you know him before?" Lawson queried as they walked further down the ravine then stopped to watch if there as any activity heading their way.

"I knew him while we were on the aircraft carrier Harry S. Truman," Gunny replied. "I was a Marine weapons man and he was responsible for the electronics on our Phalanx weapon system. So we had a chance to get to know each other. I was assigned to the Irregular Warfare Unit a year ago while Myers remained on the carrier. When we were setting up this operation to destroy the munitions going to Gaza, I was asked to find a top-notch electronics expert for the mission. I recommended Myers because he can jury rig anything electronic to meet our needs."

After a few minutes they walked back to the vehicle where they could see that Myers was still talking to himself. Without looking directly at Myers, Gunny motioned to everyone to get back in the vehicle. The fireball had made it to half the distance to where they were and had receded to where there was just a fire in the area of the ammo dump with periods of multiple explosions still going. "That will be going on for hours if not days," shouted Gunny as he started the engine.

Lawson spoke up as Gunny got them out of the ravine and gunned the engine to get moving. "The explosion just wiped out most of their force which gives us some time. Most likely they will think we were killed in the blast. However, there's the possibility that they will pursue us with everything they've got until they're sure we're either dead or captured."

Myer's phone rang at that point. "I think they're already checking," Myers proclaimed.

"Don't answer that," Both Lawson and Gunny chorused at the same time. Myers immediately opened up the settings application on the phone. "I'm making sure that all locater services are turned off."

CHAPTER 14 -- July 31, 2015, 1:45 AM – Washington, DC Time

Petty Officer Johnson walked into Admiral Roedl's office as the Admiral was lying asleep on the couch that had been moved into his office. He shook the Admiral to wake him then handed him a cup of coffee. Roedl had been up for almost forty hours before he decided to take a nap. "Five hours of sleep," he mused while taking a sip of the coffee.

"Sir," Johnson began, "we've recorded a massive explosion in northwestern Iran about a half-hour ago. There's also a significant increase in chatter coming from Iran concerning the incident."

Roedl listened for a moment then instructed Johnson to follow him to the Strategic Analysis Lab also known as 'SAL'. Walking through a series of passageways and up a flight of stairs, they came to SAL. They went to the door of the lab, with Roedl swiping his ID card then putting his head against a scanner for an eye scan. The door opened and they entered the room.

SAL was a central monitoring and command station for ground activity being captured by satellite, radio, phone and text transmissions send by other countries and for encrypting and sending rapid response messages. The center was manned at all times by no less than twelve analysts and command personnel.

The SAL center consisted of electronic stations on three walls toward one end of the room with the second half of the room laid out with seats in a theater-like arrangement. The seats were facing toward the electronics portion of the room and the associated screens. On the wall on the left was the equipment with stations for satellite tracking, assignment and recording of events. It had eight large monitors with keyboards and controls at four different stations. One station was for satellite retasking and satellite tracking. The second station was for real-time monitoring of information and video captured by satellite. The third station was assigned recording and playback tasks on demand. The fourth station was used by drone controllers for strike missions and dropping messages or small supply packages. The information and control of the satellites was provided by Schriever Air Force Base in Colorado, having over one-hundred and seventy satellites under their control with the data and control being linked to the SAL facility as well as numerous other military installations around the world.

The back wall, which the theater seats would be facing, held the large main screens used to display both recorded and real-time information. These screens could be controlled by commanders wanting to see events as they occurred or playback events that had been previously recorded. They were able to partially control what was to be displayed on the main screens once the proper station was linked to one of the main screens. They could also call up documents and information on persons, organizations, statistics and governments using controls on one of two seats in the front row of the theater seats.

The right wall held the communications tracking, analysis, recording and encryption capabilities. It supported a dozen smaller displays with eight keyboards and controls. One station was used for decrypting messages acquired from both U.S. and international sources. Another station was used for creating and encrypting messages going out to units. A third station was used for assimilating messages so that communication threads between parties could be tracked and printed. A fourth station was used for verbal capture of phone, radio and intercepted conversations. The fifth station was used for Presidential, State Department, National Security Agency, FBI and CIA communications. Three other stations were used for various tasks and to manage the overload of information during crisis times.

Petty Officer Johnson pushed a button on a hand control on one of the two front theater seats. The main screen began displaying a satellite video from a satellite that had been retasked by Schriever AFB to observe an area in northwestern Iran.

"Admiral," he explained, "this was recorded about a half hour ago. We were following a battalion-sized force moving from east to west starting from the army base located here." He pointed to the base that was located fifteen miles east of the research facility. "It appears that they had just arrived to this storage site when the explosion occurred. It looks like a good portion of the force was wiped out by the blast."

As he directed Roedl to the center screen, a line of vehicles and soldiers could be seen moving toward an outside storage area then entering the storage area. They could also see a helicopter circling the storage area. Moments later, a bright dot formed on the screen, rapidly expanded in size and brightness until the area on the screen was bright white. It remained for about fifteen seconds then slowly disappeared. The vehicles, personnel and helicopter just disappeared. Roedl looked closely at the location of the bright area.

"We thought at first that it was a nuclear detonation," Johnson continued. "Further analysis of the blast indicates that it was conventional. No radiation was detected."

Roedl continued to look at the area on the screen. "Pull up the 'Operation Tin Cup' operational files. What is this out here?" Roedl asked while pointing to a vehicle and three persons sitting next to the vehicle about four miles northwest of the blast.

Johnson looked at the area where Roedl was pointing. "Is it possible that's our munitions strike team for 'Tin Cup?"

"But there are three people. With Taylor dead, my guess is that it's Lawson with the munitions strike team. It's possible Lawson survived getting out of the research facility," Roedl observed while looking at the 'Tin Cup' roster on the second screen to see who was assigned to the air strike support teams and what teams and equipment were on the ground. "Send him a coded message to contact me. Send it to our contact in Iraq and have the contact send it by drone to Colonel Draper. His code is GOT114. Make sure the message is sealed and addressed to Lawson. Be sure to provide Lawson with the information to contact us and have Draper deliver it. Tell Draper to bring the PRC-155 ManPack radio with him so Lawson can communicate with us. Now, get going!"

Johnson jumped up and went to the encryption station. Roedl also noticed that large numbers of helicopters were moving toward the Iraq-Iran border around Highway 46. There were also a large number of vehicles and personnel on Highways 46 and 15, moving west.

Moments later, Chief Petty Officer Milkin walked over to Roedl with a handful of papers. "Admiral," Milkin said while handing the papers to Roedl, "Here's the latest on Tin Cup. Communications between the research facility and Tehran indicates that the lab at the research facility was destroyed and Dr. Polevsky was killed in the blast."

Roedl leaned back in his chair and contemplated the information. He wondered what Lawson had done to cause such destruction. "Dr. Polevsky dead," He thought. "How did Lawson pull that one off? This guy is far more creative than I give him credit for. If Polevsky is dead then the only information left on how the laser system is built and works is in Polevsky's papers." After Milkin had waited a few minutes, he interrupted the Admiral's thoughts.

"There's also communications captured between Iran, Egypt and Libya concerning the vehicle taken by the intruders at the research facility. Other communications between Tehran and Moscow indicates equally intense concern over the vehicle the intruders took. I think the vehicle you pointed to that's four miles to the northwest of the blast area is the vehicle in question."

Roedl thought through Milkin's report then asked him, "What is your assessment?"

"Well sir," Milkin started, "It seems that Iran was intending on stealing the weapons plans being developed in the research facility with an objective of selling the information to Egypt and Libya. Other than the Polevsky document, whatever Lawson took from the research facility is raising a lot of concern in the Middle East. One other thing, the Iranians appear to be moving two, possibly three mobile radar sites to the west of the research facility. Based upon what we see on placement so far, the two mobile sites being set up right now are about five miles apart from each other in a line north to south. The northern-most site appears to be about eight miles north of the research facility and just west of the road that goes past the research facility and the storage area that was destroyed. Also we can't get anything in or out of northern Iran due to the military activity, so our teams are orphaned, on their own."

Roedl listened carefully to what Milkin was saying. "Pass that information on to Draper. The radar sites need to be taken out tonight," Roedl replied. "What concerns me is the level of interest over what is in the vehicle. These communiques don't show as much concern for the loss of a lab or possible loss of the plans for the weapon system as they do for the loss of the vehicle."

"Oh, there's a lot of concern over the missing documents," Milkin added. "The Iranians and Russians are in a quandary over the loss of the Polevsky papers. They're not sure if the papers were retrieved or destroyed in the storage area blast. They're scanning for the lost vehicle for the recovery of the papers, if they still exist."

"One thing is for sure," Roedl observed, "the fact that the research facility lab and the storage area were both destroyed indicates that some of our people survived to carry out the missions. We have to assume that they have survived and have the Polevsky papers. I'm curious as to what the vehicle holds."

Roedl got up to leave the SAL center. "Get me as soon as you hear from Lawson," he said as he departed out the door of the SAL center. As Roedl left, Captain Michaels followed him out the door from the SAL Center.

"Admiral," Michaels complained, "Lawson has exceeded his authority on a number of levels. I'm recommending a court martial for Lawson. We can't have people going around making their own set of rules and setting their own protocols."

Roedl looked at Michaels for a moment then responded, "If Lawson had not destroyed the lab at the research facility, we would have to send another team in to destroy it. I can guarantee that would be a suicide mission, not to mention a serious diplomatic situation. The Iranians would be much more alert and getting inside the facility would be impossible. Lawson was given no training in our protocol. We got our best benefit from him because there were no rules for him to follow. Also, Michaels, it would look bad for the Navy to be presenting Lawson's Navy Cross medal at his court martial."

Michaels gave a short smile to Roedl. "I guess that would be bad press."

CHAPTER 15 -- July 31, 2015, 9:43 AM – Iran Time

As events were unfolding in Washington, D.C., Lawson and his team were looking for a place to hide in Iran. They headed northwest for about fifteen minutes when Lawson pulled out his map. An idea was formulating in Lawson's mind. With Myers having a phone that was still connected, there may be a way to convince both the Russians and the Iranians that both copies of the document were destroyed and the copy still in Polevsky's filing cabinet was a fake.

Lawson showed Gunny the map. Gunny stopped the vehicle to analyze the map and to see where Lawson's coordinates would take them. While Gunny was examining the map, Lawson handed each person a bottle of water along with a sandwich made from pita bread and cheese. While they were sitting, Myers phone made a dinging sound. Myers looked at the screen.

"It's a text to Rouhani and it's in Farsi," Myers announced while opening the text. He proceeded to read the text to everyone, "Colonel, we tried to open Dr. Polevsky's file cabinet. It exploded when we attempted to open it. Both technicians were killed, contents of the filing cabinet were destroyed. All we've got is a couple of burned sheets. The rest caught fire and burned before we could get to the cabinet after the explosion. You must get the photos taken by the British correspondent. And it's signed, Behzadi."

"So Behzadi is still alive," Lawson supposed. "It makes sense that if Rouhani was working with the Iranians to get the design, the firing squad for Behzadi would be a hoax. It also shows that

Rouhani was in communication with Behzadi. How else would Behzadi know that we had taken pictures of the papers?"

Gunny spent around twenty minutes looking at the map and the possible avenues of escape out of Iran while Lawson and Myers closed their eyes for a short nap. While he was fumbling with the map he spoke to Lawson. "In order to get to your coordinates on this map, we have to be heading south instead of to the northwest. Heading south as far as you show with these coordinates puts us back in the lion's den and this time we'll have to deal with aircraft overhead." Lawson lifted his head and nodded, realizing Gunny's evaluation of the situation was correct. Gunny noted that Lawson was looking at Myers and was moving his eyes back and forth as though he didn't even see Myers.

"Lawson," Gunny continued, "is it my imagination or are you planning something else?"

Lawson looked down at the map Gunny was holding and replied, "I am thinking of a plan that will convince both the Russians and Iranians that all copies of Polevsky's papers have been destroyed. That fireball we saw was sure to destroy everything within it. If so, it wouldn't be too hard to believe that we didn't get away with the plans."

Once Lawson made his assessment, Lawson and Myers spent the next hour going through several plans to get the Russians and Iranians to bite on the bait. Gunny listened to them as they talked. Finally, he inserted himself into the conversation.

"You guys forget that the Russians and Iranians are at war with each other over this thing in this region. I'd send Behzadi back a message that I, being Rouhani, decided to join up with the Russians and am heading off to Iraq." Lawson and Myers looked at each other.

Myers was first to speak. "That's a start. We need to provide something else in the mix that makes it more believable." Gunny agreed. Lawson just sat there thinking while pulling out his watch. It was 11:10 AM.

"Give me the phone," Lawson said to Myers. Myers handed him the phone. Lawson pressed the icon on the screen that showed a telephone handset. A list of phone numbers and names came up by date in Farsi. Lawson handed the phone back to Myers. "Find me a phone number for a senior Russian officer," Lawson requested while Myers was looking at the phone.

"Here's one," Myers declared. "It's the phone number for a Russian general. His name is Asimov. His note next to his number says that he speaks Farsi."

"Let's think on this," was Lawson's reaction.

Lawson turned to Gunny and laid out his thoughts. "Rouhani wanted to put the chip with the photos in the courier pouch. That's what the Russians were picking up so it is fair to assume that Rouhani was working for the Russians. If that is the case, then Rouhani would be expected to inform the Russians of the condition of the papers. I can call the Russian general and have Myers inform him that all copies of the papers were destroyed in the explosion. Gunny, you said that the munitions may be cooking off for several days. No one is going to get close to the area to check on the bodies until the fires die down and it's safe to go in."

Gunny thought about Lawson's explanation for a moment then gave his take on the situation. "It's like this," Gunny started. "If Rouhani was working for the Iranians, he would see to it that the fake papers were sent to Moscow. So it is just as possible that the pouch was being filled with false information in the chip while the papers originally in the pouch were the real papers." Lawson saw Gunny's logic. It was a dilemma.

"We do have one way to know which copy is true, or at least get an idea," Lawson observed. "Myers, check the phone to see if there are any other senior Russians Rouhani contacted over the past week."

Myers picked up the phone and started to scroll through the calls that came in and the ones that were made. Lawson continued to analyze the situation to see if any events would give him a clue.

A few minutes later, while Lawson was thinking, Myers came up with the results of his search. "There is only one person of high rank, that's Asimov, that Rouhani called and who also called Rouhani. What makes it significant is the times of the calls. The Russian general called Rouhani four days ago at 03:10 hours. That's the middle of the night. Rouhani called the Russian general back twice. Once, two days ago at 01:35 and again, yesterday at 02:14, both middle of the night calls. There is also a text from Rouhani at 05:47 this morning telling the same general that the pigeon is ready to fly and to transfer the money. Asimov appears to be the main contact in Moscow." Gunny and Lawson looked at each other, realizing that they just hit the mother lode.

"So Asimov is the money guy for Rouhani. Maybe it's worth a try," Gunny offered.

Myers then interrupted. "I've heard Rouhani talk enough that I think I can mimic his voice close enough to carry this off."

Gunny stepped back in. "If we make the call, we'll need to do it late this evening. Our pickup is at 22:00, right?" Lawson nodded his head in the affirmative while he was thinking through the process. Gunny continued, "All of their contacts were done at night. I figure that either Rouhani could have some limitations to keep the calls at night or, more likely, the general had problems that would prevent him from talking at other times, maybe because others were around him at other times."

Myers was listening while looking at other calls on the phone. He raised his eyebrows while tending to a thought. "This might work for us," Myers contemplated out loud as though Gunny and Lawson weren't there. "You see," Myers went on. "If a call were to come to the general at hours he wasn't expecting, that might add urgency to the message." Both Lawson and Gunny realized the idea was a good one.

Gunny then probed a question that had been bothering him since the discussion started. "Why is it so important for everyone to think the papers have been destroyed?"

Lawson leaned back in the rear of the vehicle. "A simple question," he thought. He picked his words carefully. "The Russians are building a weapon that can take an aircraft out of the air by cutting a wing off or through the fuselage in less than a second. It uses ground lasers rather than missiles. If the Russians and Iranians think that all of the work and research has been lost, it'll take them a couple of years to get back to a point where they can test. From what I saw, none of the information has yet been sent to Moscow. They didn't want anything exposed to possible leaks until the concept was proven."

Gunny looked at Lawson and questioned once more, "How do you know this?" Lawson explained to Gunny what he saw in the lab – the laser table setups, the metal structure at the end of the lab with long burn marks through it and servos on the laser generator that indicated rapid, well-defined movement of the mirrors.

"All of that has been destroyed," Lawson said. "But there is one more thing," Lawson expressed. "If the papers are thought to still exist, many more people will die either trying to get them or being caught in the middle. In just this effort alone, I estimate somewhere between seventeen and twenty people lost their lives from us just moving around, not counting all those that may have been killed in the blast at the facility and the blast at the ammo dump. If the weapon gets out, it can be seen as the ultimate defensive weapon which could encourage offensive enterprises. As for knowing that nothing has been sent yet to Moscow, it's a hunch I have based upon the interest everyone's got about the papers." Gunny thought it over for a moment then asked Myers when he would be ready to make the call.

Myers looked at the phone then at Lawson. "I need a basic script to work from with the major talking points listed out."

Lawson laid out the basic points. "First, you must convince the general all copies have been destroyed. Make it sound like you're going back into the blast area to get the papers if they still exist. Second, tell the general you still expect to be paid even if the papers have been destroyed. The general will probably be angry and refuse to pay. Stick to your guns on this one. Rouhani would."

Myers understood most of it but was curious about one point. "Why would I state I'm going back into the blast area to find out if the papers were still there?" Gunny was curious about the requirement, as well.

Lawson described his plan. "When everything settles down in the munitions dump, Rouhani's body will be found. There may be enough evidence around him for them to confirm his body. If the Russians find out he's dead, that's going to raise some questions unless they have some prior knowledge that he was going to take some risk to go back in for the papers. With the pouch under his body, if it hasn't been moved by the blast, they will find the courier pouch and the contents of the pouch." Both Gunny and Myers saw the logic in the plan. Myers sat down to make notes of how his call must go.

CHAPTER 16 -- July 31, 2015, 11:30 AM – Iran Time

The sound of rocks tumbling down the side of a nearby hill and the distinct clatter of horse hooves stopped all of them from their activities. They all grabbed their AK-47s and swung them in the direction of the sound.

"Hello in the camp," came a distant call before the horses came into view. Lawson knew it had to be an American, someone who was raised on a ranch in the western US.

"Come forward," Lawson shouted. The men, riding in on horses with four other horses in tow came down the hill and out into the open. The weapons were still trained in the visitors' direction.

"Compliments of Admiral Roedl," the voice continued. "I'm Colonel Draper of the 75th Ranger Regiment, U.S. Army. Is Petty Officer Lawson here?" The man rode up with three others, all dressed in native Kurdish garb.

They wore light-colored turbans with loose fitting brown pants, gray long-sleeved shirts and vests. Each man was wearing a sidearm with an M-14 rifle strung to the side of very primitive saddles. Colonel Draper was about six foot tall with a dark tan and a short brown beard. He had a rugged face prevalent with a person that has been out in the wilderness for a long period of time. One man appeared to be a local Kurd with a beard and clothes that had seen a lot of use. The other two men were shorter and less tanned, apparently Americans. Neither had beards and appeared to have come into country only a few days ago as their outfits appeared relatively new and manufactured rather than hand made.

"Let's get this vehicle into a ravine," Draper said while getting off his horse. "They're looking all over for you guys, particularly about twenty miles south of here."

Lawson motioned to Gunny to move the vehicle into the nearby ravine while Draper walked toward Lawson. "Here," Draper said while handing a small sealed envelope to Lawson. "It's from Admiral Roedl dropped in by drone about an hour ago." Lawson took the envelope and broke the seal.

"We saw the blast you guys caused," Draper went on. "It's the largest explosion I've ever seen. At first we thought that it was a nuclear blast." Lawson nodded his head as he read the note from Roedl. Lawson realized that it was a transmitted message that was packaged and sealed by someone just across the border, probably delivered by one of those drones he saw in crates on the aircraft that brought him to Iraq.

"Do you have a radio?" Lawson asked Draper.

"It's on the fourth horse back," came his reply. "The communications is secure and scrambled. By the way, your 22:00 pickup tonight has been scrubbed. Nothing is coming in or going out of the country in this area."

As Lawson walked over to the horse and lifted a blanket, Draper began taking the other horses into the ravine. Under the blanket was a battery-powered PRC-155 transceiver. Lawson looked at the note and dialed the number written on the note. Putting on the headphones and getting the sound of mechanical voice saying 'standby for contact,' Lawson waited for the 'you are connected' message and started speaking, "Coffee Rabbit Fifty this is Tango Bulldog, do you copy?"

"Tango Bulldog this is Coffee Rabbit Fifty" came back the reply almost immediately.

Lawson responded, "Coffee Rabbit Fifty code word."

There was silence for a moment then the response came back, "Code word two-six-zero Sirloin."

With the code word verified Lawson responded, "Code word Red Dawn two-seven." Lawson then proceeded with the call, "Coffee Rabbit Fifty any traffic for me?"

There was a pause at the other end followed by, "The old man wants to talk to you, stand by." Lawson waited about forty seconds before a familiar voice came on the call,

"What are you doing wiping out the whole lab?" came the voice on the other end.

Lawson hesitated for a moment then replied, "It was a target of opportunity, Sir."

Another pause and Roedl's voice came back, "You've stirred up a hornet's nest. It's not what I planned for this venture but it sure has helped us to get a lot of information by way of communications activity between the Shuyesheh Facility and Tehran. I commend you for removing any ability to reproduce the design."

At first, Lawson thought he was being chewed out but then realized he was being given a free hand and a vote of confidence from the Admiral.

Lawson said "thanks" then Roedl continued, "It appears that you've taken something of great value to the Russians and the Iranians, and I'm not talking about the original package, though that is critically important. By the way, do you have the papers?"

Lawson looked around to see who might be listening then responded, "Yes I have. I've got food and water too." Roedl knew immediately that Lawson was carefully covering his tracks about the Polevsky papers so that no one around him knew that was what he was talking about.

"This is an order," Roedl continued, "keep the package and do not give them to anyone else but me. Also, check the vehicle you have. Apparently the vehicle you took is raising a lot of talk across the channels. Not just in Iran but also in Russia, Libya and Egypt."

"Will do," Lawson acknowledged.

Roedl went on, "Colonel Draper has some items you'll need. I want you to take out the three mobile radar facilities south of you. Also, if you've got some shoulder-launched rockets or RPG launchers and rounds, give Draper all you can spare. We can't get any other teams into your area because the region is being covered like a blanket. Highways 46 and 15 are buried in checkpoints and even getting drones in is a challenge due to the radars and the number of helicopters in the air."

Lawson was surprised by the mission to take out the radar sites. He and his team were tired. They needed sleep. Once more hitting the transmit key, Lawson spoke, "Sir, we need to get sleep, clean our weapons and develop a plan. When do these radar sites need to be taken out?"

There was silence for almost two minutes. Lawson was about to ask again when Roedl came back, "We need the radar sites taken out tonight. The tribes we're supporting can't defend themselves on what they've got. We've got to get more equipment in to them but can't at the present time. Jim, the activity you've stirred up caused the Iranians and Russians to expose some secrets. We think a war is about to break out but we don't know where or who is involved. It may well be between the Iranians and the Kurds or the Iranians and the Israelis. With the horses Draper is bringing you, you should be able to kick the mission into gear late tonight and take out all three sites before first light. You have some time today to get some rest. By the way, when you find out what's so important about that vehicle, call me back. Roedl out."

Lawson pulled out his watch and checked the time, 11:55 AM. "I guess the Admiral has been up all night," Lawson thought. "It's 3:55 AM in Washington. If we can get everything in order in the next hour, we can get some sleep until about 8:00 PM."

He shut off the radio, dropped the blanket over it and walked the horse to the ravine and Draper. Draper was in the process of handing out clothing for each of Lawson's team to wear. Typical Kurdish garb.

Draper pulled out a high-powered rifle with scope and handed it to Gunny. "You're the weapons man on this team. With your ratings for long range accuracy, this should be a sweet tool for you. The rifle is 7.62 mm bolt action rifle built for maximum velocity and has a twelve-power swivel scope set for five-hundred yards. Here are four-hundred match rounds for the rifle," he stated as he handed Gunny three web belts loaded with ammo clips.

Draper then turned to Lawson. "There are three horses for you. One of the horses is carrying extra water, oats for the horses, food and ammo, oh, and some toilet paper too. Each of the horses has rifle straps for AK-47's with one horse having extra straps for the sniper rifle I just gave to Gunny." Lawson, Myers and Gunny all nodded they understood.

Draper continued as the Kurdish man stood next to him, "This is Bahram Khaliqi. He is leading seven other men to create a diversion at the main army base about twenty miles southeast of here. They're tasked to destroy one of the munitions storage facilities on the base tonight. They are particularly interested in carrying out this mission because it would destroy the whole supply of barrel bombs the Iranians have in this area."

"What's a barrel bomb?" Myers asked as he shook hands with Khaliqi.

"A barrel bomb," Draper answered, "is a fifty-five gallon oil drum filled with plastic explosives, thousands of ball bearings and an impact detonator. It is dropped from a helo and upon impact sets off a massive explosion, killing anyone in the path of the flying ball bearings or caught in the explosion. Khaliqi's family was almost wiped out by one of them so this is personal for him and his team."

Bahram Khaliqi was a small man with clothing that had seen the stresses of time and a black beard that was thick but clean. He was a Sunni Kurd and, as such, was adamantly opposed to the interference inflicted on his tribe by the Shiite Iranians. He was an expert with the knife in his belt, more of a short sword, that was sharp enough to cut through thick leather in one swipe. He was a graduate of Oxford University and, when he was speaking perfect English, it was with a slight British accent. It appeared to Lawson that he was no nonsense in his behavior and hated the Iranians. Draper told Lawson that Khaliqi thought all Iranians were evil men and had no reservations about killing them.

Draper looked at Lawson. "Do you want me to take the Polevsky papers?"

Lawson looked at the other guys and insisted, "The papers were lost in the blast at the ammo dump. We had to get out so fast we had no time to go back to the shed to get them. The Iranians were almost on top of us."

Draper walked toward the other two guys and posed, "Is this true?" Gunny and Myers both nodded 'yes' and went back to their tasks. Draper walked back to Lawson.

"So your mission was a complete failure," Draper lamented.

"Not so," Lawson said, "We destroyed the ammo dump and no one else gets the Polevsky papers. I would call that a success." Draper nodded agreement and proceeded to grab some food from one of the pouches on his horse.

As Draper was eating, Lawson called everyone together and brought up the issue Admiral Roedl addressed. "Apparently," Lawson stated, "there is some significant concern by the Russians and the Iranians over the vehicle we took. It's actually caused communications to be exchanged between Russia, Iran, Libya and Egypt. I think we need to take a closer look."

Draper walked over to Myers with a hand-held transceiver. "It's a spare satellite radio telephone we have but it eats batteries like crazy. Use it sparingly."

Lawson interrupted Draper, "We have forty RPG rounds and three launchers. Would you like to take thirty-five rounds and two launchers off our hands?"

Draper smiled at Lawson. "Would I?" he exclaimed. "We've been starved for defensive weapons. This is a gold mine!"

"Good," Lawson said, "get them now because we have to clear out the vehicle to find out what is so important about it."

They pulled all of the equipment and weapons out of the vehicle. Draper noticed the suicide vest as the materials were being taken from the vehicle. "You plan to use this when all else fails?" he asked while handling the vest. Everyone laughed at the comment. As Draper was looking at the vest, he wondered why they would take the vest with the timer and detonators but without the needed explosives. He set the vest down and went onto the task at hand.

Once the vehicle was cleared, Myers went to the back of the vehicle and felt under the floor mat. Feeling around he announced, "No wires." He lifted up the mat to expose a metal lid to a chamber. Once more, he slightly lifted the metal cover and felt along the edges for wires or switches. Once he was convinced it was safe, he slowly lifted up the metal cover all the while looking for any switches that might be toward the back. The lid swung open on hinges attached to the left side of the chamber. Now open, he looked in to see a large, canvas bag with a zipper opening at the top. Myers slowly lifted the bag out of the chamber, feeling around underneath for any wires or triggers. Convinced there were none, he lifted the bag out of the chamber.

With the bag completely out, he slowly opened the zipper. Finally the bag was open enough to reach his hand into it. He pulled his hand out to show the others the contents – diamonds. "The bag is full of them," Myers exclaimed. "There must be seven pounds worth here."

Draper took one of the largest diamonds from Myers hand and held it in his hand. Taking out his cellphone, he made some adjustments to the screen on the phone to zoom in on the diamond and took a picture. Next he dialed a number, typed in a message and attached the picture. The text was sent. "We'll see what the value of these are," He said while handing the diamond back to Myers. "Keep this diamond separate from the others until we get a response back," Draper said while Myers took the diamond.

Draper also noticed that there were several AK-47s on the ground. Noting that Lawson, Gunny and Myers already had AK-47s, he turned to Lawson and inquired, "Are these weapons extras?"

Lawson looked at the rifles and said, "Take them." Draper immediately picked up the weapons and loaded them into an empty bag on his horse. His pack horse already had the RPG rounds and launchers on it. Meanwhile, Lawson and his team changed clothes into the clothing Draper had brought. It struck Lawson how well the clothing fit each man.

The day was getting hot and the wind was picking up. Lawson began to wonder how much hotter it was going to feel wearing the turbans. First, he had to figure which way it was to go on the head. As Lawson was putting the turban on his head, Draper started laughing and adjusted the head gear on Lawson to the right position. Everyone else followed suit.

"Let me show you something," Draper instructed. "It's time to water the horses." Taking off his turban and turning it upside down, he poured water from one of the water bladders into his turban. He walked over to his horse and let the horse drink until the water was gone. "Once the horse has had his water," Draper continued, "put the turban on your head. It's soaked enough to keep your head cool for about an hour." Everyone followed his example and watered the horses.

Draper then informed them, "Feed the horses twice a day with four cups of oats. That's two times with two handfuls." He put his two hands together side by side to show them how to hold the oats. "Otherwise, let them graze the grass around them when you're not riding them."

After feeding and watering the horses, Myers walked over to Lawson. Handing the phone to Lawson, he stated, "If we're going to get the Russian General to believe that Rouhani went into the blast area at the storage area, we need to do it soon." Lawson looked at the phone then at Myers. Lawson motioned for Gunny to come over to join them. Gunny and Draper came together.

"What's the topic now?" Gunny asked.

"We're getting ready to make the call to General Asimov," Myers replied. "I've got the sequence needed for the conversation and I've been practicing Rouhani's voice. I've got the voice down well enough that I think I can pull this off."

Draper looked at each of the team members. "What's going on here?" he inquired as Lawson handed the phone to Myers.

"Myers is going to call a Russian General by the name of Asimov using Rouhani's phone to tell him that he's going back into the storage area to get the Polevsky papers," Lawson explained. "We figure Asimov will know by now about the blast and destruction that took place. If Asimov finds that Rouhani died before the blast, he will believe that we have the papers and will continue to pursue us, even inside the U.S. However. If Asimov were to believe that Rouhani died while trying to get the papers, it might make the Russians believe the papers were destroyed in a subsequent explosion from the munitions burning off after the blast."

"Let me warn you," Draper cautioned, "I know of Asimov. He's no fool. His people have been on our tail for the past year. Even though he has the responsibility for weapons development, he also has some vendetta against the Kurds in this area. He'll read right through this scam if you make any mistake. If you do make a mistake, he will certainly come after you, even in the U.S. Be sure you know what you're about to do."

Lawson, Gunny and Myers talked it over while Draper listened. They finally agreed that the risk was worth it if it would help convince the Russians that the plans no longer existed. Draper listened to their decision and stated, "I'm leaving this decision up to you three. You have your mission and your orders. I could order you not to do this but I feel that would be interfering with what you know you may have been ordered to do. You're not putting my people in danger with this stunt so the consequences are not in my kingdom. Good luck."

Myers scrolled to the number next to Asimov's name.

"You might want to make sure you know Asimov's first name. Not just what is listed but what he is known by," Draper advised as he walked back toward his horse. "Rouhani may have had more than just a passing acquaintance with Asimov."

Myers realized that Draper was right. He accessed the text sent to Asimov that morning. "It appears that Rouhani referred to Asimov as 'Sergey'," Myers stated while looking at the text. "And Rouhani is known as 'Ashkan'."

"Make the call," Lawson ordered.

Myers selected the number from the phone log and dialed. After several rings, a woman's voice came on the line in Russian. Myers spoke in Farsi, mentioning General Asimov's name. There was silence for about thirty seconds, then a male voice came on speaking in Farsi.

"I've been waiting for your call, Ashkan. Did the bird fly?" The General asked.

"No it didn't, Sergey," Myers responded in Farsi. "The area has been hit by a major explosion. I'm going back in to retrieve the information. They were going to send you a document that was fake. The real document is on a memory chip."

There was silence for a moment then the General reacted, "I heard about the explosion. Remember that you don't get the other five-hundred thousand Euros until I get the document. I've already lost a significant cache of diamonds due to the incompetence of your people. We're relying on you not only to get the document but also the diamonds. Otherwise I'm in deep trouble with my superiors. Do you understand?"

"I understand," Myers answered. "I'm leaving now to get the document. The sooner I get there, the better chance I have of getting the memory chip before it is destroyed by the heat."

"Call me back when you get it," Asimov stated. "I'm relying on you to complete this task. Since our helicopter was destroyed in the blast, we need you to go to the city Bashmaq on Highway 46 and cross over into Iraq to the city Penjwen. You'll meet a man carrying an umbrella at the Panjwin Masjid Mosque in Penjwen at 11:00 hours Iraqi time, day after tomorrow. Can you do it?"

"I can be there with the document," Myers replied. "Getting the diamonds in that time might be tricky."

"You need to get the diamonds," Asimov replied in an increasingly irritated voice, "However, the document is more important. We need it in Russian hands by day after tomorrow. You'll contact the same agent you've used before. He's the one whose code name is 'Tripoli'. Now I'm signing off." With the discussion ended, Myers phone showed that General Asimov had hung up.

Myers walked over to where Lawson and Draper were sitting. Myers face was drenched in sweat and his hands were shaking as he handed the phone to Lawson.

Draper was first to speak. "Did he buy your story?" Myers nodded his head yes and sat down at which point both Lawson and Draper responded with, "Well?"

Myers collected his thoughts and proceeded to explain. "The General appears to buy the fact that I'm Rouhani and I'm going back to the storage area to recover the memory chip with the document. I could tell he was already familiar with the memory chip as he didn't ask anything about it, so Rouhani probably already told Asimov that the real document was on the chip."

"How do you know he bought the story," Draper retorted as he fought to keep his desire to take control of the situation to keep it from getting out of hand.

"Asimov gave me instructions," Myers countered. "He told me to meet a guy at the Panjwin Masjid Mosque in Penjwen at 11:00 AM Iraq time, day after tomorrow to give him the chip. He'll have an umbrella. His code name is 'Tripoli'. I also remembered that the phone I was calling on was Rouhani's phone so I guess Asimov probably saw the phone number calling him matched the name in his phone directory for Rouhani."

Draper's face relaxed once he heard Myers' response. "He bought it, hook, line and sinker!" he exclaimed while grabbing the water bladder to take a drink. "You're to meet 'Tripoli'?" With that comment, he walked to the horse with the radio and proceeded to call someone while Lawson and Gunny proceeded to look over the map.

Later, Lawson, Gunny and Draper were talking about the terrain south of them when Draper's cellphone rang. Draper answered the call, talked for a couple minutes, then handed the phone to Lawson. "He wants to tell you the value of the diamond." Lawson took the phone and answered.

The voice on the other end began the explanation, "This is Captain Clark from the Army Logistics and Evaluation Center. The markings on the diamond that was photographed indicates that it is of highest quality. We checked some references on the value of the diamond based upon its size and the markings and came up with a value of somewhere between forty thousand and fifty thousand dollars. Basically speaking, if you have seven pounds of diamonds all of different sizes but of this quality, you've got a package worth in the range of forty-five million dollars to sixty million dollars." Lawson sat down. "Thank you very much," he said and handed the phone back to Draper.

After a couple of moments, Lawson got up and went over to the horse with the radio. Lifting up the blanket and checking to see that the frequency was still set for satellite communications when he used it last, he put on the headphone and dialed the number. He then remembered that Draper had used the radio after he did so it became apparent that Draper had called Admiral Roedl. He let that observation pass as he made the call.

"Coffee Rabbit Fifty this is Tango Bulldog, do you copy?"

He waited about thirty seconds then heard, "Tango Bulldog this is Coffee Rabbit Fifty."

Lawson responded, "Coffee Rabbit Fifty code word."

The response came back, "Code word three-six-zero Sirloin."

With the code word verified Lawson responded, "Code word Red Dawn four-seven."

There was silence for a moment then Admiral Roedl's voice came on, "Do you realize that it is 04:45 hours here. What took so long to tell me what's in the vehicle?"

Lawson laughed for a moment then responded, "Sir, meaning no disrespect, but we thought you'd like to know the specs on what we've got before talking to you."

"No disrespect taken. What have you got, sailor?" Roedl answered back in an almost churchlike tone.

"Well, Sir," Lawson continued, "we've got a load of diamonds, approximately seven pounds worth between forty-five million and sixty million."

There was silence for a moment. Roedl questioned, "million what?"

"Dollars," was Lawson's response. Again silence, this time longer.

"No wonder they're looking for you," came Roedl's assessment. "Give the diamonds to Draper and have him hold onto them until I figure out what to do with them. Meanwhile, you need to get those radar sites tonight. Our teams are hanging out there. No one can get into the country and no one can get out. We're almost blind as far as the condition of the teams are because most of them went out like you did. No communications except what they can capture to use to communicate."

Lawson acknowledged and signed off. He looked at his watch, "12:48 PM," he thought, "like the Admiral said, that's 4:48 AM Washington D.C. time. No wonder the Admiral was ticked."

Lawson walked over to Draper. Taking the bag of diamonds from Myers, Lawson handed them to Draper and said, "The Admiral wants you to keep these until he figures out what to do with them. We're all lying down to get some sleep."

Draper took the diamonds as he and his associates mounted their horses. "Cover that vehicle with brush and keep the horses down in the ravine. Also set up your defensive positions. We're going up to the top of the ravine and will cover you so that you don't have to put out a sentry. We'll watch for you. If you hear a rifle shot, get to your positions." Lawson nodded affirmative. Draper and his men rode up the ravine into the foothills.

After Lawson and the others covered the vehicle and set up their weapons to respond for action, Lawson took the sniper rifle with a clip in in it and handed it to Gunny. Next he took the RPG launcher and two RPG rounds and laid them next to Myers and himself. He positioned the AK-47s and clips next to the RPG rounds. Finally, he took the memory chip containing the Polevsky papers out of his pocket and put it in a zippered pocket in the backpack in the vehicle. He went back to his defensive position and laid down to go to sleep.

Gunny came over and checked the layout. "Good job," he said to Lawson. "I told you that you weren't a stupid squid. You're thinking more like a Marine every day." Lawson smiled at Gunny and closed his eyes. Gunny moved to the back of the vehicle after picking up the sniper rifle and ammo. Laying the rifle across his chest, he went to sleep.

CHAPTER 17 -- July 31, 2015, 5:35 PM – Iran Time

Lawson awoke to Myers talking to himself. He looked down at his watch to see it was 5:37 PM. "Well, I got five hours of sleep," Lawson thought to himself. He turned to the sound of Myers continued conversation to himself as Myers was looking over the Polevsky papers on the memory chip. Lawson looked around to see where Draper was. Looking up the ravine toward the foothills, he could see that he was not in view. "I hope Draper or his boys don't see you reading this," Lawson reminded.

Myers was looking at the last pages. "I've kept it down where he can't see me."

Myers was mouthing something from one of the formulas. "As much as I can tell here," Myers went on, "this is a design for a five-hundred kilowatt laser system that can be adjusted to different frequencies that can penetrate clouds to take out an aircraft that's way above visual range. It uses two beams. The first beam clears out the moisture in the air including clouds in its path by making a small channel of intense heat. This is followed by a second, much stronger beam that's fired a couple of milliseconds after the first beam. The second beam is the one that causes damage to the target. Each of the beams uses different frequencies. That was the reason for the frequency generator. They had to rapidly switch between two different frequencies when taking the shot. In fact, with the right adjustments, it can take out satellites in orbit by changing frequencies of the light waves to cut down on the effect of the laser being reflected off of a shiny surface. The trick is the fact that they can change the laser to set a beam that can operate at different frequencies depending on the atmospheric conditions and the surface conditions of the target. They have a method for reading cloud penetration and the unit automatically changes frequency until it detects cloud penetration. It can also adjust to surface conditions of the target so that the beam is less likely to be reflected off of the target. That was the reason for the frequency generator having twenty different frequency settings while being hooked up to the laser unit in the lab at the research facility. It also indicates that the multiple shifts in frequency creates lots of heat in the laser unit that limits the ability to be mobile due to the need for large amounts of liquid nitrogen to keep it cool."

Lawson was confused. "You can read that stuff?"

"Most of it," came back Myers. "The text is in Russian, so I can't read that, and some of the equations I'm not familiar with but I understand enough from the math formulas to know this is a quantum-leap in weapons development."

Lawson continued to look at Myers. "Are you some kind of math genius?" He asked.

Myers quietly responded, "What do you think I was doing at MIT, Basket weaving? Most of my work was done in molecular theory and energy wave generation. It's all math."

Lawson turned his attention to the mission at hand. While Myers was putting the memory chip back in the backpack, Lawson was taking inventory of what they had. Five RPG rounds, one RPG launcher, five-hundred feet of primacord, one suicide vest with a dual detonation package and timer, three AK-47s, three-thousand rounds of 7.62 mm ammo taken from the ammo dump for the AK-47s, two pistols – a Russian Makarov PB with built-in silencer taken from Rouhani and a U.S. Maxim 9 pistol with built-in silencer, one hundred rounds of 9 mm ammo, a pair of binoculars and a satellite cellphone. He also remembered that they had the sniper rifle and four hundred rounds of 7.62 match ammo for the rifle that was in Gunny's possession.

As Lawson was completing his inventory, Myers came over and sat down. Picking up one of the AK-47s, Myers began to speak, "You know, when I was in school at MIT, I had a professor in one of my energy wave classes that said that if we come up with a weapon that can neutralize aircraft and missiles, we'd be back to fighting ground wars similar to World War I and the same weapons used against aircraft can be used against armor vehicles like tanks. When he said that, I wondered what type of survival skills would we need to live through that type of a war? A war with no air support and no armor. I thought it would be a couple of generations before we got to that. I'm afraid that we are already there."

Lawson stopped what he was doing and looked at Myers. He could see real fear in his face. Lawson sat back, picked up another of the AK-47s, pulled out the clip, checked the ammo in the clip and glanced off in the distance. "I guess we're about to see the beginnings of Armageddon," Lawson said while contemplating what Myers had said.

"Being that I'm a Christian that believes in the Bible," Myers reflected, "you have no idea how right you may be. I was planning on being a minister before I ended up going to MIT. That's why killing all those people upset me so much. I wanted to be involved in bringing salvation to those that are lost, not in bringing death to them. In the Bible, Armageddon is the war that ends all wars. That looks like what we're facing if these designs work. We'll be left between using ground forces and nukes if this all goes...."

A rifle shot from up in the ravine moved the team into action. Gunny grabbed the sniper rifle and binoculars while scanning the horizon. As he scanned to the south, he could see two Hind helicopters heading their direction.

The Hind helicopter was a Russian-built helicopter that had one main overhead five-blade rotor and a second vertical three-blade tail rotor in the rear section that directed the steering of the aircraft. The helicopter was large, supporting a pilot, co-pilot and two door gunners and could double as a troop carrier. The distinctive profile of the helicopter was the wings extending off of each side of the aircraft. The wings were fitted with machineguns and rocket launchers, making the Hind helicopter one of the deadliest helicopters in the world.

"Choppers coming in!" Gunny shouted while pulling brush down over himself to hide. Lawson looked to where the horses were and saw that they had a cover of brush above them. Lawson and Myers followed Gunny's example. The helos drew closer as Gunny checked the sniper rifle for ammo and settings on the scope. Myers grabbed the RPG launcher and held an RPG round ready to insert it into the launcher while Lawson checked that he had a round in the chamber of his AK-47 and a clip of ammo.

The helos approached their position then turned toward the east and passed by them approximately a half mile from their position. The aircraft went farther north then proceeded back to the south.

"That was close," Gunny observed while putting the lens covers back on the scope of the sniper rifle. All three team members sat down and proceeded to decompress.

A few minutes later, as they were sitting there, Colonel Draper and his associates rode down the ravine to their position. "Hello in the camp. You guys alive?" Draper shouted as they rode in.

"We're here," Gunny shouted back.

Draper pulled his horse up and slid off to the ground. Walking over to Lawson he probed, "Close call. Glad you guys didn't try to challenge them. It's obvious that they were looking for you. They typically don't fly this deep into Kurdish territory except where the main roads are. You guys got a plan for what you're doing tonight?"

Gunny was first to speak, "First we have to know where the radar sites are and, second, we have to know their layout."

Draper motioned for everyone to come over. After they all set down, he broke off a branch from one of the bushes and started to draw on the ground. "This is where we are. Five miles southeast of here is the first radar site. Don't do it now, but if you take the binoculars, you can see the site over there," Draper indicated, pointing to a direction southeast of them. "The second site," he resumed, "is about five miles directly south of that. We don't know where the third one is but it's probably about the same spacing that the first and second ones have, again going directly south."

"What about the layout of the sites?" Lawson inquired.

"Well," Draper responded while rubbing out his first diagram in the dirt with his boot and drawing another, "There's a main control trailer, an eighteen-wheeler type, with the radar antenna approximately fifty yards from it. Next, there's a rocket launch assembly made up of four surface to air missiles approximately one-hundred yards from the trailer but well behind the radar antenna. Power to the control trailer, antenna and missile rig is provided by a built-in generator in the front end of the control trailer. The control trailer controls the radar signal, antenna movement, target locking, launch controls and communications to all supporting units. The control trailer is usually manned by four persons. One person is a radio man, the second a radar operator and controller, the third is a missile launch technician and the fourth is a roving security guy."

Lawson looked at Draper then at the diagram. "This is all well and good," Lawson interrupted, "but knocking out the radar sites isn't going to get rid of the helicopters roaming the area. If anything, an explosion will draw them to the location of the first strike on the radar site and we're toast."

Draper sat for a moment shuffling his boot in the dirt while processing what Lawson had said. "Lawson," Draper revealed, "As I told you earlier, we have an eight-man Kurdish team going to the main army facility that's fifteen miles east of the Shuyesheh Research Facility. They've been tasked with destroying or heavily damaging the munitions storage facility on the base where missiles used for the Hind helicopters and the barrel bombs are stored. They're scheduled to set off the blast at 02:00 hours. It would enhance your chances if you were to blow the three radar sites about a minute before that time."

Lawson looked at Gunny then at Myers. "We don't have plastic explosives or equipment to set all three of them off at the same time. We've got one suicide vest with no explosives, five RPG rounds and about five-hundred feet of primacord. On top of that, we thought we had until just before dawn to blow the three radar sites."

"This is a problem you're going to have to solve," Draper explained. "Nothing can get in or out of the western area until we all do this. We have to blow the radar sites much earlier so that our choppers can come in to pick us and the other teams up under the cover of darkness. See what you can do with what you have or can get at these sites." Lawson sat down, fatigued from the heat, the constant demand on him for solutions and the lack of needed sleep.

It was Gunny that came up with a solution. "I think there's a way to get this done," Gunny started. "We've talked about wrapping primacord around the cable to the radar, but as Myers said, they've probably got spares to bring it back up in operation in about ten minutes. Myers, is it likely that they are using complex connectors at the antenna to hook up the antenna to the trailer?"

Myers thought for a moment then replied, "They would probably have a gang connector of 64 pins or greater for the movement control and calibration, a main cable for the radar-beam transmission and another cable to handle the return signal. So yes, the connection scenario is somewhat complex. More importantly, if the connectors are damaged, they would have to take the antennas back to a repair depot to get them fixed. They might have spare antennas at the army base but it would take them a half hour to forty-five minutes to load up the antennas and bring them out to each site. Another ten to twenty minutes to set them up."

Gunny proceeded, "It seems to me that if we were to destroy the connectors on the antenna and doing as Myers just said, they would have no way to bring the site back up without taking the unit back to the depot for repair."

Lawson shifted how he was sitting as Gunny talked. The fatigue seemed to leave him as he realized that Gunny was on to something. Gunny continued, "We can destroy at least two of the antennas with what we've got. We take the explosive compounds from two of the RPG rounds, use explosives from one of the rounds to put around the connectors on the first antenna, wrap that with about ten iterations of primacord around the connectors and the explosives. Then take one of the detonators off of the suicide vest, leaving the other one on the vest. Put the detonator and timer still on the suicide vest into the combination on the antenna connectors and set the timer. That would take care of one of the sites."

Lawson began to understand the plan Gunny had laid out. "We could take the components from the second RPG round," Lawson interrupted, "and the spare detonator and set it up to destroy the second site the same way. Question is, what do we use for a timer?"

Myers was quick to speak up, "We could hook up the cell phone I have like we did with the one at the ammo dump." Lawson looked at Gunny noting Gunny was smiling. "We need to find a way to call that cellphone," Lawson stated.

"What about the satellite phone Draper gave us?" Gunny inquired. "It will still connect to Myers' phone when called." Lawson nodded agreement.

With two of the sites planned for shutdown, the focus moved to the third site. "The only thing we have left to get rid of the third site is to hit it with an RPG round," Lawson concluded after thinking through his inventory.

Changing the conversation, Draper was quick to respond, "It's best that you wire them up to destroy the farthest site from you first. If you do the farthest one last while you're at the farthest one, you'll be riding fifteen miles or more with helos on your tail. All three need to be destroyed in a timed or remote-controlled trigger with all three being set off within a two-minute period. Also, the sequence of the explosions should be the farthest one first, the nearest one second and the one in between third. This will draw the helos to the last explosion, giving you time to escape."

Myers thought through the sequence then replied, "We'll wire the farthest one with the vest timer, the one in the middle with the cell phone and we'll hit the closest one with our own attack. That will allow for us to control the sequence as the Colonel suggested."

Everyone was in agreement. Lawson posed the question of timing, "When should the sequence start?"

"As I said," Draper explained, "my team is set to detonate the munitions storage area in the army base at 02:00 hours. I would suggest you set your series to take out the sites starting three minutes before 02:00 hours with the last site destroyed a minute before the 02:00 hour. That will draw the helos closer to their base and, once Khaliqi's explosions go off on the base, their response should be to protect the base." The plan looked good. Everyone started putting the pieces together.

CHAPTER 18 -- July 31, 2015, 7:35 PM – Iran Time

Lawson walked over to Gunny while Gunny was checking out the sniper rifle. "You want something, Lad?" Gunny asked while looking through the rifle scope.

Lawson laughed and inquired, "Why is it sometimes you speak in a thick Irish accent and other times you sound like you just came out of California?"

Gunny pulled his eye from the scope and smiled at Lawson as he responded, "Sometimes I'm an Irishman and sometimes I'm a Marine."

"So what are you doing?" Lawson asked.

"You see this scope?" Gunny explained. "It has a focus sight which means ye turn the eyepiece like this and focus in on the target. That will set the elevation of the barrel to the range to the target. When the target is in focus, me lad, you should be able to hit within a three-inch area of where you'd be spottin'. If the range is above eight-hundred yards, you swivel the scope to the side of the rifle and adjust focus which will take you out to fifteen-hundred yards max. The scope also has a laser pointer that will mark the spot where the bullet will hit by simply holding down this button. It's useful at night and in close range. Ye follow me?"

"Yes," Lawson replied. "But how do you take in account the movement of the bullet when the wind's blowing. It'll push the bullet sideways."

"So, you're not so wet behind the ears as I first thought you'd be. You seem to know about windage and elevation," Gunny said abruptly while pointing to a little bulge at the top of the scope. "This little thing catches the wind in it and will show you the direction of the wind and the speed. The information is sent to a little computer in the scope that adjusts the sighting of the scope to take in account for the windage. It's so simple even you could do it. However, it's not going to be able to adjust for wind gusts between you and the target."

Lawson could tell that Gunny was bothered by something as Lawson looked through the scope then proceeded with his thought, "The reason I want to talk to you is that I'm handing off the command of this effort to you. Now before you say anything, let me explain." Gunny face relaxed as he nodded his head and motioned for Lawson to continue. "I'm more of an inside man like what we did at the facility. This thing we're about to do is strictly a military operation that requires the experience of a Marine on the ground. We've got to avoid choppers, patrols and personnel at the sites, and, I might add, we have the potential for a major shootout at the last site as we have to expose our position when we fire the RPG round into the antenna. I would like to know someone is giving the orders that gives us a chance to escape after completing the mission."

"I agree," came Myers' response. Lawson looked to see Myers kneeling off to his right, putting explosive materials from one of the RPG rounds into a bag. "We've pressed Lawson beyond what I would ask of any man over the past twenty-four hours. He's not a field combatant, he's a spy. This is turning into a field combat situation, and Gunny, you're the perfect guy to lead this team."

Gunny smiled once more then asked, "So let me get this straight. Are you guys giving me your vote of confidence that I can lead you guys in a life or death situation?"

"Yes," came the response in unison from Lawson and Myers.

"Besides," Lawson noted, "it's your plan and your experience that got us to a point of possibly pulling this off on what we've got. You've turned something improbable into something possible."

Gunny nodded agreement and asked for the ammo for the sniper rifle. Lawson pulled out three belts. "One will do," Gunny said.

Gunny proceeded to load a clip into the rifle, pulled back the bolt and watched the cartridge move into the barrel. "It moves smoothly and quietly," Gunny observed. "Unlike a lot of other rifles I've seen that have stamped parts, this one has all of its parts machined. They last a lot longer, move a lot smoother and jam a lot less." Lawson was perplexed by Gunny's sudden change of interest from the mission to that of the rifle. He then realized that it was giving Gunny time to think about the change in command before responding.

"The question, Gunny, is do you trust us to follow your orders?" Lawson posed.

"It's not much different than what we do now, is it?" was Gunny's response. "After all, all of us have taken control of situations in this effort without being concerned about command. Lawson, I was a little peeved at you for jumping in on my description of the plan I had in mind. It's very foreign to me to be taking orders from a subordinate. Particularly when that person isn't combat trained. That being said, you've performed beyond any of my expectations. Both of you have."

After he listened to Gunny, Lawson walked over to where Myers was putting together his munitions for the night mission. Both Lawson and Myers saw the change in Gunny. "He needed to vent cause he's all Marine. Giving him command is like he's won a gold medal in the Olympics," Myers observed. They both sat down, feeling satisfied that Gunny finally got some recognition for his experience and leadership, and it came from two team members he respected.

Gunny pulled the clip out and loaded it back into the sniper rifle. Checking the slide action, he sat the rifle down and contemplated what had just happened. "I guess they're not such bad blokes," he thought while looking over the area. "They sure know their stuff. I sure hope I can live up to their expectations. I wouldn't dare tell them how intimidated I am by their confidence and ability to take risks. I guess it's my turn to show what I'm made of."

A while later, Draper slid in next to where Lawson was sitting and whispered, "I just heard that you guys turned control over to Gunny. You do know that he doesn't have a day's worth of combat experience. He's been in logistics and weapons maintenance for most of his career."

Lawson smiled at Draper and responded, "Thanks for the update, Colonel. He is combat trained and he does have one day of combat experience, the last twenty-four hours. He has watched out for us and kept us out of trouble since we joined up with him. And don't forget, he's taken teams into this area for the past eight months, much of the time having to avoid patrols and reconnaissance. He deserves to lead, he's earned it."

"Point well taken," Draper replied. "He has proven himself. I think you guys have a good chance of succeeding. I was concerned you hadn't thought this through but you are one of the better teams I've worked with and you seem to be naturals at what you do. Who else could have set off an explosion so big that half the nations of the world were asking if Iran had tested a nuke. You'll do well." Lawson thanked Draper and proceeded to get oats and water for the horses.

While Lawson was watering the horses, Myers shouted out to everyone, "Hey guys, look at this, cigarettes and matches!" Lawson had forgotten about the cigarettes and matches in the backpack.

Draper ran toward Myers and grabbed the pack of cigarettes. "American cigarettes, no less," he exclaimed while pulling one from the pack. "I haven't had one of these in the past six months," he exclaimed while lighting up one of the cigarettes.

"Hold on a minute," Myers shouted, "a couple of cigarettes and the matches will give us the timing fuse we need for the final radar site." Everyone stopped and was curious as to what Myers was thinking.

"It's simple," Myers continued, "we wrap the matches together, strap a lit cigarette on either side of the match bundle, put a 7.62 mm cartridge with the bullet removed on top of the match bundle and shove an end of the primacord into the end of the cartridge. The cigarettes burning down set off the matches, the heat of the matches causes the primer in the cartridge to detonate which sets off the powder in the cartridge and the primacord." Everyone agreed to the plan.

Myers took the two cigarettes out, removed one match from the box and handed the match and the rest of the cigarettes to Lawson. Lawson handed the rest of the cigarettes out and lit the cigarettes with the match. Meanwhile, Myers was already in the process of wrapping the rest of the matches together and setting up the cartridge to create the detonation.

Lawson looked at his watch. It was 8:05 PM. He figured that they would be leaving in about another hour as darkness started to settle in. The moon had already risen just above the horizon and was full. Leaving now would allow for the moon, being low in the sky, to silhouette them as they rode across the valley and it was still too light of a sky to make a move. An hour difference would make the chances of being seen less likely.

The team went through the plan step by step as they waited for the time to leave. Lawson, Gunny and Myers went through the inventory over and over again to ensure they weren't missing anything. Everything they needed was loaded on the horses. Now it was just sit down and wait. "Hurry up and wait," Lawson thought to himself.

It was nearing 8:40 PM when Lawson watched as Khaliqi and his Kurdish team rode out on horses. They were taking a risk leaving so early but they knew they had to leave now if they were to remain on schedule. Khaliqi's team rode across the terrain at a quick pace, their years of experience riding the range at twilight became apparent to Lawson as he watched them ride off to their mission.

Seeing the terrain, Kahliqi's men on their horses and the way they were riding as they moved reminded Lawson of so many movies situated in the Middle East where he had seen riders traveling across the landscape. All that was missing was the exotic Middle Eastern music. He started laughing as both Myers and Gunny looked at him.

"The heat's getting to him," Gunny stated. "Next, he'll be dancing around the countryside singing some weird song."

"At least it won't be the Marine Corps hymn, more likely 'Anchors Aweigh' I'll be singing ye," Lawson responded back mimicking Gunny's accent with a sarcastic flair.

"All right," Gunny remarked, "ye got me with me own words. Just remember whose watching ye back when you go in to set up those radar sites." Both Lawson and Myers laughed.

"I think he's ready to lead," Lawson quipped.

"I don't know," Myers retorted. "He's going to be sitting on a hill with our backs to him. Not a good position for us to be picking on him." Gunny didn't respond. He just slammed the bolt forward on the sniper rifle then grinned at both of them.

"Just remember guys," Gunny shouted, "the Marine Corps is the men's department of the Navy." Everyone laughed as they prepared their horses.

CHAPTER 19 -- July 31, 2015, 8:17 PM – Moscow, Russia Time

At the Kremlin in Moscow, Russia, it was getting late in the evening when General Sergey Asimov removed his hat and placed it under his arm as he stood at the double doors of the conference room. The doors were heavy mahogany with engravings of working people on both doors, reminiscent of the Soviet Union era. Opening the doors, he stepped into the room where seven generals and one admiral sat. The room's walls were covered in mahogany with pillars evenly spaced out going down the length of each wall. The pillars had exquisite carvings of groups of people that were workers holding flags. Again, something of a throwback from the communist era. At the center of the room was a heavy mahogany table with heavy mahogany chairs covered in red velvet fabric on the back and seat of each chair. The eight 'interrogators' were sitting in chairs representing the Military Industrial Commission. In front of each attendee was a folder with briefing papers inside and a glass of water next to each folder on the table. General Asimov walked up to the end of the table and stood waiting for the conversation to start.

Asimov was a thin man whose uniform hung from his body. He was a junior officer when the Soviet Union collapsed. As a member of the Russian intelligence network serving in the GRU in his early years, he made connections with a number of powerful leaders in Soviet society. After the Soviet Union collapsed, his relationships with those same powerful people in Russia continued. He made many of his advancements through the ranks by destroying the careers of those that got in his way. Asimov worked through the intelligence ranks in his career and was helped by the fact that he had an advanced engineering degree from the Moscow Institute of Physics and Technology. He was promoted to the General Staff as a Major General in 2004. During this time, he served as the Director of new weapons maintenance. In 2009, he was promoted to Lieutenant General and was put in charge of new and advanced weapons development. One of those projects was the Shashka project, started in 2012, to develop a five-hundred kilowatt laser system that could be used in a variety of weather conditions. This project is what the Military Industrial Committee is inquiring about. One general opened the folder in front of him and began to speak.

"Good evening, General Asimov. We see here in our report that the plans for the laser system can't be found. From what we know, the helicopter and courier we sent to pick up the document were lost in a massive explosion at the pickup site. Now we're finding that, what appears to be a British team, has taken the three billion, three hundred million ruble diamond cache that we intended to use to pay the Iranians to get the document. If you like, that's forty-four million Euros or fifty million US dollars. Anyway it comes out, that is a loss we can't afford. What are you doing about the laser documents or the diamonds?"

Asimov sat his hat on the table. "I've talked to Colonel Rouhani," Asimov began. "He is going back into the ammo dump to try to retrieve the document. He thinks it might still be recoverable. I also gave him instructions to try to retrieve the diamonds. He is going into Iraq day after tomorrow with whatever he can recover. We will have Agent Korchagin meet him at the Panjwin Masjid Mosque in Penjwen, Iraq. Korchagin will be carrying an umbrella. His code name is 'Tripoli'. By the way, how do we know it's a British team?"

The general asking the questions turned and conversed with the others at the table. After a short discussion, he turned back to Asimov and said, "Why are you using an asset as valuable as 'Tripoli' to be the pass-through? Never mind, It's already in motion. The team appears to be led by a person by the name of Jason Kendrick that works for the London Chronicle as a cover. Now, it appears you have a plan for getting the document and diamonds. How is it that the plan to get the document out of the facility appeared to be so well set up but could unravel itself so badly? Rouhani had everything under control. What went wrong?"

Asimov fought to keep from panicking. "Our plan was perfect if this British team had not inserted themselves into the effort," Asimov replied. "I believe that we have a spy inside the research facility that was passing information to the British. That's the only way they could have known the timing of the document delivery or the presence of the diamonds."

"Who would have known both the timing of the delivery of the document and where to find the diamonds?" the general asked.

"Well," Asimov responded, "there was Colonel Rouhani, Captain Behzadi, the security chief and Salnikov, the Senior Sergeant at the facility."

"It seems that one of these guys is a spy." The general replied. "Rouhani is working for us. Behzadi possibly would have known about the delivery plans but not the diamonds. The security chief would have known about the diamonds but not the delivery plans. Salnikov would have known about both the delivery plans and the diamonds. It looks like Salnikov may have been our spy. However, from the briefing I have in front of me, Salnikov was killed inside the security vault going to the scientists' offices before the diamonds were taken. So what happened to the diamonds? He couldn't have taken them if he was dead."

"I wouldn't know," Asimov nervously stated as the others looked on. "We will be hearing from Rouhani in a couple of days. Then I should have some answers. Remember that we lost over seventy percent of our Russian personnel at the research facility this morning. The explosion in the lab was devastating and caused most of the casualties. The Iranians also lost a lot of their people, it appears, before the blast. So getting information out of the research facility is very difficult and confusing."

"Thank you for your time, General," the admiral at the table said. "Please keep us updated on anything you find out about the document or the diamonds. By the way, the Iranians have the whole northwestern Iran area covered and are searching for this British team. There is some belief that the team died at the time the ammo dump blew up but we don't have confirmation on that yet."

General Asimov picked up his hat, tucked it under his arm, clicked his heels together, turned and exited out the double doors. Picking up his weapon from the security guard at the entrance to the building, he exited and went to his waiting car. He was once more at the mercy of General Serov's direction and he was tired of Serov's interference that had made its presence known throughout his career.

Once Asimov left, General Serov, the General heading up the inquiry, spoke to the others in the room. "If we don't get the document, it will result in three years of lost research and money. If we don't get back the diamonds, it will be a significant loss of money and trust. If we don't get either of them, there will be a major shakeup by the Duma and we may be a part of that shakeup."

So what was the conflict that defined Asimov's and Serov's relationship? General Georgy Serov's career ran a parallel course to General Asimov's, but that is where the resemblance ended. They both graduated the same year from the University and entered the intelligence community at the same time. While Asimov joined the GRU, Serov joined the KGB. The KGB was responsible for international spying operations in other countries while the GRU was responsible for internal Russian spying. The leadership of the KGB looked upon the GRU as an interference to the KGB's work and the GRU leadership looked at the KGB in the same way. They tended to get into each other's business, which lead to significant conflicts.

Asimov and Serov held each other in contempt which bordered on hatred. Asimov felt that he should have been promoted to the position that Serov received as the General in command of the Military Industrial Commission. Serov felt that Asimov was incompetent and wanted to get Asimov removed from any position in the Russian Army. Serov went so far as to recommend his brother-in-law, General Goremykin, for the position that Asimov ended up being promoted to as Commander of Advanced Weapons Development. They both had played politics with each other's career and were cutthroat in their methods.

As Serov finished his comments, the other committee members all nodded their heads in agreement and proceeded out of the room. Each of them knew the damage if Asimov failed. It would probably result in their resignations and the end of their careers.

CHAPTER 20 -- July 31, 2015, 8:55 PM – Iran Time

It was nearing full darkness when Gunny and his team got on their horses. Draper walked over to wish them luck. "I'll be here when you get back," he said while shaking their hands then continued. "Something to remember. The command trailers are in constant communications with the Iranian ground and air forces. If you have a shootout at one of those sites and you wipe them out before they can get off a call for help, their silence will result in helos looking for you within a few minutes. If they get a message off before you get them, you'll have choppers breathing down your necks almost immediately, choose wisely." They all nodded their heads understanding Draper's warning.

They left the ravine and proceeded at a fast gait across the land, slowing down at each ravine to slowly cross through them. The ground appeared to shimmer as the moon light struck the ground and the heat rising gave the appearance of rippling waves coming up from the ground. A light wind was blowing the patches of grass into waves that reminded Lawson of the ocean. Lawson thought about the level of wind and the possible impact it might have on the bundle of matches when they set them up for the destruction of the third radar site. Lawson was struck by the silence. He saw the millions of bushes and trees spread across the landscape, the mountains in the west turning into plains to the east and the little swirls of dust rising in the distance. Night birds were calling once in a while and, at times, he could hear a helicopter but they were too far away to break the silence for very long. The smell of moisture from the plant life left a sweet scent in the air. Lawson found it distracting as he watched for any movement ahead of them.

When they got near the farthest radar site to set explosives, the sound of helicopters was almost continuous. They were constantly watching as some of the helicopters came within a mile. As they arrived at the radar site, Lawson looked at his watch. It was 11:40 PM.

While Gunny and his team were approaching the first of the radar sites, Khaliqi and his men had arrived at the southwest corner of the Iranian army base.

It was a sprawling base with twenty Hind helicopters, numerous trucks, personnel vehicles and other support vehicles. It also sported three older T-72 Russian tanks. There were twenty-seven large storage facilities running the length of the south side of the base next to the fence and, about a mile away to the north on the other side of the runways, were large support facilities, hangers, an air traffic control tower, fueling stations and an ordinance supply area.

The middle of the base had a large cement pad with runways where the helicopters, vehicles and fueling trucks were parked. There were fighter jets here at one time but they had been moved near Tehran. The field was brightly lighted with numerous spotlights. About half of the helicopters were gone as they were involved in keeping the western border sealed.

Khaliqi and his men had been scouting the base for the past six months and knew the layout, the timing of sentries and the safest places to get into the base. They expected that someday, the knowledge of the base would be essential for the survival of their tribes. That day had come.

Khaliqi had one of his men cut the chain-link fence at the southwest corner of the base where it was darkest. Cutting one link at a time, the man would stop for a moment to listen for any movement before cutting the next link. Link by link, the opening was made. Once they created an opening, the eight men slipped into the opening in the fence with their bags of materials and worked their way down the south edge of the fence. The area was covered in tall grass that stood about three feet high with the ground being muddy in spots and slippery at times. They walked carefully through the area moving to the south fence line.

The progress was slow as they would move a few feet then stop. As they watched for sentries, it was obvious that there was more security activity than normal. Several times a roving sentry would come within fifty yards of where they were at which would cause them to stop and slowly shift to the ground as the sentry came nearer. The sentry would walk to the edge of the cement but not into the grassy area. It was too much work to clean their boots for morning inspection if they ended up with mud on the boots. Khaliqi's team were careful going to the ground as the mud made a squishing sound as they laid down. The full moon didn't help them except to aid them in seeing where they were going and where the sentries were. But the moon was also bright enough to make them visible as they moved to the first of the storage facilities.

The storage facilities were old and made of corrugated metal. They were built when the Shah of Iran was still ruling. Each storage facility stood about forty feet high, fifty yards wide and one-hundred yards long with dirt floors and no windows. Each of the storage facilities had large main doors at the north side of each building. The doors were double doors that would slide open to each side as the buildings were originally built to house and maintain fighter jets.

Khaliqi's team moved slowly to the south of the buildings, walking next to the southern fence. They made it to the back side of the third storage building while watching for sentries that were roving around. As they came to the center of the back of the third building, Khaliqi started feeling around on the corrugated metal for the edge of one of the metal plates. Finding the edge, he felt for the lag screws that held the plates together.

Once he found one of the screws, he pulled out a socket wrench with a properly fitting socket and proceeded to turn the lag screw. As the screw turned, a screeching sound was heard. Kahliqi stopped while everyone hoisted their weapons and waited for the sentry to show up. They heard footsteps coming between the second and third building, the sound of boots walking on gravel. The men laid down on the ground in the shadow of the building, out of the light of the moon. The sentry stopped at the corner and looked down the backside of the storage buildings, looking toward the first two buildings then toward the opposite direction down the row of the other buildings. Taking his flashlight from his shoulder strap, he switched the flashlight on and scanned the area where the first two buildings were. Just as he was ready to scan the ground behind the buildings in the other direction, a small gust of wind came up causing a metal sign on the fence to make a screeching sound followed by a clang. Satisfied that it was the sign making the noise, he switched off his flashlight and walked back toward the airfield.

Khaliqi and his men waited a couple of minutes. Seeing the guard was well outside the range of listening, they got up as Khaliqi pulled a small plastic tube of oil from the bag then oiled the screw. He handed the oil to one of his team members to oil the rest of the screws they were to remove. One by one the screws were slowly removed. The oil cut down a lot of the noise but there were screeching noises made at times but not as loud as the first one. When a screw made a sound, the team would stop and watch for the sentry. Finally, all of the screws for the metal plate were removed and the steel corrugated plate was lowered and laid down on the ground in the shadow of the building in front of the opening they had just made.

Khaliqi entered the building first. It was pitch black. He looked first for any indication that light would leak from openings in the metal walls or the doors at the front. Once he was satisfied that it was safe to turn on a light without being seen from the outside, he pulled a flashlight out of his bag and turned it on, walked in slowly, observing where everything was situated. To the right, row upon row of rockets for the helicopters were stacked in groups of four with wooden spacers between them. They were stacked eight sets of rockets high. This went the whole length of the building. Khaliqi realized that this was probably their whole complement of rockets for the base and the helos being supported at the base. In the middle was ammo used to resupply the helicopters. There were crates marked with the ammo type. Some were linked ammo used for machineguns and some were individual rounds used for rifles. The crates were stacked ten high and were in rows from the back to the front of the storage building. To the left were the fifty-five gallon barrel bombs in rows and a quick count indicated there were approximately two hundred barrels. Forward on the same side of the barrel bombs was a munitions carrier vehicle.

Khaliqi went about halfway down the row of barrels and, using a drum wrench, removed the plug from the top of the drum. He motioned to one of his men to bring over a sack from which Khaliqi pulled out a two-hour kitchen timer with a detonator attached and a battery. He pushed the detonator into plastic explosives in the opening of the drum, looked at his watch to see that it was one minute after 12:00 AM, turned the timer to its maximum setting of two hours and attached the battery.

Next, Khaliqi pulled out a spool of plastic coated wire. He went to the far end of the line of drums, toward the front of the building and, with the help of two of his team members, took out the plug from the drum and laid the drum on its side. It was heavy.

Just as they were doing this, one of the team members came in and flashed his flashlight. Everyone stopped moving except to move their rifles to a firing position. "Sentry heading to the back," whispered one of the men.

Khaliqi moved quickly but quietly toward the back of the building and looked out the opening they had made. He could hear footsteps in the graveled soil but saw no one. Suddenly, a uniformed man with a rifle came to the south corner where, standing in the moonlight, he lit a cigarette.

The team noticed that the moon had not yet got high enough in the sky to shine on the back of the building. The opening and metal piece that was taken off were still in the shadow of the building. They waited for what seemed like an eternity. Finally, the sentry threw down his cigarette and turned to walk back. Everyone waited until he was away from the building.

Two members of the team moved back to the drum they were working on and proceeded with the setup. Khaliqi grabbed a two-inch thick piece of wood broken from one of the pallets and stuck it in his pocket. Back at the drum they had laid on its side, he took a detonator from the sack and another battery and laid them next to the drum. Running two lengths of wire out to the opening of the building, he moved the metal plate taken off the back of the building and pulled it toward the opening until it was difficult to get out of the opening without stepping on the metal plate. Then, grabbing one of the lag screws, he scraped the plastic off of the end of the first of the lengths of wire, wrapped the scraped end of the wire around the lag screw and, using the ratchet wrench, tightened the lag screw down into a hole in the metal plate. He went back to the drum and connected the battery to one end of the detonator and set the other end of the first wire going out to the metal plate next to the detonator. Having placed the end of the wire and the detonator next to the barrel, he went back out to the opening. Khaliqi picked up another piece of wood and one of the lag screws and twisted the screw into the wood. Taking the end of the second wire, Khaliqi scraped off the plastic coating from the end exposing bare wire. He wrapped the bare wire around the lag screw in the piece of wood and put the piece of wood under the metal plate, positioning the plate so that there was a quarter-inch space between the metal plate and the screw in the wood.

Khaliqi waved his flashlight, motioning his men to come to him. Once they were there he instructed them, "I'm going to connect the wiring at the barrel. Do not get anywhere near the metal plate at the opening. It is set up so when someone steps on it the whole building goes up in a massive explosion. So watch your step."

He went back to the barrel, scraped the plastic from the end of the first wire and attached it to the other lead of the detonator. Completing this, he pushed the detonator into the explosives in the barrel. Two of his men lifted the drum to an upside down position with the battery on the outside. Before letting the drum down into position, Khaliqi took the piece of wood from his pocket, put the wood down where the edge of the drum would rest on it and strung the wires alongside the wood. They let the drum down the rest of the way while Khaliqi checked to ensure the edge of the barrel would not crush the wires. He also checked to ensure that there was no possibility of the wires shorting out and setting off the explosives.

As he was checking over the layout of his wiring, he noticed a stack of crates in back of the munitions carrier vehicle marked with 'Tondar-69' and 'To: Hormuz Defense Site' in Farsi on the crates. Khaliqi remembered that the Tondar-69 missile was a medium range, anti-ship missile and was launched using a towed, mobile launch platform. In his conversations with Lawson, he remembered that there were mobile missile sites recently set up in the Strait of Hormuz area. This was information he had to pass on to Lawson.

He went out to the opening. Creating a groove in the dirt floor, he put the wires into the groove and covered the wires with dirt that were going out of the building. He motioned to his men to take several cases of the AK-47 ammo which required two men on each case to carry the wooden boxes using the rope handles on the side of the cases. Each case had one-thousand rounds (fifty boxes of ammo with twenty rounds in each box). His men carefully exited the building while carrying the ammo. Once the men were out of the building, he went back to the barrel bomb that had been laid upside down and attached the final wire going out to the metal plate to the other terminal of the battery. Satisfied with the setup, he exited the building.

Khaliqi and his men slowly moved along the southern fence. The moon had risen higher which made hiding in the shadows more difficult. They would move across the back of each building at a quick pace but when they came to the open areas between the buildings, they would move two by two, carrying the ammo cases while watching for the sentry to make sure he wasn't looking their direction.

Once they got to the open area between the first building and the opening in the fence, they got down on their bellies and crawled slowly toward the opening in the fence while laying each case of ammo on their backs. Every time a sentry would start walking their direction, they would freeze until the sentry had turned and walked far enough away to be out of hearing range.

As they got to the opening in the fence, Khaliqi looked at his watch, an hour and forty minutes to go until detonation. Covered with mud, they got through the opening and to their horses where they loaded up the ammo and quietly proceeded away from the base.

Once they were beyond the lights and hearing of those on the base, they rode at a pace that covered the fifteen miles from the base to the research facility in about an hour and twenty minutes. At the end of their ride, Khaliqi checked his watch. It was 1:38 AM. Getting off their horses above the area where the research facility resided, Khaliqi and his men slowly walked toward a three-inch opening in the side of the mountain that was the exhaust outlet for the generator providing power for the facility. There was a second, smaller opening that was the air intake to the generator room. Three of the men were carrying bags with materials to pull off the mission. As they neared the exhaust opening, they could hear the generator from down inside the facility and could smell the exhaust fumes of the diesel oil-fired generators.

"Lawson and his team don't know about this part of the mission. We've got less than twenty minutes to complete this." Khaliqi whispered to his men. They all watched for any movement of guards but knew the outside guards would be staying near the entrance doors to the facility, far away from where Khaliqi and his men were setting up.

"Give me the bonnet," Khaliqi requested while his men dug into their bags to pull out materials needed for the mission. They had practiced this sequence they were about to execute over and over again until they could do it in their sleep. One of the men handed Khaliqi a very narrow piece of metal and fabric crushed together to appear like a rod. He went to the opening of the three-inch vent made of steel. About ten inches into the pipe was a grate that was made of steel rods that were welded to the inside edges of the steel pipe. The steel rods were formed in a mesh that allowed for the exhaust fumes out of the pipe but created numerous little square openings that were less than an inch wide and high. This was done so that no one could roll a grenade or explosive charge into the generator.

Khaliqi took the bonnet and shoved it through one of the openings in the grate. The bonnet was supplied by Draper taken from the drone drop that also supplied Lawson with his orders from Admiral Roedl. The bonnet was made of fine spring wire and high-temperature resistant fabric. Once Khaliqi pushed the bonnet past the grate, he pulled the bonnet back toward him which caused the bonnet to open up into a cup-like container.

Khaliqi explained to his men, "Remember that this is needed so that the explosives put into the cup won't leak out because of the heat of the generator's exhaust. We're putting Semtex 10 explosives into the cup and lowering the cup down into the manifold area of the generator. It is hot enough there to melt the Semtex 10 causing it to run as a semi-liquid unless we have something to keep it from flowing away from the detonator. We have a short window to do this." Although the team members were very familiar with this step, Khaliqi was so used to lecturing as a college professor, he slipped into his teaching role as a means to reduce the tension he was feeling.

He took a pack of Semtex 10 explosive compound from the bag and proceeded to roll it into lengths that would clear the grating and go into the cup. As he did so, he pushed the rolled Semtex 10 into the cup, using a wooden stick to press the explosives down to the bottom of the cup. Once the cup was half full, he pushed the detonator through the grate and into the explosives in the cup and extended the detonator wires toward him. Pulling a diagram out from the bag, he looked at the layout of the facility for the horizontal length of the pipe and how far the cup would need to drop down vertically to be in the area of the manifold.

He needed to determine the distance from the grate to the generator. The diagram indicated that, once the pipe turned downward from the top of the pipe where he was at, it was a straight run down to the exhaust manifold. Taking a wire, he pushed it into the opening and down until it would no longer go further. Calculating the length of wire he would need, he strung two wires out some fifty feet and wrapped a piece of tape around them at the forty foot mark. He attached the two wires to the detonator, one wire for each lead and pushed the detonator into the explosive compound in the cup. Once finished, he continued to fill the cup with the Semtex 10 until it was full.

The cup had been designed to be narrow enough to make the turn where the pipe went from running horizontal to dropping vertical. Khaliqi attached both wires using clips to the top of the cup to hold the wires and detonator in place in the cup. He checked his watch. It was 1:47 AM. They had to finish quickly.

He pushed the bonnet deeper into the pipe using the wires to push it inward, continuing to push on the wires until the taped part of the wire came up to the pipe entrance. Going to the end of the wires past where they had been taped, he cut the wires at the forty-five foot length, stripped the wires at the end and attached one of them to the battery and timer. Once he completed the attachments, he clipped the wires to the metal grate and hooked up the other wire to the timer after setting it for eight minutes. Motioning for the men to run down the hill to the horses, he checked his watch. It was now 1:52 AM. "We've got to get out of here now!" he exclaimed while jumping onto his horse.

"With all the training we did on this part of the mission, you never explained why we had to set that up?" one of his men quietly called out while getting on his horse.

"We've got to convince the Iranians they're under attack if we're to get the western borders open. It was Draper's idea. The more attacks, the more the Iranians will panic," Khaliqi responded back as he turned his horse to leave the area.

CHAPTER 21 -- July 31, 2015, 11:41 PM – Iran Time

While Khaliqi and his men were doing their work, Gunny, Lawson and Myers were at the start of their mission. They were approximately three-hundred yards away from the farthest control trailer as they looked over the situation. They were at the first of three radar sites they needed to disable. The layout was close to what Draper had told them.

Using the binoculars, Gunny saw that there were two windows in the trailer with a door in between the windows. The door was at the central point of the side of the trailer. In one window, Gunny could see the communications set with a man sitting in front of the unit. In the other window was a man sitting at a radar screen and a panel to his left that appeared to be indicator lights and launch buttons for the missiles. The lighting inside the trailer was a dark blue which would make the control trailer hard to see unless a person had night-vision goggles.

As they were scoping out the site, the sound of a helicopter was approaching and getting louder. The team ducked down and pulled the horses down to keep a low profile while the helo flew toward them, turned about a half-mile away and proceeded back in the opposite direction.

Gunny proceeded to set the sniper rifle up in position and adjusted the scope for the proper range. Lawson and Myers walked down to the radar site moving in short shifts, watching for the sentry that should be outside of the trailer. Carrying their bag of materials, Lawson and Myers neared the control trailer when they spotted the sentry at the end of the trailer near the generator smoking a cigarette and looking away from them toward the road that was east of the control trailer. The sound of the generator running had made it easier for them to talk without the sentry hearing them.

The gray shirts and light brown pants Lawson and Myers were wearing blended in well with the shadows. Their turbans, although originally light colored, had become more subdued by the water and dirt that had gotten on them during use.

They crawled the last twenty yards to the antenna. The antenna created a shadow area that they could stand in and not be seen as long as they didn't move. The antenna was a large dish, approximately twelve feet wide, with the cables bundled together going from the trailer to the antenna. There were three connectors on the back of the antenna grouped within about three inches from each other. The antenna would move back and forth from side to side for a couple of minutes in a 180 degree swing, then stop for several minutes. Myers was wondering why they were using a dish arrangement rather than the metal screen-based antennas he was used to. He figured that they were using higher frequencies for their radar setup but wasn't sure as to why.

Hiding in the shadow of the antenna, Lawson slowly removed the primacord from the bag. Myers pulled the explosive compound taken from one of the RPG rounds and proceeded to press the material around the connectors. While they were doing this they were watching the sentry for any movement in their direction. Each time the antenna was actively swinging, the sentry would look in the direction of the antenna. Lawson and Myers would freeze at that point until the antenna stopped moving. Once the antenna stopped moving and the sentry turned to look at other directions, they would continue working on setting up the charges while they restricted their movements to very slow actions so as not to be visible to the sentry.

Lawson wrapped ten turns of the primacord around the explosive materials while Myers got ready to set the timer taken off of the suicide vest. "What time is it?" Myers whispered. Lawson looked at his watch, "It's 11:50," Lawson replied. Myers did a quick calculation and set the timer for two hours and five minutes.

As Myers was doing so, the sentry turned and looked their direction. Something they were doing had caught his attention. They both froze. The sentry began to walk toward them. Gunny was watching the action from the hill through his scope and realized that in another thirty yards or so, the sentry would see the two men. Gunny thought fast. At the missile launch site, approximately one hundred yards from the antenna, were red reflectors on the missile launch trailer. He turned the sniper rifle to sight in on a red reflector and pressed the laser button on his scope. The laser light, used for marking a target with a red dot to show where the bullet would hit, caused the red reflector to glow as though it was a bright red light. Gunny hit the reflector for two seconds, drawing the sentry's attention away from the antenna. Gunny knew that the angle of laser beam would make it difficult for the sentry to see its source. The sentry walked slowly over to the missile trailer. As he did so, Myers completed the setting of the timer and turned the timer face down against the explosives so the light from the display on the timer could not be seen. He pushed the detonator in between two lines of the primacord and into the explosives.

Lawson and Myers backed away slowly from the antenna while watching the sentry. The sentry finished looking at the missile trailer all the while wondering where the red light came from. Not able to discern the cause of the red light, the sentry walked toward the antenna. Lawson and Myers dropped to their stomachs when the sentry turned. About twenty feet from the antenna, the sentry saw that everything seemed normal and went back to the front end of the command trailer. At that point Myers and Lawson crawled back toward Gunny.

When Lawson and Myers felt they were far enough away from the sentry, they proceeded to walk back to where Gunny was waiting. Getting to Gunny, he handed the horse's reins to each of them and whispered, "Walk the horses for a few minutes until we're far enough away that they can't see or hear us," as they headed north to the next radar site.

Once they were well out of hearing range, they rode the horses at a fast pace, slowing down to go through each ravine and watching for helos approaching their area.

They were just entering a ravine when a helo moved directly toward them. Gunny stopped and told them to get off of their horses. "He might have seen us in the moonlight," Gunny said while unslinging his sniper rifle. The helo came within one-half mile and turned on its spotlight. The men waited to see what the Hind helicopter would do. The helo turned about a quarter mile from where they were at and proceeded back to the south.

"It might be that the sentry reported seeing some unusual lights and the guys in the helo were checking it out," Gunny assumed while they watched the helo withdraw.

"I hope they didn't discover our setup and that's the reason they came to check things out," Myers countered.

It was 12:40 AM when they reached the next radar site. They set up in the same position again and saw that the layout and lighting was the same as the first site.

Lawson and Myers approached the antenna all the while watching for the sentry. There was none seen. They proceeded to setup up the explosives the same way as they did on the first antenna.

As Myers was checking the phone and detonator wiring setup a thought occurred to him. "This is Rouhani's phone," he whispered to Lawson, "what if the general decides to call him or he gets a text. It could all go up before we want it to."

Lawson thought of what Myers was saying then replied, "Then I suggest we get out of here."

Myers pushed the detonator into the explosives, checked the battery level on the phone then laid the phone face down so that the light from the display could not be seen. They walked back slowly until they felt they were safe. As they got back to Gunny's position, they saw the sentry come out of the door to the trailer, hoisting up his pants. "I guess he had to go," Gunny whispered as they proceeded to walk their horses away from the site. Lawson checked his watch. It was 12:55. Helicopters kept getting closer with each pass toward their direction. "Is it possible someone saw us? Maybe they did find the first site's setup and are scanning for us." Lawson thought. Time was running out.

They rode to the third radar site, taking less time to ride through the ravines as the moon being higher in the sky made the ravines easier to see. It also meant that they were easier to see on open ground which caused them to slow down between ravines. They arrived at the third site at 1:40 AM. Fifteen minutes before the first charge is to go off. They positioned themselves once more like they did with the first two sites.

Lawson and Myers moved slowly down to the antenna at the third site while Gunny sat with the sniper rifle. They watched the sentry as they got out their gear as this sentry seemed more attentive. It was difficult to hide in the shadow of the antenna as the moon had risen higher in the sky. Myers set up the explosive charges and wrapped the primacord around the charges. While he was doing this, Lawson was keeping close attention on the sentry. Each time the sentry turned their direction Lawson would whisper, "Freeze." They both would stop until the sentry turned back around. Myers took the cartridge, matches and cigarettes combination, pushed the end of the primacord into the end of the cartridge, then pressed some chewing gum into the entrance of the cartridge. The gum would help keep the primacord in place and aid in setting off the primacord as it would help to create a more definitive explosion in the confined space of the cartridge.

Suddenly, he realized they had a problem. "What are we going to light the cigarettes with?" he whispered. "Also, any light coming from here will be seen by the guard." Lawson was at a loss.

"What about taking one of the matches from the bundle and lighting it in front of us with our backs turned to him," Lawson whispered back. Myers nodded and reached for the match from the bundle. Now, how to hide lighting the cigarette from the sentry as there may be reflected light even with their backs turned. At that moment, the antenna swung back and forth a couple of times then stopped. As it did so, there was movement at the trailer. The sentry had raised his AK-47 toward the antenna. Apparently the sentry saw Myers move to get the match or was drawn to the movement of the antenna. Whatever it was, they were exposed.

Lawson swung around, leveled the rifle toward the sentry and fired. The sentry fired at the same time then fell. Lawson felt his right leg kick back but thought nothing of it. Almost at the same time, a rifle shot was heard as a bullet shattered the window on the left side of the door and the radio operator inside the trailer slammed forward into the communications equipment. Gunny's shot ran true. A second man inside the trailer pushed the radio operator to the side as a second rifle report was heard. The second man lurched forward and fell to the floor. A third man came out of the door with his AK-47 firing full automatic. Both Myers and Lawson opened fire as he came out the door. The man took two steps and dropped.

Lawson took the match from Myers. He noted the wind had died down to where the air was still as he lit both cigarettes. He blew on them several times to ensure they were burning, put the matches and cigarettes combination back under the cartridge then turned to head back to Gunny and the horses. As he turned, his right leg felt like dead weight and he had trouble moving it. As he looked down, there was a hole in his pants. Tearing the pants open where the hole was, the moonlight exposed a small stream of gray fluid coming from his leg. He knew it was blood.

In a quick flash of memory, he remembered a verse from an old Moody Blues song, 'Nights in White Satin'. He started thinking through the verse in the song concerning how the color of things looked in moonlight, " 'cold hearted orb that rules the night removes the color from our sight, red is gray and yellow white' or something like that," he thought. The moon did make red look like gray. He limped back slowly to where Gunny and, now, Myers were. Gunny recognized immediately that Lawson was wounded.

Helping Lawson onto the horse, all three set out at a gallop to the northwest. After about four minutes of riding, Gunny felt they were far enough away to tend to Lawson's injury. Going down into the next ravine, Gunny told Lawson to stay on his horse, Gunny ripped off some cloth, taking a long strip from the lower part of his undershirt. Gunny checked the wound. 'You're not losing much blood," he said while wrapping the bandage around the leg. "Both entry and exit wounds are barely bleeding. No major veins or arteries have been hit and no bones have been hit." Gunny tightened down the bandage while Lawson winced then looked at the time.

"We're almost out of time," Lawson said while looking at his watch. It was 1:57 AM. As Gunny was finishing, a helicopter was approaching their position. It was hard to see it in the dark but they could make out the shape of a Hind helicopter in the moonlight. The sound was coming closer and it wasn't turning.

Lawson was wondering what happened to the first explosion that should have occurred at the first radar site two minutes ago.

Lawson slipped off his horse and dropped to the ground with his AK-47. At the same time, Myers had picked up the RPG launcher from his horse, grabbed an RPG round, dropped the round into the launcher and turned it around until it lined up in the launcher. "Don't fire at the chopper unless they fire first," Gunny said while picking up his AK-47.

The helicopter passed within one-hundred yards south of them turning to line up with the ravine they were in but moving away from them. Suddenly, the helicopter spotlight turned on and followed the ravine going away from them. There was a flash in the ravine about fifty yards from where Gunny and his team were and a trail of flame moving almost too fast for the eye to follow went toward the helicopter. There was a loud bang sound as the RPG round bounced off the bottom of the helicopter followed by an explosion on the ground on the other side of the helicopter as the RPG round hit the ground. Machine gun fire could be heard with tracers coming from the helicopter toward the ravine about fifty yards from where Gunny, Lawson and Myers were hiding.

The helo turned in a circle with the pilots positioning the helo to fire their rockets. Gunny raised his sniper rifle and, as the helicopter turned to where the right side of the helicopter was facing them, Gunny sighted in through the gunner's side door, focusing on the pilot sitting in the left seat of the aircraft. He waited for a clear shot then pulled the trigger. The bullet crashed through the pilot's helmet as the pilot lunged forward into the helicopter's console. The aircraft swung upward as two of the rockets from the Hind fired, passing high over the head of the other people in the trench.

Myers lifted the RPG launcher to his shoulder. Gunfire could be heard coming from farther up the ravine and hitting the helicopter. The helicopter started to turn when Myers got the aircraft in his sights.

"Aim for the lowest part of the rotor," Gunny shouted. Myers aimed just below the spinning blades, wondering why Gunny would tell him to do that. "RPGs tend to fire low," Gunny continued.

Myers pulled the trigger. Half-a second later, the front of the launcher flashed while, at the same time, a 'swoosh' sound could be heard. The RPG round went through the doorway of the helicopter and detonated in the cockpit of the aircraft.

Gunny saw two bodies fly out, one from each side of the helicopter as the RPG round detonated. He knew immediately that the door gunners had been blown out of the doors and were dead. The helicopter plunged to the ground, turning to its side just before hitting the ground with the main rotor blades breaking off, flying in all directions. There was fire everywhere. All of this took less than a minute.

Gunny grabbed some of the cloth left over from fixing Lawson's leg and ran to the aircraft. He disappeared for several moments, finally coming out with a machinegun over his shoulder, his hand holding the barrel with the cloth. In the other hand were two metal boxes of ammo. He dropped the weapon into the ravine along with the ammo.

Jumping into the ravine, he shouted for the others to get ready. Looking up over the edge of the ravine, Lawson could make out the outlines of five or six helicopters coming their way. Lawson looked at his watch. The action with the helo and Gunny's retrieval of the machinegun and ammo took all of two minutes. It was 1:59 AM. The first charge should have gone off four minutes ago!

Gunny grabbed the binoculars and moved them to his eyes. Scanning the horizon in the area where the farthest antenna should be, he looked for any indication of a flash. He waited about thirty seconds then exclaimed, "The first antenna just blew. Lawson your watch is off."

Looking around toward the south then southwest toward the mountains, he could see helicopters in large numbers moving toward the point of the flash. "Let's get ready," Gunny said as they started to set up the machine gun. "That second one should have gone off by now," Lawson stated as he look back toward the antenna closest to them. Looking at his watch, he saw that the explosions on the base would go off less than a minute. Suddenly there was a brilliant flash followed about two seconds later by a 'boom' sound. They watched as the antenna closest to them slowly moved forward and crashed to the ground. "That was a bigger blast than I expected," Myers said while watching the scene.

"Let's get out of here," Gunny shouted. "Helos heading this way, lots of them!"

"Wait," Myers shouted back. "Let's turn their interest to other areas." Myers pressed in the numbers on the satellite phone then held up the phone to his ear. "It's ringing." A bright flash along the horizon was seen and the helos farthest away immediately swung toward that direction, However, the five helicopters originally coming for them were still coming.

"That's all three sites," Gunny declared. "Let's get out of here." Gunny, Myers and Lawson grabbed the machinegun and ammo, quickly loading them onto the horses to resituate themselves up the ravine to where the others that had been firing. Gunny boosted Lawson up onto his horse before Gunny got on his horse. They began to move quickly to where the other people were sitting.

CHAPTER 22 -- August 1, 2015, 1:51 AM – Iran Time

At the Iranian army base, the sentry had gone back for another cigarette. As he lit up he looked around. The moon shined just enough in the area where the opening Khaliqi made in the third building that it was seen by the sentry. As he walked toward it, he immediately saw that the building had been breached. Getting on his radio, he called out for an alert and informed them which building had been breached. It took the emergency team five minutes to arrive.

As the emergency team was entering the building, the Iranian colonel in command of base operations arrived then stepped into the building and looked around with his flashlight. Nothing appeared to be touched in the rocket storage area. They had all side-stepped the metal sheet that had been removed from the back of the storage facility.

One of the men from the emergency team called him over to the barrel bomb area. A timer was sitting on top of one of the barrels showing it had two minutes until it would detonate. The colonel walked over to the barrel bomb and examined the setup. He gently pulled the detonator from the barrel and looked at the timer, definitely a primitive but most effective setup. He pulled the detonator from the timer, disconnected the wires and handed both to the emergency team leader.

Satisfied he had prevented a major disaster, the colonel radioed the results to the headquarters building. He could hear the timer 'ding' as he stepped toward the door. Everyone laughed. He ordered everyone out as he sat down while the soldiers leaving were sidestepping the metal plate in the doorway. The Iranian Colonel pulled out his notepad, looked at his watch and seeing that it was 2:02 AM, wrote down the time, date and a note on the event. Once he finished his note, he got up and walked toward the back opening. Stepping out of the opening the colonel stepped on the metal plate. The plate shifted down and made contact with the lag screw in the piece of wood completing the circuit to the other barrel bomb.

Back at the ravine, Lawson looked at his watch, it was 2:03 AM. "I guess the Kurds weren't successful with their mission," Lawson said while they rode up the ravine.

Just as he said that, the sky lit up behind them. Turning back to look, they could see a large fireball far off in the distance to the southeast followed by a second, much larger explosion that turned the whole area into daylight for several seconds. Draper's Kurdish team was successful.

The five helicopters were still moving in the team's direction. They had slowed down their movement forward as they had turned on their spotlights and were swinging back and forth, scanning the area underneath them.

Gunny's team continued to ride up the ravine knowing it had to be Draper's American team that had come under fire. Lawson's leg was starting to throb. As they neared the point in the ravine where they saw the fire being exchanged with the helo, Draper came out to meet them. They got off of their horses and Draper had one of his men tend to Lawson's wound while the rest of them set up weapons. The oncoming helicopters, with their spotlights on, continued to sweep back and forth as they moved, getting closer and closer to the ravine. At the same time, a low rumble was heard. Lawson thought it was the sound from the military base explosion.

"That would be the detonation at the research facility," Draper said while carrying the machinegun ammo over to

Gunny. Lawson looked at Gunny and Myers, questioning Draper's comment. Both Gunny and Myers shrugged their shoulders, indicating they had no idea about the explosion at the research facility.

Everyone situated themselves for the oncoming attack. Draper and Gunny were stationed at the machinegun Gunny had taken from the helo. Myers had loaded an RPG round into the launcher that Draper had brought while Lawson had taken Gunny's sniper rifle and quickly practiced sighting on a target. Draper now wished that he had brought the other RPG rounds and launcher that were near the vehicle. Except for the rounds and launcher he had brought with him, he had taken the rest of the RPG rounds off of his pack horse so that he and his team could move quickly.

Suddenly, the helicopters turned and headed southeast. "The helos are leaving," announced one of Draper's men, located at the horse with the radio. "They got some message but it was breaking up." Just after the report about the helicopters departure, a loud roar that lasted for about five seconds was heard. "Based upon its distance from us, that would be the sound from the explosions at the army base," Gunny surmised. "It takes five seconds for sound to travel a mile and the base is about fifteen miles from us so that would take about a minute and fifteen seconds for the sound to reach us which is about right."

One of Draper's men was lying on the ground. "He's dead," Draper said rather bluntly. Draper had his code book out and was writing a message which he took and tucked it in the dead man's pocket. "You aren't done with this mission, Lanstrum," he said to the dead man as he stood over him. He then turned to Lawson. "The Iranians will find him. They'll decode the message. It says, 'mission failed for papers, successful for ammo dump' which will be one more item convincing everyone that all records associated with the research facility have been destroyed which, I'm convinced, is not the case. I figure you're operating on Roedl's orders. Now let's get out of here."

"Wait a minute, Colonel" Lawson shouted. Draper stopped in his tracks. "There's no logic to what you just did," Lawson continued. "This dead guy is an American. Don't you think the Iranians will figure the Americans were involved if you leave a dead American here."

"Besides," Gunny added, "it's our practice not to leave anyone behind, dead or alive."

Draper thought over what both Lawson and Gunny had said. "You guys pick him up and bring him along. I guess I've gone native for too long in this country and don't think about standard military practices." Gunny and Myers picked up Lanstrum and laid him on one of the horses.

As Draper was talking, his other associate was listening to the radio. He shouted to Draper causing him to walk over to see what all the excitement was about. "The Iranians have called a general alert!" his aid shouted.

Draper turned back to the others and said, "A general alert is a recall for everyone in the field to go back to their base to defend their bases. That leaves the way open for our choppers to get in and pick up our teams."

"Looks like their air cover is going back to the base," Gunny interjected, "Looks like Draper's gamble paid off."

CHAPTER 23 -- July 31, 2015, 6:10 PM – Washington, DC Time

Admiral Roedl was at a dinner with several senators and other military officers when Commander McMahon, Admiral Roedl's nighttime aide came into the room. Roedl was talking to a group of naval officers when McMahon walked up to him.

"Excuse me, Admiral. We've got activity in western Iran that you need to see."

Roedl excused himself from the conversation and turned to McMahon, "What's up Mac?"

"Sir," McMahon answered, "your presence is needed immediately at the SAL center. We've got events unfolding that may need your attention."

Roedl excused himself and left with McMahon. It was a ten minute drive. Roedl looked at his watch. It was 6:25 PM. "That would make it 02:25 hours in Iran," he thought to himself.

"Mac," Roedl asked, "any change in conditions on the ground in western Iran?"

"Well, Admiral," McMahon responded, "that's the whole reason you have to get back to SAL. A bunch of things started happening which is the reason I came as quick as I could to pick you up."

"What things are happening?" Roedl demanded.

"Sir, there have been attacks against Iranian assets all over northwestern Iran," McMahon responded. "There were radar sites knocked out, which you know, but there were also major explosions at the army base east of Shuyesheh and communications indicating the Shuyesheh Research Facility was hit again. It looks like the Kurds are involved in an uprising."

They arrived at the Kennedy Irregular Warfare Center about ten minutes later. Both Roedl and McMahon ran through the doorway, showed security their IDs, put their sidearms on and went through a series of passageways to the biologic scanners that would grant them entry into the SAL Center.

As they entered SAL, a Petty Officer handed Roedl three sheets of paper. Two were reports on the status in the area and the third was a message from Colonel Draper. Roedl went to Draper's message first.

The message stated, "Admiral, we have Iranian forces going back to defend their bases and we are heading back to our vehicle at point Whiskey November. Need pickup by 03:30 our time for the team with me." Roedl thought over Draper's request for a moment and was about to give orders for pickup as he began to read the first report.

The report stated, "We have identified a hostile force of ten to twenty Iranian soldiers between your Shuyesheh Team's location and the Whiskey November pickup point. Furthermore, picking up the team where they are at is highly risky as there is too much activity in the area. Advise team to go back to the Whisky November point but inform them that they may need to fight their way through. Enemy positions set up approximately two miles northwest of team's present location. Also inform command that Lanstrum was a casualty."

Admiral Roedl sat down in one of the theater chairs in the SAL center and requested the live satellite feed be brought up for western Iran. Moments later the picture came up on the main screen. Next Roedl asked for them to zoom in north of the Shuyesheh area. As the picture zoomed in, he could see that there was a small group with horses next to a burning aircraft and a second group approximately two miles to the northwest comprising of twenty-one or more individuals that appeared to be on foot.

"Issue this message to Colonel Draper," Roedl instructed. "His code is GOT114. Tell him pickup delayed but he's not to tell the team that until they get to the pickup point. Also let him know about the Iranian force located between the team and the Whiskey November point of approximately twenty people. Let him know we're sending munitions and medical supplies on the pickup chopper. That's all."

The radioman took the message and typed it in. Draper should receive the message in a couple of minutes.

About three minutes later, Roedl asked the radioman to come back over to him for another message. "Issue this message to Marine Lieutenant Jake Corey, code GOT118. He's the pilot that's going to do the pickup of the Tin Cup Team. Tell him to get two cartons of American cigarettes from supply and give them to Draper when Corey arrives to make the pickup." The radioman looked perplexed but figured that it was some type of code that only Corey and Draper would understand. He sent the message.

Roedl took stock of where the missions in the area were sitting. As he was ascertaining the conditions of each team, the woman doing strategic assessments came over to report on the communications going on between the western Iran area and Tehran.

"Admiral," she started, "there has been a massive explosion at the army base near Shuyesheh. They have lost seven or eight

Hind helicopters, several storage facilities including most of their munitions, a significant quantity of their spare parts and a portion of their fuel storage. At the Shuyesheh Research Facility, they've lost all power due to an attack on their power generation system and all radar sites are down, which means they can't launch any missiles at our helicopters attempting to do team recovery operations. We can't use any of the roads for extraction as they are covered with Iranian vehicles and personnel. They're covering all of the roads and trails going across the border into Iraq. Our only hope is to fly them out."

Roedl was surprised with the results of the operation. What was supposed to be a relatively quiet set of operations, except for the ammo storage facility, turned into a well synchronized series of attacks that would convince any government that they were under general attack. Roedl began to believe that Michaels may have been right about Lawson exceeding his orders. However, it appeared to Roedl that Lawson had a lot of help and that Lawson and Draper were two peas from the same pod. He smiled while he thought about the events so far. Leave it to the Navy to turn a simple operation into a major confrontation. Lawson's team appeared to have a considerable amount of good sense and timing to pull off all that they had accomplished so far. It was time to tell the President what was happening and the result of the efforts though they weren't out of the woods yet.

CHAPTER 24 -- August 1, 2015, 2:40 AM – Iran Time

Draper's aide came up to him while Draper was planning his next move. "Sir," the aide stated, "Roedl's comm guy is on the horn for you." Draper went to the horse with the radio and proceeded to talk to the person on the other end. After a couple of minutes, he came back to the team where the three of them were talking. "We're not finished yet," He said while looking at Lawson's leg and adjusting the bandages. "We've got to go back to the vehicle in the ravine. Our choppers should be coming in about half an hour and they want to pick us up there. This area is too active for a landing and we have a small force of Iranians between us and the vehicle. Those Iranians will be a threat to any pickup unless we can drive them out or take them out. Gunny, this is your mission on orders from me. Clear out that force. They're about two miles northwest of here, directly in line with our path to the vehicle. By the way, the staging point where our vehicle is located has been designated as Point Whiskey November."

"Yes, Sir," came Gunny's response. "Lawson, Myers, on me," Gunny shouted as he picked up the sniper rifle. "Myers, you take the machinegun and the ammo on your horse. Lawson, you take the extra AK-47 ammo on your horse."

"Colonel," Lawson asked, "where again was this force last seen?"

"They're about two miles in that direction," Draper said while pointing to the northwest. "You'll be needing this. You left it in the vehicle," he remarked as he handed the Maxim 9 pistol to Lawson. "The weapon is loaded, one round in the chamber and a full extra clip. Here's an additional box of ammo for the weapon." Lawson took the pistol and ammo while pulling himself upon to his horse. Once Lawson was on the horse, Gunny handed the extra AK-47 ammo to Lawson and they proceeded to the northwest.

Lawson realized that they would have to go back to the vehicle anyway as the backpack with the Polevsky papers were still there. He began to wonder who Draper left at the vehicle to secure the area. He also realized that they had too many barriers to cover the two and one-half mile distance in thirty minutes particularly if there was a force between them and the pickup point, yet Draper didn't seem to be all that concerned about it. Lawson figured that the pickup was scheduled to be later than what Draper had said. He wondered why Draper would keep the information secret about the pickup time.

As they started out, Lawson saw that the position of the moon was past its peak causing the terrain to look as though there were small dirt mounds all over the area. Anywhere there was a clump of grass, there was a dirt mound that was higher than the surrounding ground. A small force could use those mounds as cover to keep from being seen. Lawson was shaking due to his wound and the night was getting chilly. As they rode forward, Lawson noticed how the shadows from the moonlight were making the team more visible as their shadows could be seen to the front of them. The moon was behind them and they would be more visible to anyone north of them meaning they would stand out like silhouettes. This made Lawson particularly alert and, as he looked at Gunny, he could see Gunny was realizing the same issues.

Lawson rode up next to Gunny and expressed a concern. "Gunny, can I give you a historical perspective?"

Gunny looked at Lawson. "I thought you didn't like a little bit of history."

"Actually," Lawson replied, "I use a lot of my concepts of how the enemy may work based upon history."

"Go ahead, give me your take using a historical example."

Lawson pondered for a moment then explained, "In 1759, Rogers Rangers attacked Saint-Francis in Quebec during the French and Indian War. His raid was successful but the retreat after the raid was costly. He lost around half of his two-hundred men during the retreat. One of the tactics the French used against him was to send small groups of men into the lower areas of the landscape to wait to ambush his men. They would go in twos and threes into the ravines to sneak upon Rogers men while they were marching forward. This terrain reminds me about the similarities of what Rogers faced and what we are facing."

Gunny looked over to Lawson in the moonlight. "What would you recommend?" he stated while adjusting his weapon.

"I suggest that we spread out and move slow," was Lawson's answer. Gunny motioned to Myers to move farther to the left as Lawson moved farther to the right.

They had gone about two miles when Gunny raised his hand for them to stop. They quietly sat on their horses as they waited to see what caught Gunny's attention. "There it is again," Gunny stated, pointing to an area where the ground dropped lower into a small valley while, at the same time, he was attempting to get his foot out of the primitive stirrup. Lawson looked but saw nothing. His leg was beginning to hurt at a level where he was having trouble concentrating but still he continued to look. Suddenly, there was a momentary flash off in the distance. It was obviously a reflection of the moon on a shiny piece of metal or glass. Lawson swung off his horse and dropped to the ground as the pain in his leg suddenly seemed to fade. Myers saw Lawson drop and did the same thing. A moment later, there was a snapping sound. Gunny kicked the stirrup loose, jumped off his horse with his sniper rifle in his hand and landed face-down in the dirt.

"Damn, that was close," Gunny said while looking at the hole in his vest. "That damn saddle almost got me killed." The bullet hit his vest but missed his body. He stuck his finger in the hole in the vest and declared, "7.62 round, AK-47." Lifting the sniper rifle scope to his eye, he scanned the area in the valley to see if there was movement. He could see none.

Lawson reached up to the saddle of his horse and pulled down the binoculars. Scanning the area where the flash of light originally came from, he focused on the area. A flash again. Lawson focused the binoculars to where the flash came from. He could faintly see a man's head above a mound of dirt with a pair of binoculars. "Gunny, the flash is coming from a man's binoculars. The moonlight is catching the lenses on his binoculars."

"Where," Gunny replied while moving his scope back and forth.

"Do you see the tree next to that ravine?" Lawson asked while pointing to a spot near the next ravine. Gunny searched in a swinging motion with the sniper rifle scope. He saw trees and finally focused on a tree that appeared at the edge of the ravine and stood out more than the rest of the trees around it.

"I think so," Gunny responded.

"Now go right about two degrees where there's a mound of dirt." Lawson directed. Gunny swung to the right very slowly until he saw some motion among the mounds of dirt.

"There's lots of mounds of dirt. Wait, I've got it." Gunny replied. "I see three people, one with binoculars and two manning a machinegun. I'll take out the guy with binoculars first." Gunny scanned back and forth between different people in his sights until he assured himself as best he could that the uniforms were Iranians. He didn't want to open fire on friendlies. Sighting in on the guy with the binoculars was difficult as it was hard to get a good focus with the light so low. The man with the binoculars lifted the binoculars again. This time, the way the man held his binoculars also exposed his wrist watch to Gunny's view. It was a watch that had glow-in-the-dark numbers and hands. Gunny set the scope focus to where he could see the glow of the watch in focus and pulled the trigger. There was a loud report from Gunny's rifle and a moment later, the guy with the binoculars disappeared from view.

"You got him, Gunny," Lawson whispered.

Gunny turned his sights to the person manning the machinegun and pulled the trigger. Another report followed by the gunner dropping down and the machinegun barrel pointing into the air. The third man pushed the machine gunner aside as Gunny pulled the trigger again. Another shot, another kill.

Lawson grabbed the bridle of his horse and pulled himself up to a walking position. Limping along, Lawson walked toward a ravine that was about fifty yards ahead of him, all the while watching for any other movement. Myers and Gunny followed. Once at the ravine, Lawson handed his reins to Myers and told Gunny, "As I said, other people in the Iranian patrol will probably use the ravines to get closer to us. They may get up to go from ravine to ravine but my guess is that they are trying to sneak up to the area where they think we might be. If we can smoke them out, it may give you a shot to get them as they leave the security of their ravine to get to another ravine."

Gunny thought about it for a moment then agreed. "Ye goin' to be ok with that leg?" Gunny asked.

"As long as I keep moving, the pain stays down," was Lawson's response. Lawson moved into the ravine toward the mountains to the west hoping to flank the Iranian patrol with Myers following him. As he moved, he checked the Maxim 9 pistol for a round in the chamber. He looked at both walls of the ravine on either side, noting how the shadows were covering the floor of the ravine and the left wall. He gave careful attention to those areas as it would be easy for someone in dark clothing to hide in the shadows.

After traveling approximately two-hundred yards, he stopped as he could hear some rustling sounds. Moving slowly around a turn to the right in the ravine toward the sound, he saw a rabbit chewing on a bush at the bottom of the ravine. At the same time, the rabbit saw him and took off up the ravine and disappeared where the ravine turned to the left again. Seconds later, there was gunfire as the rabbit had startled men moving down the ravine toward Lawson and Myers.

Lawson could hear quiet footsteps coming toward him. He crouched down causing his leg to give a sharp pain. "Uh," was the sound he made as the pain hit. The footsteps stopped. Lawson slowly backed up around the turn he had passed by where he had startled the rabbit. There was the sound of a metallic click, a 'thump' sound then an explosion. Lawson's ears were ringing from the grenade going off but the explosion had happened on the other side of the turn in the ravine. Lawson laid waiting and not moving.

Myers pulled himself beside Lawson and motioned that he was going to move forward. As he did so, a rifle shot broke the silence. Seconds later, a body dropped at the top of the ravine just around the corner from where Lawson was lying. One hand was laying in view at the top of the ravine. Lawson realized that as one of the Iranians had gotten out of the ravine and was checking from above Gunny picked him off. Lawson continued to wait and as he did so, a grenade rolled out of the dead soldier's hand and dropped just in front of Lawson at the bottom of the ravine. As Lawson tried to reach for the grenade, Myers leaped over him, grabbed the grenade and threw it to the north, in the direction where the Iranian soldiers were. Both Lawson and Myers rolled against the right wall on the north side of the ravine just as the grenade went off in the air. The move saved them from being hit by shrapnel from the grenade. After the grenade went off, Myers and Lawson moved back into the shadows on the left side of the ravine.

It was another couple of minutes and the footsteps started again. Drawing closer, the steps would start then stop and start again. Lawson and Myers waited. They could see the partial feature of a man's boot standing near the edge of the turn in the ravine. They knew that if they opened fire now, they'd be on the receiving end of a grenade. Feeling around him, Lawson found a clump of dried clay. Knocking the loose particles off of clump, he rested it in his right hand while calculating where the second turn in the ravine was. He figured he'd have to throw the clump about fifteen yards to clear the ravine and get the other guys focused on the noise in the opposite direction. They were moving toward him. A few seconds more and they would be coming around the turn to his location.

Lawson threw the clump of clay into the air careful not to make any noise while he was throwing. The clump landed farther than he expected but the noise of the clump landing resulted in the footsteps stopping. Lawson slowly pulled himself across the bottom of the ravine to the turn while in the shade. Myers pulled himself next to Lawson up to the turn in the ravine, also keeping himself in the shade. As he did so, he could see three men looking away from him with their rifles pointed to where the noise came from. Both Lawson and Myers didn't know how many more people there may be but they had to hit these three before they turned around or the enemy would be firing at them. Lawson motioned to Myers with the Maxim 9. Myers understood. Firing the AK-47 would tell the others in the ravine exactly where they were. Using the silencer would make it much harder for the enemy to find them.

Lawson raised his pistol and pulled off three shots. The silenced rounds struck each man in the back, dropping them to the ground. Lawson pushed himself up and half-ran, half-limped back in the direction he came from as Myers helped Lawson along. He grabbed Myers and pulled him down to a laying position just as he heard a thump followed by an explosion. The explosion was about twenty yards away.

As the dust settled from the explosion, Myers jumped up to the edge of the ravine and rolled over the top onto the ground above the ravine. Pulling himself on the ground alongside the length of the ravine toward the enemy position, he came back to the edge of the ravine where it turned north and pointed his rifle into it. Two men were in the ravine. Myers fired four times, hitting them both. He jumped up and ran to the place where the ravine turned farther to the west. Sliding to a stop and at the edge of the ravine, he pointed his rifle down and opened fire even though he had no idea what was there. One man was just getting ready to throw another grenade when Myers hit him. Recognizing that the grenade in the man's hand was live, Myers rolled away from the edge of the ravine as the grenade went off. Checking to see that there were no other people in the ravine, Myers crawled back into the ravine and walked back to where Lawson was sitting.

"What's the situation?" Lawson asked.

Myers pulled the clip out of his rifle and loaded another clip in. "It appears to be clear. I'll signal Gunny," Myers said while realizing the impact of what he had done. He realized his hands were shaking and he couldn't control them. "So this is what combat is all about," Myers said to himself. "It's nothing I want to do. Someone else can be the hero." Myers got out of the ravine and waved his hands over his head for Gunny to see that it was clear, then dropped back into the ravine.

CHAPTER 25 -- August 1, 2015, 3:10 AM – Iran Time

Gunny came over and sat down in the ravine. Looking at both Myers and Lawson he pulled out a bottle of water and handed it to them. "You guys would make some good Marines. I watched you back there. A good team ye are even if ye are wounded." he commended them while looking around for any other potential surprises. "Now we need to get to the pickup point. Don't act like we're out of the woods yet. There still may be other combatants around that broke off from the group we hit." Both Lawson and Myers nodded affirmative and drank the water.

As Myers was finishing off the water, they could hear the crackling sound of someone stepping on dried weeds on the ground above the ravine. "Spread apart," Gunny whispered as each man moved apart from each other and pointed their weapons toward the edge of the ravine where the sound was coming from. A shot rang out and an Iranian soldier with a radio strapped to his back fell into the ravine along with his rifle. The men in the ravine looked at each other while wondering where the shot came from. They waited as more footsteps could be heard.

"Bad men, evil men," Khaliqi stated as he looked down into the ravine. Gunny and Myers stood up then helped Lawson stand as they looked over the top of the edge of the ravine. There was Khaliqi with his men carrying a body that turned out to be Lanstrum.

Myers turned to where the Iranian soldier's body was laying and pulled the radio off the man. The radio had not been damaged and was an FM-based radio. This was an older style

American radio called the PRC-25 that Myers learned was used during the Vietnam War and during the Granada incursion. Myers held the handset to his ear and listened while noting the frequency they were on. There was a lot of traffic going over the air and Myers was following the conversations that were being transmitted in Farsi.

"They're arguing about sending choppers back out to determine if we're the people the patrol ran into," Myers said while continuing to listen. "They say they can't send any choppers out because all local bases are under attack and they are on general alert. They say the base was hit and there is extensive damage to the storage facilities and aircraft on the base. They also say the research facility was hit and their power was knocked out. There is also a fire in the facility and they're attempting to manually open the main door to get all of the people out. All of their radar sites were also knocked out. They believe they are under a full, synchronized series of attacks."

"Who hit the research facility," Gunny asked while looking at Khaliqi.

"Draper gave orders," Khaliqi exclaimed in response to the question. "He knew that any additional attacks would help to convince the Iranians they were under a full area-wide attack."

"I thought you were Iranian?" Lawson queried.

"You must understand the makeup of this country," Khaliqi answered. "We are in Kurdistan, and take pride in being self-ruling. We are Sunni Kurds in this area while most of Iran is Shiite Muslims. That guarantees we'll have conflict."

"Where did you learn English," Lawson asked. "I hear hints of a British accent in your voice."

"I studied at Oxford," Khaliqi said. "I spent seven years studying about the production of clean water and distilling water and other chemicals. I selected specific courses that would provide knowledge on how to recover clean water for our families, those people you call tribes."

"Ok," Gunny began. "We need to get to the vehicle as we're already past the time for the pickup. Khaliqi, you put your men out in front on their horses since you know the terrain. We'll follow about fifty yards behind on our horses. Everyone spread out so that they can't take us all out with one strike if they try to hit us." Khaliqi smiled then agreed and ordered his men into a sweeping formation.

Khaliqi turned to Gunny and said, "Our job is to get you three out of here. Don't become heroes just because you feel you have to protect us. Protect yourself first. You give us much greater benefit by finishing your mission."

"Wait a minute," Lawson exclaimed. "If this guy has a backpack radio and he is dead, then who is asking for air support over the radio?" Myers and Khaliqi looked at each other while Gunny motioned for everyone to get on their horses.

"That means more of their force is out there and they have another radio," Gunny said. "Let's go with our plan of going in two waves with Khaliqi's people leading us since they know the terrain and probably see better at night than we do."

They had traveled half a mile when a rifle shot was heard. One of Khaliqi's men fell from his horse. The others leaped off their horses and set up firing positions while Gunny and Myers ran to the wounded man. He had been hit in the side and was losing blood. Gunny proceeded to check the wound for any foreign material and once he was sure it was clean, put compression on the wound to slow the bleeding. Once he had the wound fixed, Gunny grabbed the sniper rifle from his horse and set up his position.

Myers had his AK-47 ready while Lawson was crawling forward toward where the rest of Khaliqi's men were. Finding Khaliqi, Lawson set his AK-47 pointed forward and set for full automatic. "Who are these guys and where did they come from?" Lawson asked while looking through the binoculars to see if he could catch any movement.

"These guys, as you call them, are part of a larger contingent of Iranian soldiers," Khaliqi explained. "They appeared to come from the north as additional support for the forces south of us. They don't appear to be too large a force or they would be charging forward. My guess is there are ten to twelve of them. They are probably part of the same force you ran into earlier in the ravine. We saw them earlier but thought they were just passing through. Don't underestimate them. They are well trained and work well as teams. The Iranian Army is nothing to take lightly, they are good and they take pride in that fact. I know because we have had to deal with them at various times."

Just as Khaliqi was finishing, Lawson realized that if they were part of the same force then they were using the same frequency as the other unit that was hit earlier. Lawson crawled back to Myers and asked, "Where is that radio we picked up in the ravine?" Myers looked at Lawson for a moment and Lawson could tell Myers was having trouble. "You OK, Nick?" Myers laid on the ground looking at Lawson.

"I think I'm having a heart attack," came Myers' response. At that moment, Gunny crawled back to Lawson.

"What's up?" Gunny asked.

"Myers thinks he's having a heart attack," Lawson responded. Gunny grabbed Myers hand and felt his pulse.

"He's having a panic attack," Gunny observed. "This happens a lot in combat. You finally realize you could have died and can die at any moment. The mind picks it up and…" A rifle shot interrupted the conversation as Gunny watched one of the horses fall.

"They're shooting the horses!" Gunny shouted as he pulled down two of the horses into a laying position. Khaliqi and his men followed suite. Just as Gunny's horse was down, Myers pulled his horse down then pulled the radio off of his horse. While still heavily breathing and turning on the radio, Myers listened to the conversations going back and forth. The force ahead of them was trying to get helicopters in the air to hit Gunny and his team. It sounded like the army base was going to release two helicopters to provide support which Myers relayed to Gunny. Gunny crawled back to his position, convinced that Myers had gotten past his panic attack.

Lawson crawled up next to Myers and proceeded with his idea, "Remember when you talked to that Russian general? Well, could you do the same thing to confuse the guys ahead of you into thinking we are the other unit and not the ones they're looking for?"

Myers looked at Lawson for a moment and smiled, "Sure thing. Let the other guys know I'm doing this. Maybe we can catch them by surprise." Lawson crawled over to where Gunny and Khaliqi were setting up as Gunny was setting up the machine gun taken from the helo.

"Gunny," Lawson started. "Myers is going to tell the force in front of us that they are firing at friendlies. He's going to give them orders as though he's Colonel Rouhani. Remember that Asimov bought Myers' voice of being that of Rouhani."

Gunny immediately put the concept in motion. He sent Khaliqi to tell his other men to hold their fire until the Iranians were almost on top of them. Then Gunny held his hand next to his ear as a motion to tell Myers to make the call. Myers brushed some ants and sand off of his face, held the handset up and proceeded to make the call. After listening to the call-signs during previous conversations, he was able to discern which groups were talking.

In Farsi and imitating Rouhani's voice he transmitted, "Section Seven this is Section Four, do you hear me?" There was silence for a moment then a response.

"Section Four this is Section Seven, is that you Colonel?" Myers knew he had them by the string. Now he had to reel them in.

"It is me," Myers continued. "Why are your people firing on my people? Tell the army base to stand down as you are firing at your own people."

"We're sorry Colonel," came the response. "We'll call off the air support against you." At that point, Myers monitored the enemy's call to the base and confirmed that the base had recalled the helos. He motioned by hand to the others to stand by. They laid and waited while Myers listened to the radio. Myers rubbed his face where the ants had been. Apparently they were biting ants and his face itched from the bites. Realizing he had been lying next to a large ant hill, he shifted his position and noticed that the three foot shift made the reception much better on the radio.

During this time, two of Khaliqi's men had moved about fifty yards to the left and right. Gunny was positioned forward of everyone else while manning the machine gun. He knew that, if they were seasoned soldiers, only a few would come forward while the others waited with rifles and grenades. So they waited. "Hurry up and wait," Gunny thought to himself.

Myers moved slowly up to where Gunny was, all the while listening to the radio. It was two minutes later when the radio went live again. "Are you going to come out?" came the request from the Iranians facing them.

Myers was quick to respond, "We can't come out. We were in the process of setting up an ambush position when you fired on us. We have one man wounded and we are already in position for an ambush if the attackers come this way."

"Ok, we'll come to you," came the answer.

Gunny watched through the sniper rifle scope as he could see men standing up and walking toward them. He counted eight men advancing toward their position. Gunny figured that they were not veterans as they were making a major mistake by all coming over at once. Just as Gunny was getting ready to open fire with the machinegun, Lawson pointed to a reflection to the left that looked like moonlight reflecting off of polished brass. The men advancing toward their position were about twenty yards away. Gunny and Lawson switched positions while Gunny sighted in with the sniper rifle on the reflection. It was a machine gunner with the belt of his ammo making the reflection. The enemy was set up to respond if it turned out to be an ambush.

"OK, so they're seasoned veterans. When I shoot, open fire," Gunny told Lawson. Gunny sighted in the target and set the scope into focus. Slowly he pulled the trigger. The rifle kicked as the round headed toward its mission. As the round struck the man at the machinegun, Lawson opened up on the group approaching him. He swung the machinegun left and right as he sprayed the area ahead of him. Suddenly, he noted a second shot from Gunny's rifle. This was followed by gunfire from both sides. The force ahead of them appeared larger than they had estimated.

Lawson had already used up the ammo from one metal box and was reloading the machinegun with the second one. As he was reloading, several explosions went off about fifteen yards ahead of him. "Those are grenades," Gunny shouted. "They haven't used RPGs."

Lawson realized that the enemy in front of him wouldn't move any closer as long as his machinegun was operational. They were also out of range to throw any grenades into Lawson's immediate area. It appeared to be a standoff except that he knew it was only a matter of time before the helos from the army base would become airborne again. Then the advantage would be all the Iranians.

Myers recognized the predicament they were in. He could already hear radio calls for air support. Myers countered the request by telling the army base they weren't needed. He figured by doing so, it would delay any action by the base until the commanders could figure out what was going on. So to enhance the situation, Myers radioed the base and told them that "the enemy has got our frequency and are trying to lure more helos into the area to shoot them down just like they did the first one earlier tonight."

The trick worked. The commander at the base refused to put any more of his assets in jeopardy. Myers reported the results to Gunny and Khaliqi.

Meanwhile, the two men from Khaliqi's group that had moved to the flanks of the action had been able to bypass the Iranian force and come up behind them. They were able to get a count on the number of Iranian soldiers involved in the action. There appeared to be another fourteen men hiding behind mounds of dirt.

The two men moved to the back of the force, using their knives to quietly take out the first two of the soldiers they came upon. Once they accomplished that task, they took the grenades from the soldiers and moved backward to a position where they could not be seen. Pulling pins on the grenades, they threw the grenades to spots where they could see soldiers laying. As the explosions started happening, the men got up to escape the attack and Gunny proceeded to pick off men that were jumping up and running. Lawson started firing with the machinegun. The two men at the back of the enemy force were forced to dig in quickly as machinegun rounds were flying everywhere. Gunny tapped Lawson on the shoulder which caused Lawson to stopped firing.

"We've got friendlies out there and you're making them targets too. So stop that noise!" Gunny shouted as he sighted his rifle once more at a uniformed soldier trying to make his escape. Lawson grabbed his AK-47 and proceeded to crawl forward with Gunny following. Every once in a while, Gunny would raise the sniper rifle and catch another fleeing soldier. After about three minutes the shooting stopped.

Khaliqi went forward with his men to check on the situation. There were no Iranian soldiers alive in the area though five or six had escaped. Lawson limped back to where Myers was sitting. He was still monitoring radio calls going on between Iranian commands.

"There is a lot of confusion out there," Myers reported. "We've got at least three commands in lockdown and two others trying to recover personnel in the field. If we want to get to the vehicle in the ravine, now's the time to go." Lawson waved to Gunny. Gunny came running while watching around for any other movement.

"Myers thinks it's safe to go. What's your thoughts?" Lawson posed as Gunny watched Myers' and Lawson's expression. In the moonlight, the facial features were more subtle but Gunny could tell both men were anxious to get moving.

Gunny moved forward to inspect the area and make sure there were no more active adversaries. Going slowly toward the back part of the area where the Khaliqi's men had first located the enemy, he walked while checking to see if anyone was still alive. Even in the moonlight, it was hard not to catch a foot on one of the dirt mounds. Gunny tripped on a mound and as he was catching his balance, two Iranian soldiers popped up about forty yards from where Gunny was walking and charged toward him. Both men were firing their AK-47s on full automatic. As they charged, Gunny realized that they couldn't get an accurate shot at him as the weapons would be kicking all over the place.

Gunny charged full speed toward them with the sniper rifle leveled at the first man. His shot hit the man in the shoulder causing the man to reel back for a moment but he kept on coming. Bullets were kicking up dirt near Gunny's feet as their distance closed. Gunny lunged to the right just in time as rounds from the first man's AK-47 went past Gunny clearing just inches from his body. The first man lunged at Gunny with the bayonet on his rifle. Gunny used the sniper rifle to block the move of the bayonet while, at the same time, pulling the K-Bar knife from its sheath on his web belt. Gunny plunged the knife into the man's chest while he used the man's body to block the second man's bayonet thrust. Gunny swung around, released the grip on the knife from his right hand and threw the sniper rifle from his left hand to his right hand. He swung the sniper rifle and caught the second man's head with the butt of the rifle resulting in a crushing blow. The man fell limp to the ground.

As Khaliqi and Myers arrived at the scene, Gunny was leaning on the sniper rifle trying to catch his breath. Myers checked out both men and handed Gunny back his knife. "You trying to be a one-man Marine unit?" Myers asked while checking Gunny for any wounds. While the discussion was going on, a shot rang out. Twenty feet from Gunny and Myers, a man fell with his AK-47 falling to the ground followed by his body. Both Myers and Gunny looked to where the shot came from.

They saw Lawson lowering his weapon as he began to limp toward Gunny and Myers.

"I think the area is more active than we would like to admit," Lawson said. "I think we should work in teams of two so that one man can be checking out the area while the other man is watching for surprises." Both Gunny and Myers agreed.

They checked the area for any survivors and, once convinced that there was no one else alive in their line of vision, they proceeded to plan their next move. Lawson was still concerned that there were at least a couple of soldiers that were unaccounted for. "We may have a problem in that we could still be followed by those that escaped," Lawson said while looking over the area.

"Why should we worry about them?" Myers questioned. "As long as we're alert, they probably have no interest in continuing the fight." Gunny agreed.

"The reason I'm concerned," Lawson explained, "is that we know they had a radioman. We communicated with him. Yet I don't see any of these dead having a radio on them." Both Gunny and Myers realized that Lawson's observation was true. It also meant that the radioman could just follow them and report on their whereabouts to his command. This indicated that there was still a real threat that they could be hit by an air attack or a rapid ground movement at their vehicle's location.

"We should get moving but after we collect the weapons left behind by the Iranians," Gunny instructed. "I noticed several bags of grenades. Leave them alone. They may have pulled a pin on one of them and left them in the bag for some poor sucker to pick up." Myers and Lawson both gave an affirmative and began to pick up the AK-47s and machineguns. Khaliqi's men took the machineguns and ammo, putting them on their horses while Myers put the AK-47s on his horse. Lawson and Myers got on

Myers horse as Lawson's horse was killed in the initial action. Khaliq went back into the combat area and appeared to do something on the ground. Shortly afterward, he came back and got on his horse.

"What was all that about?" Lawson questioned.

"Well," Khaliqi responded, "Gunny said that it was possible that the bags of grenades may have one grenade with a pin pulled to act as a booby trap. I just want to make sure he was being truthful so I pulled the pin on one of the grenades and set it up so that if anyone picks up the bag, the whole lot goes off."

"You've been doing this stuff for a long time, haven't you?" Lawson remarked. Khaliqi nodded his head 'yes' and smiled as he turned his horse to go forward. "Evil men," he said as he spurred his horse.

Gunny pointed toward the direction they needed to go and shouted, "Follow me! I always wanted to say that."

CHAPTER 26 -- August 1, 2015, 3:45 AM – Iran Time

With Gunny's orders, they moved forward to the ravine where the vehicle was parked. Lawson was feeling the weakness from the long day, the wound and the constant demand on his body and mind. Once in camp, Lawson had Myers bring him the backpack. Myers came back holding nine DVD disks in his hand. "What's this?" he asked while waving the disks. "Were you going to watch movies while you were waiting in your prison cell?"

Lawson took the disks and put them back in the backpack. "They are the videos from each of the cameras in the research facility," Lawson explained. "They had us on those videos and, without these, they have no way to identify us."

"What about the pictures in our files?" Myers inquired. "They can still identify us from those."

"I've got those files," Lawson responded. "They're in the backpack as well." Gunny looked in the backpack for a moment then handed it to Lawson.

"How many miracles have you got left in this bag?" Gunny inquired while watching the sky to see if any helos were in the area.

As they talked they could hear horses moving at a fast pace toward them from the south. Each of them grabbed their weapons, sat down in the ravine and waited for whoever was coming.

"Hello in the camp," came the familiar voice of Colonel Draper.

Gunny stood up and shouted, "Come on in!"

Draper and his aid came riding in with two horses in tow. He said something to Khaliqi which Lawson assumed was a question concerning Khaliqi's team picking up Lanstrum while Gunny walked over to Draper and handed him the sniper rifle.

"I take it you've got communications with the extraction teams to get us out of here," Gunny questioned while everyone else looked on for the answer.

"The choppers have been delayed about half an hour. We'll just have to sit and wait," Draper replied while checking out the sniper rifle. They all sat down and waited for the time to pass. Gunny grabbed the binoculars and proceeded to scan the area for movement.

Lawson and Myers sat next to each other, relieved that the end of the mission was almost finished. "You still wrestling with the deaths caused by our actions?" Lawson asked Myers.

"I am," Myers responded. "It's not exactly what I signed up for." Lawson sat thinking for a moment as he thought back to the assessments he had done on the intentions and movements of the Islamic State also known as ISIS or ISIL.

"If you were ordered to Israel to defend them from attack by several nations, would you do it?" Lawson posed. Myers wondered where the question was coming from then gave an affirmative. "From what I could see of my previous assessments," Lawson continued, "ISIS was building and capturing land as a goal of forming a Caliphate that would be directed by Iran. They had a second goal. To capture Syria, which borders on Israel, for the intent of being able to set up forces to invade Israel."

Myers looked perplexed. "And you know this how?" he challenged Lawson.

Lawson shifted his position to get the pressure off of his wounded leg then explained. "I know this because the assessments I made and the strategies ISIS was using appeared to be focused on gaining control of Syria. The only reason why chaos broke out in Syria was because ISIS wanted to get a foothold in a country that shared borders with Israel. The U.S. gave them that capability when we went after Assad. The U.S. instigated the fighting in Syria with the intent of overthrowing Syria's government and ISIS saw it an opportunity to replace it with their own. That would make Iran the most powerful entity in the Middle East which would allow for Iran to draw other countries into an alliance with them. That's also the reason we had to get these plans and stop Iran's ability to build the laser weapons. Their intent with this weapon was to neutralize Israel's air force. By getting the plans and destroying the ammo dump, we delayed Iran's plans. There were enough munitions at the storage site to supply a full military division. I figure the plan was to use the munitions to launch an attack on the southern area of Israel from Gaza while the forces from Syria hit Israel from the north at the Golan Heights, thereby splitting Israel's defenses." Myers began to put the pieces together.

"So what you're saying is that we just gave Israel some breathing space to set up a defensive plan," Myers observed. "We killed some to save many others. I know in the Bible, Christ told Peter to bring a sword with him on the night Jesus was betrayed. I think Christ was telling him this to emphasize that he had the right to defend himself. Israel has the right to defend itself."

"If you extend that further," Lawson replied, "then you had the right to defend yourself when you set off those explosives, wiping out a good portion of the force moving against us. You didn't set up the timing of their arrival at the ammo dump, they did. Had they come later, they would have continued moving toward us and we would most likely have been captured or killed. Maybe God set up the timing. Who knows. See my point?"

Myers began to see the difference in just taking lives and killing to defend oneself. He was still struggling with the concept but it was all beginning to make sense to him. "What makes the actions right or wrong….," Myers started as Draper came over to where Lawson and Myers were sitting.

"It looks like you two are having an in-depth discussion." Draper said while Gunny joined the group. "We'll have to break it off. We've got choppers coming from the southeast. Looks like three of them and they aren't ours."

"OK, Colonel," Lawson started while Gunny and Myers looked on. "We're just totally exhausted and trying to get our minds back on focus. A side note that maybe important and maybe not. In our fight with the Iranians on our way here, we took out most of them but we know that the radioman got away because none of the dead had a radio on them and we had communicated with the group before the real fighting broke out."

"Why didn't anyone tell me this!" Draper exclaimed. "I was wondering why helos would be up this early after all that had happened. That might be the reason. Anybody got any ideas. Those choppers will be here in about nine minutes based upon their search movements. We can hold them off with RPGs and machine guns but we have limited ammo and once we start shooting, other helos will follow. Think fast!"

Myers was the first one to speak up, "Colonel, we still have the radio we captured from the Iranians which means I may be able to jam the radioman's signal if they're following his instructions."

"What radio?" Draper queried.

"We have an Iranian radio," Myers answered. "It's set to their frequency. I can speak Farsi and can also add confusion to their communications by telling the choppers that they are running into a trap. The requests for support and the location given is fake and is set up to take numerous helos out."

Draper looked to the southeast. He could see the helos getting larger as they were getting closer. "Get on the horn and do your thing," he shouted. "The rest of you, get the RPG rounds and launchers from my horse, set up the machineguns and get ready for a fight. Meanwhile, Khaliqi and I are going out to see if we can locate this radioman if he's there."

Everyone started putting the defensive setup together with Myers, assuming the Iranian radioman was giving the helo pilots directions, got on the radio while speaking in Farsi. "Air support this is Section Seven, you're running into a trap. Turn back. They're setting you up."

Both Lawson and Myers watched as the helicopters kept coming then turned and headed the other direction. "That will hold them for only a short time," Lawson said. Myers ran over to the vehicle and pulled off the antenna from the rear of the vehicle. Pulling the antenna and cable from the vehicle, he ran back to the backpack radio. Pulling off the antenna from the backpack radio, Myers screwed in the cable attached to the vehicle's antenna into the backpack radio's antenna connector. The radio was now connected to a much larger antenna giving them greater range.

"This should allow us to jam the other guy's signal," Myers explained. "He would have to be close enough to us to see what we are doing. By continuously transmitting something that will create more noise than he does, it should keep him from hearing what his command unit is telling him. At the very least, it will force him to move to a position where he can communicate which should give Draper a chance to see him."

Myers started transmitting continuous radio calls with no breaks. Lawson knew he couldn't keep this up for long and looked around as to what could be used to create noise. Digging through the stuff in the back of the vehicle, he came upon the radio telephone Draper had given them. "What's the phone number for the International Coordinated Time phone number?" Lawson asked, knowing that a Navy ET would probably know the answer.

Myers was perplexed by Lawson's question but answered anyway, "It's 303.499.7111, but it's in the U.S. so you'll have to use the international calling code."

Lawson dialed the number and proceeded to hear the message, "At the tone, zero hours thirty-one minutes, Coordinated Universal Time" followed by a tick, tick tick for ten seconds followed by the next announcement of time in Zulu time zone hours.

Lawson brought the radio telephone over to Myers. Once Myers heard what was being picked up on the phone, he activated the speaker phone on the radio telephone and held down the mike button on the Iranian backpack radio. Next he switched the backpack radio to full power. "I don't know how long the batteries will hold up on either unit but this should create problems for the moment," Myers declared while holding the mike and the phone.

Draper and Khaliqi had moved out in a slow crawl until they were approximately one-hundred yards from the ravine. They lay waiting for any sign of movement.

The Iranian radioman was hearing nothing but the Universal Coordinated Time transmission. He dug around in his pocket for the notes that would instruct him on the second frequency to go to if he could not communicate on the first frequency. As he dug around, he couldn't find it so he figured he'd have to move from where he could see the ravine and the people in the ravine to a location where he could communicate with the army base. He sat and thought it over.

Myers stopped the transmission long enough to listen to what was going on. It appeared that the helicopters were going to go back out to investigate what was going on. There was some argument between the chopper pilots and the command as to the wisdom of the decision. One of their helicopters had already been shot down in what appeared to be an ambush and the pilots were convinced that this was a ruse to bring more helicopters out where they could become targets. After all, the attack on the army base appeared to be targeting the munitions, spare parts and helicopters on the base. The Iranian pilots felt that the Kurd's real targets were to take out as many helicopters as they could. The night was not the pilots' friend and there was still some time before daylight.

Myers heard enough to know there would be at least two helos coming out. He told Lawson of the potential for two helicopters approaching their area then went back to transmitting the Universal Coordinated Time message. Both Myers and Lawson wondered what happened to Draper and Khaliqi. While Gunny continued to scan the area for any movement, Lawson hobbled over to Gunny and told Gunny his concerns.

"Myers thinks that the base is going to send two choppers out to see what's going on. We need to take some of Draper's launchers and RPG rounds and get them up the ravine about one-hundred yards to keep the choppers occupied if they come. That way they'll be firing at us and not the camp."

Gunny thought for a moment then said, "Help me load up two of the horses with the machinegun and last can of ammo, grab a couple of AK-47's and ammo. I'll get the launchers and RPG rounds Draper was given." Lawson went back and told Myers what was going on.

"You'd better hurry," Myers exclaimed. "The helos are just taking off and should be here in about ten to twelve minutes. I figure they'll do that spotlight sweeping back and forth thing as they get close to this location which should give you some time to be ready. Now go!"

Lawson grabbed the machinegun and ammo and loaded them on his horse. As he was doing so, Gunny led his horse, already loaded up with the launchers and RPG rounds, over to Lawson and helped Lawson load the last of the ammo as Lawson's wounded leg was getting weak.

"Enemy choppers on their way," Lawson stated. Gunny helped Lawson on to his horse then Gunny got on his horse. They took off up the ravine, traveling about a quarter mile, a little bit farther than Lawson planned. Getting off of his horse, Gunny put the binoculars to his eyes and scanned to the southeast. The fires were still burning at the base and, with the helos being silhouetted from the fires, he could see them as two black specks heading their direction. They pulled the weapons and ammo off of the horses and set up to put some firepower at the helos. Lawson loaded both RPG launchers as Gunny loaded up the machinegun.

As they were preparing for the helos, the Iranian radioman decided he had to move away from the ravine as it was obvious he was being jammed by something. Getting out of the ravine he was in, he slowly crawled toward the southeast with the backpack radio on his back. Draper was scanning the area with the sniper rifle's scope when Khaliqi tapped him on the shoulder. Draper looked to where Khaliqi was pointing. At first he saw nothing, then he saw what looked like a blade of grass moving among other blades of grass. It suddenly hit him. It was the antenna from a radio. Draper watched as the antenna moved. "This guy is good," he thought. He turned to Khaliqi but Khaliqi was no longer there.

Draper scanned the terrain to figure out where Khaliqi had gone. After scanning a couple of times, he could see Khaliqi crawling rapidly in a line that would intercept the radioman. At the same time, he could see the outlines of two helicopters coming from the southeast. "Just what we need," he thought to himself.

Scanning the ground where he saw the antenna, Draper picked the movement again, following the antenna along the ground. Suddenly, the antenna stopped moving and he could hear a voice speaking in Farsi. The antenna moved a little higher until Draper could see a part of the radio. The man was trying to get a better position to communicate with command. He wondered why the man would have problems communicating then suddenly realized that Myers and Lawson must have found a way to jam his signal. He raised the sniper rifle and focused in the scope while scanning to the right to see where Khaliqi was. Once satisfied that Khaliqi was out of the line of fire, he sighted back onto the radio.

Draper knew that the top of the radio was where the transmission circuitry existed. It was designed to be in that place in the radio to make the line from transmitter to antenna to be as short as possible. He put the crosshairs of the scope on the radio about two inches below the top. Slowly he pulled the trigger. The bullet pierced the radio at the point he intended to hit.

Once the shot was fired, Khaliqi jumped up, took several running steps and dived onto the radioman. There was a quick flurry of activity that reminded Draper of a wolf pouncing on a rabbit. Moments later, Khaliqi stood up and walked back to where Draper was laying. "Bad men, evil men," was all Khaliqi said while he wiped the blood off of his knife, put the knife back in its sheath, picked up his rifle and proceeded back to the ravine and the vehicle. Draper picked up the sniper rifle and followed Khaliqi back to the ravine, all the while watching around for any movement and the progress of the oncoming helicopters.

Once at the ravine, Draper told Myers he could stop transmitting. "You realize, of course, that they can vector onto your location with that transmission and, with choppers coming in, they may be using your signal as a beacon," Draper said while he lifted the blanket on the horse to get to the ManPack radio. After talking on the radio for a few seconds, he turned around to Myers. "The other teams are being picked up as we speak. Our choppers will be here in ten minutes. We've got to help Gunny and Lawson if those enemy choppers get too close."

Draper told Myers to stay where he's at while he grabbed another belt of ammo for the sniper rifle, jumped on a horse and headed up the ravine. He rode up and got off the horse where Gunny and Lawson were set up. As he got off his horse, the two helicopters turned on their spotlights and proceeded to swing back and forth searching for the team. Gunny took the sniper rifle from Draper and sighted in on one of the helicopters. Setting the focus, he announced, "They're about half a mile away."

"Sight in on the spotlights and take the shot," Draper shouted as the helicopters were getting louder. Gunny put the crosshairs on the spotlight of the closest helicopter and pulled the trigger. There was a bright flash from the spotlight as the light was hit then it went dark. Gunny sighted on the second helicopter's spotlight and pulled the trigger again. The second light went out.

The helicopters turned and came back forward pointing to the right of where the men sat, each firing two rockets. The rockets hit about two hundred yards short of the ravine and about three hundred yards to the right. It became apparent to those in the ravine that the helicopter pilots had no idea where the shots were coming from.

The helicopters were now laying down machinegun fire as they moved forward toward an area about three hundred yards up the ravine. Gunny motioned to Lawson to load up the RPG launchers.

"They're already loaded," Lawson said as he handed one of the launchers to Gunny. Then he picked up the second launcher and handed it to Draper. Once he finished that task, he picked up four additional RPG rounds and dropped two RPG rounds each at the feet of Gunny and Draper. Completing this effort, he moved over to the machinegun and swung the barrel toward the closest helicopter.

The helicopters had turned and were heading back toward the ravine. They each fired two more rockets at the area they had been hitting before. The rockets exploded about two-hundred and fifty yards away from the men. Gunny set the launcher down and picked up the sniper rifle. Sighting on the closest helicopter, he waited until it started to turn. Once he had a clean shot through the door gunner's door to the head of the pilot, he pulled the trigger. The pilots head kicked forward.

"It won't be long before they figure where that came from," Gunny said as an RPG round left Draper's launcher with a swoosh and a fiery trail, hitting the same helicopter whose pilot was hit by Gunny. The helicopter turned to the southwest and, after traveling about five hundred yards, crashed into the ground.

"The second chopper is going to come for us now!" Draper shouted. Lawson opened fired on the helicopter, hitting the rear of the helicopter as it attempted to make a turn. There was smoke coming from the rear of the helicopter as it turned to line up its rockets on the men's position.

"Let us be truly thankful for what we're about to receive," Gunny shouted as he loaded up another RPG round. The helicopter lined up with its nose down. As the pilot was bringing the nose up to fire his rockets, there was a bright trail to the right and a flash as an incoming missile struck the helicopter. Parts of the wing and the rocket launcher attached to the wing fell off as the helicopter turned and headed southeast with smoke coming out of the doorway. Seconds later, another helicopter flew over the heads of the men and swung around to land while a second helicopter circled overhead providing cover. They were friendlies.

"That was close," Gunny said as he sat down. "I think I'm going to say some prayers right now." Myers came over to see what was happening. He tossed the backpack to Lawson as he looked over the scene of the burning helicopter off in the distance.

Draper set down the launcher and motioned everyone to head for the helicopter that was landing. "You guys did a great job. Now get out of my territory." Everyone laughed at Draper's comment.

Lawson raised the question on everyone's mind, "Colonel, aren't you going with us?"

Draper looked each one of them over then spoke, "This is my mission and my territory. These hill people don't stand a chance without us giving them aid and support. These are my friends. No, I'm not going and the Admiral understands that. Yes, I've got a one-hundred thousand Euros bounty on my head but that's been there for a long time. You guys give Roedl my best."

Lawson picked the backpack, opened it and took inventory. The papers taken from the shed were there. He pulled out the memory chip and Rouhani's jump drive and put them in his pocket. Next, he checked to make sure the papers taken off of Rouhani were there. After verifying he had everything he zipped the backpack closed and swung it over his shoulder. Getting back on the horse, he rode to where the evacuation helicopter had landed.

Crewmembers were pulling off munitions and medical supplies from the chopper as Lawson arrived at the landing site. As the materials were being removed from the helicopter, Khaliqi finished a conversation with Draper and walked to Lawson.

"Lawson, my friend," Khaliqi began, "Colonel Draper says I have a piece of information that may be pertinent to your needs concerning missiles for Hormuz." Lawson watched the removal of items from the helo while Khaliqi was talking. Lawson immediately turned his attention to Khaliqi.

"Did you say missiles for Hormuz?" Khaliqi nodded 'yes'.

"You do not have to worry about them," Khaliqi continued. "They were destroyed when the blast happened at the army base. They were anti-ship missiles."

Lawson realized that the Iranians were one step closer to engaging ships in the Persian Gulf in warfare. Even though they didn't get these missiles, it wouldn't be long before they got others. The crews in the Persian Gulf must be told about the threat.

After the supplies were removed from the helicopter, Myers and Gunny climbed on board the helicopter as they helped Lawson on board. Khaliqi's men laid Lanstrum's body on the deck of the helicopter. The pilot yelled out, "Where's Draper?"

"He's not coming," Lawson shouted back above the sound of the aircraft's engines.

Draper stuck his head into the doorway, "What do you want Jake and thanks for the supplies?" he yelled to the pilot.

"Here are the saddle straps and bags to carry that stuff on your horses. Oh yea, they told me to give you this," the pilot shouted back while handing Draper the materials along with two cartons of American cigarettes.

"Wow, this has been a great day!" Draper exclaimed.

Lawson grinned at Draper, "I hope you have matches to go with that. By the way, send a message to Roedl and tell him that the Iranians are on the verge of arming the missile sites at the Strait of Hormuz. I figure it should be a week or two before they're fully operational."

Draper slapped Lawson in the back of the head and said, "I'll send that to Roedl with your compliments. Get that leg fixed. You've got a good sixth sense. You sure you're not Kurdish?" Turning to Gunny he shouted, "You've done great on the mission, Semper Fi!"

Gunny smiled and shook hands with Draper as the helicopter started to take off. Lawson looked down to see Draper tearing open one of the cartons of cigarettes. "I guess he's good for a couple of days," Lawson thought.

Lawson looked at Gunny and Myers. It seemed to him that they had aged since he first saw them. He wondered how he looked to them.

"Everyone get strapped in," said the pilot. "We've got to clear the mountains and with daylight coming, there may be some larger caliber rounds being fired at us." The helicopter went up to ten thousand feet and proceeded west with the escort helicopter in tow. They had several rounds fired at them but nothing came near as they cleared the border into Iraq.

CHAPTER 27 -- August 3, 2015, 09:22 AM – Moscow, Russia Time

General Sergey Asimov found himself walking once more to the conference room at the Kremlin to have another discussion with the inquiry board. Colonel Rouhani never showed up at the mosque in Iraq and the document and diamonds were never recovered. He figured he would probably be removed from his position and transferred to some minor command away from Moscow.

As he walked through the door to the facility, he turned to the guard signing in each of the persons coming into the facility. Removing his weapon from its holster, he handed the weapon to the guard and received a claim ticket to pick it up on the way out. Walking down the hall, he opened his briefing folder and proceeded to read once more the issues brought up by the inquiry board. The usual complaints about failure to perform. He had been through this process numerous times throughout his career and this was nothing new. None of the officers ever completed their assignments to anyone's satisfaction and this was no exception.

Asimov came to the double doors that led into the conference room. Once more stepping into the mahogany-covered room, he walked to the head of the table and laid down his hat and briefing papers. The same seven men he had talked to days before were there again. General Serov was probably going to ask the same questions with nothing changing.

Asimov waited for the general to speak. All of the board members were busy reading the information in the briefing papers while several were marking specific areas in the report. 'Hurry up and wait," he thought while the board continued to make markups and notes. General Serov turned to Asimov. "Sergey, we've had a difficult week with all the activity and problems going on in Iran. What is your perspective of the problems?"

General Asimov opened up his briefing report and scanned it briefly. "General Serov, as you know we had a plan that was a two-phased approach. If Colonel Rouhani of the Iranian Army could get the document to us through underground channels, we would pay him one-million Euros for the document. If he couldn't get the document in the underground fashion, we would pay three-billion three-hundred million Rubles in diamonds to the Iranians directly for the document."

"I understand that Sergey," Serov replied. "What happened to the deal with Rouhani?"

"Rouhani never showed up for the meeting in the Iraqi mosque," Asimov stated. "We have no idea where he is. I suspect that he couldn't get into the ammo dump to get the document or found the document destroyed and left Iran with the diamonds. When we tried to get in contact with Tripoli later that day there was no reply. That is unlike Tripoli not to respond. Our backup man, Sergeant Taylor of the U.S. military, was found dead in the research facility, so we had only Rouhani to rely upon."

"We got a message about an hour ago," Serov replied, "that Rouhani's burnt body was found inside the remains of the shed at the munitions storage area with the courier pouch under his body. It appears to have had both the document and a memory device in the pouch. Both were destroyed. There was no sign of the diamonds."

"So it looks like we lost on all fronts," Asimov observed.

"The Iranians are upset with us because our people didn't join in the fight or the search for the group that made the attacks." Serov commented.

Asimov was starting to feel nervous as the charge appeared to be pointed toward him. "Actions at both the research facility and the munitions storage area on July 31st didn't warrant activating our troops, besides a major number of our people at the facility were killed in the first attack so we didn't have Russian resources to respond," he said while wondering why this was having greater significance than it should. Loss of the documents was significant and so was the loss of the diamonds but neither of these events required the Russians to intervene in an Iranian response.

Serov appeared to be getting more agitated. "You apparently didn't realize that there were attacks against the Iranian military base near Shuyesheh causing significant destruction including eight Hind helicopters. Also three radar sites were knocked out and a second attack was made on the research facility that resulted in their power units being destroyed and a fire wiping out essential equipment, weapons and munitions."

"When did all that happen?" Asimov inquired as he began to realize the magnitude of the attacks.

"I know you were out of the loop," Serov explained. "With your people at the research facility all but wiped out and the casualties at the army base taking out your reporting people, I would expect that you would not have known about the later attacks. I can't fault you for that. However, the plan miserably failed. We not only lost the plans but also the money and some good-will with the Iranian government, not to mention that, according to our base-sharing agreement with the Iranians, we will also have to bear the cost of replacing the Hind helicopters and the munitions that were lost. Oh, I almost forgot. The Kurds ambushed and brought down three other Hind helicopters which we will also need to replace. Even though the Iranians will pay for the munitions replacements, they are very unhappy with our support to them. This past week has cost us as much or more than our retaking of the Crimean peninsula. And what did we get for it, nothing!"

"I can't be to blame for all of this," Asimov protested. "You cut me out from any information that would have allowed me to properly respond! How can I make a response for something I have no control over. If you knew what was going on, why didn't you move to intervene?"

Serov looked at the other members and responded, "We are dealing with information after the fact. We had no way of knowing what was going on in Iran on the ground. That was your responsibility. You had a backup plan for getting information for such a situation as this and you didn't follow it."

"I guess that means that this committee would like for me to resign," Asimov said dejectedly, realizing that the deck was stacked against him. After all these years, Serov had won.

"No Sergey, we will reassign you," Serov responded. "You will be reassigned to the Crimea peninsula as the Crimean District Commander. General Goremykin will replace you as commander of weapons development since he is the senior person reporting to you." Asimov saw the real reason for his reassignment. Serov had finally gotten his brother-in-law into a high command position and it was Asimov's position. However, Asimov saw that there was a silver lining to the bad news. He had been trying for the past two years to get the Directorate position in Crimea so it seemed like a positive turn of events for him.

"I guess that should work. When do I go?" Asimov stated while feeling the animosity building once more toward Serov but glad he got what he wanted. Maybe Serov realized that the information Asimov had on Serov and his brother-in-law about their corrupt dealings with the Russian Mafia would be less of a threat to Serov if Asimov was in Crimea.

"In a few days. Then it is done," Serov announced. "Thank you General Asimov for your time. I'm happy we could come to some agreement. You'll be getting orders. Go home and wait there until you get them."

General Asimov picked up his hat and briefing papers from the table, saluted and turned, exiting from the conference room. Once past the doors, he felt the anger well up in him. Serov was playing his usual round of politics. Asimov went to the guard at the entrance, handed his claim check and had his weapon returned to him.

Leaving the facility, Asimov went to a public phone a couple of blocks down from the facility and dialed a number. Once the person answered, Asimov instructed, "Serov must be stopped. I know your relationship with him but our hands are being tied too much by his lack of keeping us in the loop for information. Deal with him." The voice on the other end of the call acknowledged and hung up.

It was a week later when General Asimov took his dog out for a walk in the back of his sprawling estate which sat on the outskirts of Moscow. Covering some eight-hundred acres, it was beautifully covered with trees, gardens, trails and a pond. The mansion was ornate with a circular driveway, a pillared entrance and, in the back, a raised terrace that looked over the beauty of the valley and the pond.

The warm, fresh air added life to the early morning as Asimov walked the trails. He reflected on the events of the past couple of weeks and wondered what type of crack unit could pull off such a well synchronized series of attacks. He also wondered how they knew about the diamonds. "It couldn't have been luck," He thought. "Everything happened with such coordinated detail."

After an hour of walking, he went back to his mansion while servants were setting out his daily breakfast of a soft-boiled egg, toast and coffee on the terrace. As he looked to see them setting up, he could see another man in uniform standing at the top of the steps, obviously waiting for him.

Asimov went up the steps to the terrace to go to the table with his dog while the man waited while holding a manila envelope. Asimov reached the top of the stairs as the man handed him the envelope and saluted. "Compliments of the District Commander, Sir." Asimov saluted, took the envelope and opened it. As he did so, the man left.

He read the orders. They specified for him to leave in ten days to Crimea. "Well, Sorby," Asimov said while talking to his dog. "It says here that I'm to report in ten days to the Crimean port of Sevastopol to replace the District Commander. It looks like I'm getting a job that won't hurt my career." Looking around at the view around him, he continued his thoughts, "I'm sure going to miss this place but we won't be dealing with Moscow politics anymore."

Asimov headed to the table with his breakfast sitting in perfect order. He took the leash off his dog and pulled up a chair to sit down in front of his breakfast. He had finally gotten what he wanted, command of the Crimean Peninsula. He was at peace, breathing the fresh air, watching the dancing bounce of the butterflies as they went from plant to plant and he rested with the knowledge that he wouldn't have to deal with Serov any more as the bullet pierced the back of his head. General Sergey Asimov's services were terminated.

Asimov's face fell forward knocking the breakfast dishes off of the table creating noise that brought one of his security officers to the terrace. As he pulled his weapon, a second shot was fired and the officer's body fell lifeless to the terrace floor.

Stepping out from a hedge at the edge of the driveway, the courier twisted the barrel from the rifle, removed the silencer and put the parts of the weapon into its case. Looking around to see if anyone else was watching, he stepped to the other side of the hedge, put on his helmet, strapped the weapon case to his motorcycle and drove away.

Fifteen minutes later, General Serov was sitting at his desk when a phone call was transferred to him. "So it is done," Serov stated as he received the report from the courier. Hanging up the phone, he thought to himself, "Finally, I'm rid of Asimov. A day to celebrate."

Serov left his office to tell his brother-in law, General Goremykin, the good news. Asimov would no longer be able to challenge Goremykin's appointment. He rang the doorbell to Goremykin's apartment at which point Goremykin opened the door and welcomed Serov in.

"Viktor, why are you still in this apartment?" Serov asked while looking at the small but plush surroundings that were Goremykin's apartment. "You know the General Staff officers have access to much better living conditions." The room was decorated with a Louis the Fourteenth couch and a Russian desk from the Czar Nicholas era. There were collectable paintings on the walls, captured in World War II when the Russians entered Germany. The carpets on the floors were Persian rugs from the sixteenth century.

Goremykin just shrugged about Serov's comment about his apartment and offered Serov a drink. Serov sat down and began his news.

"Asimov is no longer with us, he is deceased," Serov began. "You now have the commander's position that was Asimov's without having to worry about challenges to your position. We've now got to work on recovering from the disaster that was experienced in Iran a couple weeks ago. What we found out from our agents in Washington, D.C. was that an American team of three people were responsible for all of the destruction. We don't know who they were and there appears to be no record in Iran of who they were. I have trouble believing that three people did all this damage."

"Well, Georgy," Goremykin responded, "the Americans have always been very effective with small, well trained units. As you know, we are just as effective when it comes to dealing with military units in third world countries. Why should they be different?"

"That is true Viktor," Serov said while drinking the shot of vodka. "This is good stuff, where did you get it?"

"I don't know," Goremykin replied. "Your sister, my wife, bought it a couple weeks ago. I thought a goodbye drink should be of the finest." Serov pulled his glass from his mouth at the comment. "What does he mean by goodbye drink?" At that moment, Goremykin leveled a pistol at Serov and two shots rang out. Serov fell to the floor while trying to grab at Goremykin. One more shot was fired into Serov's head.

Once Goremykin was sure Serov was dead, two men came from another room, dressed in mover's coveralls. Rolling Serov's body into a rug, they carried him out the door and put him into a van.

Goremykin sat down to another shot of vodka. "Sergey's right, this is good vodka. Asimov's order that Serov had to go is finished. I did what Asimov ordered. Too bad Asimov wasn't around to rescind his order," Goremykin thought as he drank the vodka. "Now what to tell my wife?"

Several hours later, inside a Kremlin conference room in Moscow, Russia, a second evaluation team made up of generals and admirals were looking at an evaluation report of the Iranian situation.

"General Glazkov," Admiral Kapustin started, "since you are the chairman of this review board, why don't you start off with your thoughts." General Glazkov looked at the briefing notes on the table while he thought about his words.

"First," Glazkov began, "we appear to be up against a new U.S. intelligence protocol that we haven't seen before. It appears to be light-years ahead of what we are doing with our foreign agents." The other members of the evaluation team looked at one another, perplexed by the General's comments. Glazkov saw their confusion and decided to address the most obvious of concerns.

"Gentlemen, as head of strategic intelligence analysis, what we experienced in Iran over the past couple of weeks was one of the best coordinated operations we have ever seen. It is hard to believe that a team of three agents could operate with so well a developed, synchronized set of actions." The general looked down at his notes then continued.

"Here is the summary of the coordinated actions. First, an agent is able to penetrate the security of the Shuyesheh Research Facility, destroy the research lab and, through some excellent planning, kill the only person that understands the methods and formulas, thereby making it impossible to reproduce the design that Doctor Polevsky had put together. After that, they take the vehicle that has the diamonds, inside the half-hour period that the vehicle had the diamonds in it. Next, they time the destruction of our Gaza munitions with the arrival of the Iranian battalion and the Helicopter with our courier on board and, in the process, destroy the only copy of the Polevsky documents." Glazkov stopped for a moment to let the observations sink in.

"What about the attacks on the Iranian assets?" Admiral Kapustin asked while the others nodded in agreement to the question.

"I was about to get to that," Glazkov responded. "I just wanted to cover the first part to show how well coordinated their operation was. The attacks you're referring to in Iran added to the level of understanding of how highly planned and executed the operation was that was carried out by the U.S."

"Are we sure it was a U.S. team and not a British team as we originally thought?" one of the other generals questioned.

"We know now that it was an American team," Glazkov continued. "The attacks on the Iranians in the early morning of July 31st when all this went down was well coordinated and carried out. The American team took out three radar sites in quick succession, demolished most of the munitions and most of the spare parts at the Shuyesheh Army Base, shut down the Shuyesheh Research Facility power and lulled three of our Hind helicopters into an ambush. On top of that, they methodically took out an Iranian infantry company and had access to the frequencies the Iranians were using to move their troops around, using that information to create confusion among the Iranian troops. One or two of these items might be coincidence, but all these things happening in such a well, coordinated way leads me to believe it was all planned."

"There is also the question of Iranian Commander Rouhani's death," Kapustin interjected.

"From what I read in the report," Glazkov answered, "Rouhani's autopsy indicated that he had been shot in the back before his body was burned. We're still trying to determine how that all fits in the picture. However, they did find the courier pouch with the burned papers and memory chip under his body. The memory chip was destroyed as well, so we don't know what information was on the chip except that Rouhani had indicated to Asimov that the chip contained the photos of the real document. We also know that another copy of Polevsky's document was destroyed at the research facility when some idiot tried to open his cabinet without realizing the cabinet was booby-trapped."

"Is it possible that the American's got a good copy of Polevsky's papers and the pouch under Rouhani was just a setup?" Kapustin asked.

"That's a possibility," Glazkov responded. "However, looking at satellite video of the moments up to the explosion at the Gaza munitions area, the Americans were running away at a very rapid pace from the area just before it blew up. It appears as though they were in confusion and were about to be overrun by the Iranian force arriving at the area. On the satellite replay, we saw a man go into the building at the corner of the ammo storage area, then come out moments later. We figure that was when Rouhani was shot. There wasn't enough time to get the documents and the chip and set up a fake set of papers and chip. If Rouhani was shot in the back, which it appears he was, we've come to the conclusion that whoever shot him was doing so on the way out. We figure that they finally determined that Rouhani was working against them but didn't realize Rouhani had the courier pouch in front of him. If they realized he had the pouch, he should have been shot from the front, facing the shooter and they would have taken more time to set up a red herring. Besides, they had the Iranian force breathing down their necks and they had to get out of there immediately. Again, from the satellite info, they barely had enough time to set the charges before they would be overrun."

"I heard some rumor that Rouhani was in contact with Asimov after the destruction of the ammo dump and that he was going back in to get the document if it still existed," another general brought up. "It was also mentioned that Rouhani was supposed to meet one of our agents 'Tripoli' in an Iraqi mosque,"

"I've heard that rumor too," Glazkov responded. "We've checked into it and can't find any evidence that it was the case. We think that Asimov was lying and trying to buy time by making us think that Rouhani was still alive. We also just heard that one of our agents may have been killed at the same mosque in Iraq but we are waiting for confirmation. This also seems to be a direct result of the American operation."

"So why do you think the Americans have a new type of agent foreign protocol for their spies?" Another general asked.

"It's simple," Glazkov explained. "First, the sequence of events showed excellent planning and coordination. Second, the timing of the events was done with such precision, in minutes rather than hours. Third, they have done nothing that even comes close to matching our understanding of the operational training and books they use for operations by their agents. They're doing something new. I recommend that we ask our contacts at our embassy in Washington, D.C. to find out where the training is taking place and how they are being trained. We might also contact our information collection center in Virginia to see if they can come up with anything relating to these new procedures."

All of the generals and admirals agreed. The operation in Iran was too perfect and too well executed. Now it was a matter of picking Russian agents that could penetrate the intelligence hierarchy in the U.S. and find out what the Americans were doing different.

As they were getting ready to leave, a Russian officer came in with a message which he handed to Glazkov. The General opened the message and addressed the team, "Gentlemen, I've just received word that General Serov has committed suicide. I guess the failures in Iran were just too much for him." It was no surprise to anyone.

The evaluation team closed their folders and proceeded to leave the conference room.

"So General," Kapustin queried after the others left, "what if everything that American team accomplished was just lucky timing?"

General Glazkov looked at Kapustin for a moment, then closed his folder and answered, "If it was lucky timing, Admiral, then we've just witnessed the most improbable operation in history. I don't think that's the case. By the way, something I didn't want the others to know concerning who the agent was in Iraq that was shot. We've got confirmation and I don't want this leaked. As you know, for years the Americans have been trying to find and take out our agent 'Tripoli'. He was one of our best sanction agents, having taken out several key U.S. operatives and being responsible for sowing numerous effective disinformation efforts. When Tripoli was at the mosque in Iraq after he reported Rouhani as a no-show, he was gunned down by someone with a silenced weapon. I feel that was a key part of the plan in this whole thing, and maybe the key target of their plan. As I said, it was supremely well coordinated and carried out. It also proves that Asimov was telling the truth about Rouhani being ordered to Iraq by Asimov."

They both left the room with many questions unanswered.

CHAPTER 28 -- August 12, 2015, 1:30 PM – Washington, DC Time

Lawson had reported to Admiral Roedl when he got back to Washington, D.C. Lawson turned over both copies of the Polevsky papers, the DVD disks, ID's and files he took from the Shuyesheh Research Facility to the Admiral. Now he was ordered back again eight days later for who knows what. Lawson sat in the chair facing the Admiral while the Admiral was reading reports on the mission. Roedl just nodded his head up and down as he read the report, smiling once in a while at points while he read. Lawson wondered what made him smile.

About a half hour into the waiting, the door to Roedl's office opened. Lawson saw Petty Officer Norman escorting three men in then leave and close the door. Lawson glanced up for a moment to see the three men dressed in suits with intelligence portfolio folders under their arms.

Each of the portfolio folders had the seal of the Office of Naval Intelligence on them. Lawson looked back down at his papers in his lap. "Good afternoon to you Admiral," came the voice of the first man.

Lawson recognized the voice almost immediately and started to pull his pistol from its holster. The voice was that of Captain Hamid Behzadi. Lawson stood up with the pistol behind his back. The voice was Behzadi's but the face looked different except the eyes were the same. Then Lawson realized that Behzadi had shaved and the beard and mustache were both gone. "Could this be the mole?" Lawson thought to himself.

Roedl's voice broke in, "May I present Navy Commander Blaine Samoylev also known to you as Captain Hamid Behzadi." Lawson swung his pistol to his side and holstered the weapon. Commander Samoylev saw Lawson's motion and realized Roedl may have spoken just in time.

"To use your own words, you've got some explaining to do, Commander," Lawson insisted.

"You're right, Admiral," Samoylev observed, "He does exhibit a weird sense of authority."

Roedl nodded his head in agreement and told Lawson to sit down. Lawson did so and Roedl continued, "I brought Commander Samoylev in here to answer questions and to explain some things to help you understand what went on with your operation." Lawson looked around and nodded understanding.

Samoylev began the explanation while Lawson sat and listened. "The first thing I want you to understand, Lieutenant Lawson, is that you wrecked havoc on our plans and the work we had been doing. That being said, we were caught in a rut with no way out. You came in and shook things up to a point where everyone started showing their true colors. By the way, I'm the inside man, not Rouhani and not Dr. Polevsky."

"One correction, Sir," Lawson interrupted, "I'm not a Lieutenant." Samoylev looked at Roedl and smiled.

"The orders are in but not official yet," Roedl explained. "You'll have your commission in about two days. As always, Myers refused his and you can refuse yours if you want to but I would advise against it. Now you may continue Commander."

Samoylev pulled out the memory chip from his portfolio. It held the photos of the Polevsky papers from the research facility.

"These are the real papers," Samoylev continued as he held up the chip, "and you were right to keep it hidden from Rouhani. He was in the process of selling the design to the Russians for one-million Euros. Now before you get confused and believe the Russians already had control, they had control in the lab but couldn't get the papers out of the Iranian facility until the Iranians were paid fifty million dollars for the papers. Rouhani would save them forty-nine million dollars if he provided them with the plans. With me so far?"

Lawson stated, "Yes," then added, "What about the little show in your office where Rouhani had you arrested and how did that come about?"

Samoylev sat down in a chair and thought back through the situation. "The scene you saw in there was set up to convince you that Rouhani was the inside man," Samoylev revealed. "It was a plan set up by Staff Sergeant Mike Taylor to get you to a place where you could be duped. Taylor probably suggested that the Commander's office was the best place to hide?" Lawson nodded 'yes'.

Samoylev continued, "We had suspicions that Taylor was a turncoat. He was paid twenty-thousand dollars by the Iranians to set you guys up so you could be captured with the papers. Thereby the Iranians would have the real papers with no options for the Russians but to pay the fifty million. The Russians thought Taylor was Rouhani's backup. We knew that you were sent to collect the papers and that Taylor would be captured. He also knew he would be captured. I already was planning to put you into the cell with the other men when they were captured. Rouhani messed up my plans when he had you put in the cell across the hall from them. When you changed cell numbers that made my job easier as I figured you had a plan to get out of the cell. I was just hoping that you would discover the rest of the guys were in the other cell. No one knew yet that Rouhani was working with the Russians, though we suspected that someone in the facility was working with them. When you shot Taylor, it scared Rouhani. He saw you as a cold-blooded killer that would take out anyone in your way. That was probably the best move you could've made because it put Rouhani on the defensive. My arrest was part of the agreement between Rouhani and myself to get the papers out of Dr. Polevsky's office. I needed a person to come in that could get past all of the safeguards and retrieve the papers. You were on your own once you got the papers. I couldn't risk exposing my role in this. For myself, it would be easier for me to get the papers once they were out of Russian control. Once that happened, I planned to lift the papers off of Rouhani at an opportune time and pass them on to Colonel Draper. However, neither Rouhani or I knew which set of papers were the real ones. In fact, until you breached the scientists' offices, we didn't realize that there were two different versions of the document. Dr. Polevsky played a shell game with us, knowing that Americans were coming to get the plans. He created two sets of plans, one fake and one real and was manipulating the moves of both plans so that no one would know which one was real. You see, everyone knew you were coming. The security was that porous. That's the reason the second team was picked up just after they dropped you off on the road. However, Rouhani heard the other copy of the plans were there at the ammo dump and were to be picked up by a Russian courier. So realizing that the plans on the memory chip were the real ones, he encouraged you guys to take the chance on completing the mission at the ammo dump so he could switch that copy with the real copy. It would put you at the place where the pickup would occur, and you, having the chip with the real documents, was Rouhani's way of getting the real documents to the Russians by way of the photos you took of the papers. You screwed that whole thing up. Blowing the ammo dump left everyone with questions on whether the papers survived or not. Almost everyone assumed that the papers were destroyed in the blast. There were some senior officers in Tehran that felt it was possible you could have escaped with the papers and they didn't want to take a chance, so they closed off the border. By the way, message intercepts we got between the Tehran and Moscow yesterday indicated they found remnants of the courier pouch with evidence that both copies of the Polevsky papers had been destroyed."

Lawson's curiosity was increased by Samoylev's explanations. "What about the copy in Dr. Polevsky's office? Lawson asked. "We got a message from you to Rouhani's phone just after we blew the ammo dump that the papers in the cabinet were destroyed."

Samoylev motioned with his hand as he started to explain, "I knew by this time that the copy in the doctor's office was also a real copy and you had a photocopy of it. I got two of the guards to go in and open the file cabinet. I took the cabinet keys off of Dr. Polevsky's body in the hallway, gave them to the soldiers and they went in to open the file cabinet. Knowing that the file cabinet was wired, I stayed outside of the vault while they went inside. As expected, they turned the key on the file cabinet and immediately opened the top drawer. There was a rumble sound and then the vault door opened up with the Russian guard in the security room screaming at the top of his lungs and alarms going off as he left his chair. Looking at the inside of what remained of the pouch, I could see that the pages had all burned. By the way, Polevsky didn't want the papers to end up in Russian hands and he sure didn't want the Iranians to get them. Polevsky was a Russian Jew with part of his family in Israel. He knew the weapon would end up in Iran's hands and Israel would be the target. Try to figure Israel with no air power. By the way, you guys made one major amateur mistake. You destroyed the lab but left the original papers in the file cabinet. I know you wanted to leave without them realizing that you got a copy of the papers but destroying the lab kind of went against that concept. I had to destroy the papers in the file cabinet to complete the job at great risk to myself."

Lawson was impressed by the effort Samoylev had put into destroying the evidence and agreed that Samoylev had covered for their mistake. Lawson posed the next question, "When you were in your office, it appeared that you were going through Rouhani's desk. Was that part of the act or were you really looking for something?"

Samoylev looked at Roedl and back at Lawson. "That was one of the areas where I failed," Samoylev said. "It was part of the act but it also was an opportunity to get an item out of the desk that I felt would tell me if Rouhani had sent any part of Polevsky's work to Russia. He came in too fast for me to get the item."

"What was the item?" Roedl inquired.

"It was a jump drive," was Samoylev's response.

At that moment, Lawson gave an excited stare then jumped up surprising everyone, almost falling over as the wounded leg was not ready for such a quick move. Catching his balance, he dug around in his pocket and pulled out a jump drive. "I was bringing this in today. I found it last night when I went to wash the clothes from the operation and return those clothes back over to supply. I took this out of Rouhani's pocket after Myers shot him at the ammo dump!"

Samoylev grabbed the jump drive. "Put this in your computer!" Samoylev exclaimed while handing the drive to Roedl. Roedl put the jump drive in his USB port and waited for the operating system to identify the drive and install the proper drivers. Once it said the jump drive was ready, he double-clicked on the external drive icon and saw the files were encrypted. There was a message on the screen with an entry box requesting the password to decrypt the files on the drive.

"Oh, great!" Samoylev exclaimed, frustrated by the discovery of the file protection. "This will take us days to determine the password and it will probably only give us several tries before it automatically deletes everything then we'll never know if the Russians have any preliminary development information."

Lawson looked at the screen and thought about what was a likely password for the drive. He remembered the layout of Rouhani's office, the way he dressed, his mannerisms and language. He figured that it would not be something in Farsi or Russian. That would be too obvious. Since the documents on the jump drive would be something Asimov would need as part of his final report, it had to be something that both Rouhani and Asimov would know, something Rouhani would not forget.

Looking once more at the screen, Lawson asked Roedl to let him have access to the keyboard. "I remember when Myers was talking about his call to Asimov while pretending to be Rouhani," Lawson started, "There was one word both men would know and remember. A name of an agent Asimov used before with Rouhani." Lawson looked at Roedl as he made his thoughts known.

"Well, Lieutenant, type it in," Roedl ordered as Lawson looked at him.

"Just remember Sir, if I'm wrong, my guess is that we've only got two more tries to get it right," came Lawson's response. "You really want to take the risk for me to do this?"

"I've considered the risk," The Admiral tersely remarked. "Just do it."

Lawson reached for the keyboard and typed 'Tripoli' as he spoke out each letter. As soon as he did, the screen opened up to show the files on the drive. There were a bunch of photos of documents. Samoylev clicked on several of the photos and read the contents of each he opened as Roedl looked on. A smile grew on Samoylev's face.

"This proves it," Roedl said after examining several of the documents. "Rouhani never sent anything to Moscow. The messages here show that he convinced them nothing would be of value until the final papers were finished. This also proves that the Polevsky papers are the proof of a working system as what we have are the final papers."

"I forgot to tell you," Samoylev interjected. "I just remembered something else when you typed in 'Tripoli'. When we found out that 'Tripoli' was to meet with Rouhani, based upon what Draper told us, and we had a time and date, I went to Iraq. Tripoli was a target that we have been trying to get for years. I was able to take him out with a long range shot using a rifle with a silencer thanks to the effort you guys made in covering up Rouhani's death. He was the only person with an umbrella at the mosque which made it easy to get him."

Lawson looked at Roedl and wondered if the whole operation was to get Tripoli. He let the thought pass as he realized that everything had been a 'flying-by-the-seat-of-the-pants' series of events. It couldn't have been known that this opportunity would have availed itself.

Samoylev inquired of Lawson, "What do you know about the system they were developing?"

Lawson responded, "I know that this system is a 500 kilowatt laser system that has the capability of taking aircraft out of the air at a very rapid rate. I know it can target long distances as aircraft come over the horizon and can probably take out a full squadron of aircraft and all their missiles before they make it halfway to target. It might even be capable of taking out satellites in orbit. It does so by changing frequencies to allow for the laser beam to penetrate clouds, other atmospheric conditions and adjusts for the surfaces that beam must strike. There is also the thought that it may be a double beam system where the first beam penetrates the clouds to form a clear channel to allow the second, more powerful beam to hit the target."

"How do you know all this?" Samoylev asked.

"I saw the layout in the lab," Lawson replied. "The laser system itself was small with high-resolution servos that made it very accurate. The sheet of metal across the other end of the lab had a three foot cut in it that was a clean cut with no slag around the cut. That meant that the cut was made in a split-second and the beam was not reflected back meaning that the reflective surface was considered in the equation. There was a frequency generator attached to the laser system that might explain the adjustment for clouds and reflection of the target."

Samoylev and Roedl took in everything that Lawson was saying. Samoylev spoke first, "What type of metal was the target made of?"

"It was aluminum about a quarter-inch thick," Lawson offered.

"How did you figure all this out? You're not a mathematician," Roedl questioned.

"I was an engineering student before I joined the Navy," Lawson replied. "Myers looked through the formulas and diagrams. Even though he couldn't read Russian, he was able to figure out what it was for, how well it would work and would it work from the formulas in the papers. With my experience in motor-driven machines and his experience in energy wave sciences, we were able to determine the use and potential of this design."

Roedl interrupted, "You realize that what you and Myers know is way beyond top secret." Lawson nodded his head affirmative.

"One question," Samoylev intervened, "Does Myers know to keep his mouth shut on this?"

"He does," Lawson replied.

"If he does," Samoylev continued, "then how is it he shared the information with you?" Roedl could see Lawson's face getting red and his temper about to go ballistic.

"I can vouch for both Myers and Lawson," Roedl said while looking at Samoylev.

"One thing you've ignored, Commander," Lawson barked, "we went out of our way to ensure that all copies of the document were found at great risk to ourselves, except for the part you did with the file cabinet! You should consider the fact that we went way beyond our orders to make sure the design could not be reproduced by either the Russians or the Iranians."

Samoylev thought over Lawson's comment for a moment, then reached out and shook his hand. "You guys did an amazing job, considering what you didn't know and what you were up against," Samoylev complimented. "By the way Lieutenant, you've got six months of Russian language training to go through."

Lawson looked at Roedl as Roedl looked down at his desk. "You might as well know, Jim," said Roedl, "you're reporting to me directly from here on out. So is Myers and Glendenning. School starts Monday for all of you." Lawson smiled at both Roedl and Samoylev.

"With your permission," Lawson said as he picked up his hat and cane and turned toward the door.

"Permission granted, how's the leg?" Roedl asked. Lawson gave a thumbs up and slowly walked out the door.

"Well, you wanted a good penetration team. We found our team," Samoylev said to Roedl as Lawson closed the door.

"What designator do you want to give them?" Roedl questioned.

Samoylev looked into his portfolio at a list of designators. He gave his opinion. "This is such a new method of intelligence that we have no designator for this type of team. I've been thinking about a designator for them. Since their key skills are getting into difficult areas, I've decided to designate them as the Creative Access Team or CAT. We'll give them the next number on the teams list which is 205. So they have the designation of CAT205." Roedl thought for a moment then nodded his approval.

Lawson stopped at Yeoman Norman's desk and rubbed his leg. Handing her his travel voucher, he smiled at her.

She smiled back and asked, "You feeling better now that your leg is healing?"

Lawson said, "Yes, thanks for asking. Though it may take a month before I get full strength back in this leg."

"By the way," Norman continued, "Gunny Glendenning left me a note that he wants to meet with you after you see the Admiral for some drinks. He says that Petty Officer Myers will be joining him."

"Thanks," Lawson said, smiling as he walked out the door and past the Marine on security. Lawson met Myers outside of the Admiral's office.

"How are you feeling now?" Myers asked.

"I feel like I've been through a totally surreal experience," Lawson answered while looking at his watch. "I wonder where Gunny is right now?" Lawson asked Myers as they walked down the golden hallway. "I think the Marine would like to go for a drink and maybe Petty Officer Norman would like to join us."

"I'd like to as well," Myers replied, "but the Admiral wants to see me."

CHAPTER 29 -- August 12, 2015, 2:47 PM – Washington, DC Time

Just as Myers finished his sentence, alarms started going off and lights were flashing in the hallway. Both Myers and Lawson drew their weapons. As they did so, the vault door to the Admiral's office opened and Roedl, Samoylev and Norman came running out of the door with their weapons drawn.

"Get into my office," Roedl shouted as he and the others raced down the hall. Lawson and Myers jumped through the doorway into the room where the Marine was sitting. The Marine pressed the button under his desk which caused the outer door to close and the inner door to open. Lawson and Myers went through the doorway, around Petty Officer Norman's desk and into the Admiral's office.

"Why does Roedl want us in here when he said that all of the personnel must respond to an alert?" Lawson asked. Myers just shrugged his shoulders. Both Myers and Lawson checked that they had a round in the chambers of their weapons then holstered their weapons as the alarms continued. Lawson could see the portfolio on Roedl's desk that held the reports and the memory chip with the Polevsky papers in it.

As Lawson was noting the presence of the portfolio, a man came through the side door and into the Admiral's office. He was dressed in a Lieutenant Commander's uniform standing about five-foot seven inches tall with a trim build. His uniform had no nametag on it which Lawson thought peculiar. Lawson also noted that his complexion was light, his voice was higher pitched, probably because he was nervous and his English was perfect. What concerned Lawson even more was that he was pointing a pistol at both Lawson and Myers.

"Well, I've got both of you, not just Myers," he shouted above the alarms while motioning Myers and Lawson away from the desk. "I wondered how long it would take me before I met the two people responsible for stealing state secrets from my country. I wasn't expecting I'd get you both at the same time but I'll take what I can get. With you two where I want you, I have only one more person to be concerned with. Now, why don't you tell me where the memory chip is."

"What memory chip?" Lawson shouted back.

"Don't play games with me!" he shouted. "I'm not stupid and I've been working long enough in this facility to know who you are and what's been going on! Now where is the memory chip?" At that moment the alarms stopped.

Knowing that the man, being Iranian, probably was not familiar with the culture or the history of the American west, Lawson looked at Myers then back to the man. "You remember how things were done in the old west?" Lawson posed to Myers. "I think we should give him what he wants."

"If we do that," Myers responded, "once he gets it he will just kill us both."

"I can just kill you both now and look for it myself," the man yelled back. "Now where is the memory chip?" Lawson felt like he was replaying the whole scene when he faced Rouhani in the shed at the storage area in Iran.

"Regardless, I don't know where the memory chip is and, besides, how do you plan to get out of here once you get it?"

Lawson said while he glanced toward the desk. The man saw Lawson's glance and looked toward the desk.

"Ah," he said, "I'm sure the Admiral would have something like that in a report portfolio. One similar as to what's on the desk. And as to how I get out of here, it's all planned out." The man said as he looked down at the desk while pointing to the items on the desk.

As the man pointed to the desk, Lawson saw that he was left-handed. Lawson knew that a person would point at something with the hand that was their dominant hand. He guessed that, being left-handed, he would shoot from left to right, shooting at Myers before he shot at Lawson. That would give Lawson a short period to draw his weapon and make sure his shot would make a motion-stopping impact on the man. Lawson hoped the man's first shot at Myers would miss him. Myers looked at Lawson then back at the man confronting them. He could tell from the looks on both their faces that they both had gone beyond talking.

"Oh, damn," Myers shouted as both Myers and Lawson drew their weapons at the same time. It was a western-style fast draw with Lawson dropping to one knee to fire as Myers drew the weapon and pulled the trigger. Both Myers' and Lawson's shots hit the man while the man's shot hit Myers in the chest. Myers fell backwards to the floor as Lawson fired a second shot, hitting the man in the head. He slumped to the floor, dying as he hit the ground.

Lawson stepped past the desk and kicked the man's weapon away from him. It was obvious to Lawson the man was dead. Lawson turned his attention to Myers. There was a bullet hole in Myers white uniform jumper just about where the heart was. Myers was unconscious. Lawson ripped open Myers jumper while yelling at Myers, "Don't you go and die on me. We've been through too much to end it here."

Myers suddenly sat up screaming, "Man that hurt!" Myers sudden return from the dead startled Lawson.

Lawson looked to see a bright piece of brass stuck into a dark fabric where Myers' chest was at. "Why are you wearing a bullet-proof vest?" Lawson exclaimed as the Marine from the desk dashed in. At the same time they could hear someone hammering on the outside door. The Marine went through the door, past Norman's desk, back to his desk and pushed the button. The door to the inside closed and then opened a moment later. Roedl, Samoylev and Norman came running in as Myers got up from the floor.

"Well, it looks like we found our mole," Samoylev stated while looking at the dead man on the floor. Lawson and Myers just stood there as Lawson wondered what this was all about.

"Lawson," Roedl exclaimed, "what are you doing in here?"

"Well, Sir," Lawson responded, "you told us to get into your office when you came running out the door."

"That was meant for Myers, not for you," Roedl shot back. "Myers has a bullet-proof vest, you have nothing."

"Sir?" Myers interrupted while picking up his weapon from the floor and clearing the round from the chamber. "Had Lawson not been in the room with me, there was a good chance I would be dead right now. When that guy shot me, it knocked me out. I'm not sure that my shot would have stopped him. He could have finished me off while I was unconscious. And Lawson, couldn't you use some better analogy to tell me how you were going to respond to this guy than saying we need to do it like in the old West. I didn't understand what you were getting at until we were just ready to draw. Wouldn't it have been better to say 'like at the OK corral'."

"Well, Nick, it's not like I had a whole lot of time to come up with some statement to tell you what I planned to do," Lawson exclaimed. "I could have just asked the guy to wait while I sat down and thought through a series of possible scenarios to give you a hint of what I was going to do. Why was Myers wearing a bullet-proof vest?"

"Enough of that you guys," Roedl said. "He was wearing a vest because I suspected that Commander Colman was the mole. We had no way to prove it but we figured that if he was the only one left to guard my office while the alert was on, he would take the chance to steal the Polevsky papers. The commander knew Myers was on duty today and was to stay in my office if there was an alert. This was to secure the documents on my desk. Myers volunteered for this effort as he told me of the suspicions you guys had that there was a mole in the facility, a fact we already knew. Captain Michaels and I had already suspected that but didn't tell anyone else. What the Commander didn't know was that Myers was going to wear the vest. We arranged the alert to put Colman and Myers in my office at the same time with no one else here. Now, take this outside and get a fresh breath of air. We'll do a debrief in about half an hour. Myers, get another uniform. Your jumper is a mess."

"Admiral," Lawson questioned, "Why would you leave the chip there where the guy could get it? And, before we go out, the guy we killed said he had a plan to get out of the facility after he got the memory chip."

"That's right," Myers added. "He seemed confident he would have no problem getting out of the building."

"That's not the real chip," Roedl replied. "Now what's this you both are all excited about?"

"He said he had a way of getting out after he got the chip," Lawson explained. "The way I see it is that he either had help that would get him out or he had some type of exit that would enable him to escape that we don't know about. Keep this in mind, his plan would require a fast exit. He would only have maybe a minute or so to collect the memory chip and exit the building before you guys returned. I figure that he expected the Marine guard to come in, so maybe he was counting on killing the guard as well and expected some delay before you guys would come back in."

"Your point is well taken," Roedl responded. "Like I said, the chip on the desk has nothing on it. It was a plant to get Colman to act and the delay to get back in wouldn't take that long as I would just need to swipe my card in the reader if the Marine on security wasn't able to open the door. Your point of a quick exit seems to make sense and that is what alarms me. Do we have a second mole in the facility or has he made some breach in the physical layout of this facility that would allow for him to make his escape?"

"Admiral," Norman interjected, "Maybe he was planning on taking a hostage to get out of the facility and had other plans to get away once they were out."

"I don't think that would have gotten them very far, Commander," Roedl said.

Lawson and Myers looked at each other. Lawson moved next to Myers and whispered, "He called her Commander, I thought she was a second class Petty Officer." They both looked at each other while Lawson began to put the pieces together.

"Admiral," Lawson said while turning to face the Admiral, "I think I know how he planned to get out." The Admiral looked at Lawson and Myers while Samoylev and Norman eyed each other with questioning looks.

"Well, you've got my attention," Roedl declared. "Go ahead with your thoughts."

"It's like this, Sir," Lawson began. "You mentioned that your top female agent was not known by our adversaries. I would guess your top female agent would have to be an officer. I think that top female agent is Petty Officer Norman. You see, Sir, you just called her 'Commander'. This is what I think was planned. This guy on the floor had plans to take us both out, like dead. He stated no less. Follow me so far?"

"You're doing good," Roedl remarked. "Keep going."

"Well, Sir," Lawson continued. "I think our assailant had two missions. One was to get the memory chip and the other was to take out your agents involved in the Iranian mission as well as taking out your top female agent. He mentioned that once he was finished with us he had one more person to take care of. The guy would know that Norman is your top female agent as he worked in operations and would see the communications going on within the office. I think Norman was the 'one more person'."

"Aren't you stretching things just a bit," Samoylev complained.

"Commander, let him finish. He sees things we miss. Let's hear him out," Roedl fired back.

"Yes, Sir," Samoylev conceded.

Lawson thought for a moment as he gathered his thoughts. "As I was saying," Lawson resumed, "once this guy got rid of both me and Myers, he would take out the Marine guard next then wait for all three of you to get into this room and take you out in quick succession. Having done that he would change into Petty Officer Norman's clothes."

"That's quite a story," Samoylev interrupted. Norman nodded agreement.

"Will you let him finish," Roedl admonished. "One more interruption and I'll bust you down to a Lieutenant!" Samoylev looked sheepishly at Roedl and said 'ok'.

"Thanks," Lawson continued. "If you notice, both the assailant and Petty Officer Norman are about the same size and build. I suspect that once he took you three out he would dress in Norman's uniform and walk right out the front door. After all, we have good security checks coming in but just cursory checks going out. Most times they're looking at briefcases and purses going out, not even looking at the person's face. If he were to walk out dressed in Norman's clothes without carrying anything, they would have not noticed him."

Samoylev looked at Roedl for approval to respond. Roedl nodded 'yes' at which point Samoylev raised a question.

"Ok," Samoylev queried, "wouldn't they have noticed his short hair? That would have given him away no matter what he was wearing. Then, there's the question of the facility being under a lockdown. He wouldn't be able to get out until the lockdown was released."

Roedl looked to Lawson for a response. Lawson walked over to the door in the left wall that went into the conference room. Everyone watched him open the door and go in then looked at each other, questioning his move.

"I guess that answers that question," Samoylev quipped. "He has no answer so he walks out."

"Blaine," Roedl observed, "if he was leaving, he would be going out the office door, not into the conference room."

They heard some rustling and moving of chairs as Roedl started walking toward the door of the conference room. As he looked in he could see Lawson opening cabinet doors of the oak cabinets against the far wall. Looking at each of the cupboard areas he changed his attention to the flat-screen display on the center oak shelf. Lawson reached behind the display and pulled out a black gym bag. Walking back to the Admiral's office, he walked past Roedl and dropped the bag on a chair in the Admiral's office. Unzipping the top of the bag, he pulled out two boxes of 9 mm ammo, a key card that would allow for an exit from the building and a brunette wig. After looking at the key card, he handed it to Roedl. On the card was the identity of Petty Officer Norman but with his face and the necessary codes to allow him to scan himself out at the exit.

Samoylev picked up the wig and held it next to Petty Officer Norman's head. A perfect match both in color and style.

"I can't believe it," Samoylev exclaimed. "The story sounds like a fairy tale but this is real world. You can't make this up. But what about the lockdown, Lawson?"

"With the Admiral dead, and since the Admiral was the one that ordered the lockdown, he would just have to take the Admiral's clearance card, swipe it on the computer card scanner and select 'Release from Lockdown', then he would be free to walk out the door of the facility," Lawson said while he continued to look through the bag for a moment then looked toward Samoylev and Roedl. At the same time, there appeared to be a flash of realization on Norman's face.

"This guy had to get away fast," Norman observed. "It would be just minutes before our bodies would have been discovered in this room. He's got to have someone waiting for him outside the building, most likely in a parked car."

Roedl jumped to his desk and grabbed the phone. He punched a button on the phone. He waited a moment then said, "I want you guys to check the front of the facility for anyone sitting in a car. Do it immediately and report back to me as soon as you know one way or the other."

"I just called central security. We'll see if there is someone waiting for him. However, there is a chance with the amount of time we've spent talking, if there is an escape vehicle, it may be gone," Roedl explained to the people in the room. A moment later Roedl's desk phone rang. He answered the phone, listened for a moment then said, "Have the security team surround the car and apprehend the guy."

Roedl turned back toward those in his office and proceeded to update them on what was going on. "Security spotted a man in a vehicle about four cars up on the opposite side of the street. It was obvious he was waiting for someone. This might be our man or an embarrassing situation. The car has consul plates so the vehicle is owned by one of the foreign embassies in the area. We'll know soon who he is and if he's involved in this scenario."

A few minutes later, an NCIS forensic recovery team came in to take pictures and recover the body of the foreign agent that was killed.

"Hello, gentlemen and lady," Roedl said while looking at their badges. "I guess Gibbs is not going to be showing up." Everyone laughed while the NCIS lead investigator responded, "You don't know how many times we hear that. Now to our questions."

Roedl was answering questions from the NCIS investigators when the phone rang. He answered the phone, talked for a couple of minutes then sat the phone down.

"You've got another crime scene," Roedl said to the NCIS lead investigator. "The guy down in the car in front of the facility just shot himself when our security team approached the car. Apparently, he was part of the plan. Lawson, Myers and Norman, get out of here. Any questions to be answered will be answered by me."

As Lawson, Myers and Norman all got up to exit the office, one of the NCIS investigators called out, "Sir, look at this. It looked like this dead guy shaved his legs."

"Get pictures of it," was the lead NCIS investigator's response.

Lawson and Myers looked at each other and laughed as they were going through Norman's front office with Norman leading the way. One of the NCIS investigators looked into the Admiral's office to see if they could go. The NCIS lead investigator gave a thumbs up and the three of them were sent out the door to the Marine's checkpoint and out to the hallway.

"Well," Norman said, "now that you know who I am, what do you say we go find Gunny and get that drink you guys were going to offer me."

Lawson and Myers looked at each other then at Norman. "How did you know we were going to invite you out for a drink," Myers asked.

Norman smiled back at them. "Didn't the Admiral say I was his best female agent? I can put pieces together too, you know. By the way Lawson, that was a good piece of detective work you did in there. I'm impressed."

"I'm impressed too," Lawson said while smiling back. "Let's get Gunny." They all laughed as Norman put her fist into Lawson's arm.

"No humility there," she said as they went to join Gunny and think about the day.

As they walked down the corridor, Myers rubbed his hand against his pocket and felt something there. Reaching into his pocket, he pulled out the large diamond he was given to hold onto by Draper. Showing the diamond to Lawson and Norman he remarked, "I brought this in to give it to the Admiral. I need to go back and give it to him."

"Do that later," Lawson advised. "We need to get a drink and the diamond will be around when we go back." Myers looked at the diamond for a moment then put it back in his pocket as Gunny approached them.

"My guess you guys are looking for me," Gunny stated as he met up with them. Looking at Norman, he smiled then said, "Drinks are on me. Myers, what happened to your shirt?"

"It's a jumper," Myers replied being irritated that the jumper was ripped. "I've got to go to my office and change it. By the way, Gunny, you are one stupid Marine if you don't even know what this piece of a naval uniform is called, though you are smart where you need to be. I'll meet you guys at the restaurant. "

"Ye got me there, sailor," Gunny quipped. Looking at Lawson he continued, "What goes around, comes around. It's amazing how different we are in our branches of the service even as we work with each other day to day." They all laughed as Myers turned to change his uniform.

As they exited the building and entered the courtyard, Lawson wondered what Draper did with the other diamonds. They took off their belts that held their side arms and put them in the briefcase Gunny was carrying.

"Another typical day in the Navy," Lawson thought as they stepped onto the sidewalk.

EPILOGUE -- March 27, 2016, 11:36 AM

Although the operation was successful, the result of the operation delayed rather than stopped the Russians from continuing the development of the advanced laser weapon. They were significantly delayed because the only person that knew how it worked, Dr. Polevsky, was killed during the operation. He knew how the laser system worked, what frequencies were needed and when to change frequencies to account for weather conditions. The Russians were hard pressed to find another scientist with the expertise and creativity comparable to Dr. Polevsky.

There was a period of confusion in the Russian's new weapons development group that added to the delay in the start of a new laser weapons development project. General Asimov's records mysteriously disappeared after his death. The Russians blamed the loss of records on American agents but it is more likely that Asimov burned the documents once he was relieved of his command. The records were believed to contain some information on Dr. Polevsky's work but according to the files the Americans found on Commander Rouhani's jump drive, no such records were sent to Asimov.

The Naval Intelligence Office never found out the real name of the Iranian mole that was killed in Admiral Roedl's office. All they knew from the evidence was that he was an Iranian national that was able to go up through the ranks in the U.S. Navy and entered the Intelligence Branch as a low-level officer that wouldn't attract any attention. During additional investigations and reviews, the U.S. Navy found another mole in the Intelligence Branch that was from China. After that discovery, several rules in the authorization of allowing personnel into the Kennedy Irregular Warfare Center were changed and all personnel internal to the center had to go through full analysis of their personnel records every six months.

Lawson, Myers and 'Gunny' Glendenning were each awarded the Navy Cross for their actions but were informed that they could not wear anything on their uniform that would indicate that they received the award. Even their personnel records didn't show it. This was so that it would not raise any questions by anyone as to how they earned such an award that was second highest in the Navy, with only the Medal of Honor being higher. Lawson received the Purple Heart for his wound in the operation. All three men spent the next six months in Russian language training. Lawson and Myers had no problem picking up the language and, in the words of Commander Samoylev, both spoke like native Muscovites. However, Gunny could not seem to lose the Irish accent even in his Russian words.

Colonel Draper continued his work in the mountains of northwest Iran, aiding the Kurds in obtaining food, drilling for water, buying weapons and setting up defenses. The fifty million dollars in diamonds seemed to add some help. Draper was suspected of setting up the operations that relieved the Russians and Iranians of the Polevsky papers and, as such, the Iranians raised the bounty on him to two-hundred thousand Euros. Admiral Roedl arranged for cigarette drops to Draper by drone. The cases of American cigarettes were the Kurds most favorite type of delivery. Areas north of Draper's area, in the very northern part of Iran, found cigarettes more available but expensive by Iranian standards. Cigarettes were also a great trading currency.

Inside the Iranian government, Colonel Rouhani was recognized as a military hero, sacrificing his life by going back in to the munitions storage area to get the Polevsky papers. He was buried with full military honors and a statue was erected to his honor in Tehran. The Iranians didn't know of Rouhani's actions because Asimov had been killed and Rouhani's records of his activities were all on the jump drive that was in the possession of the U.S. The U.S. was not about to share any information with the Iranians on what they knew really happened at the ammo dump.

About The Author

Mr. T. James LeDoux is a U.S. Navy Vietnam veteran, having worked on river operations on the upper Mekong River with the Mobile Riverine Force and, at times, supporting the Office of Naval Intelligence in Vietnam in 1969 and 1970. His military experience extends from years 1968 to 2000, in both active and reserve service in the Navy, Army, Air Force and Coast Guard. In Coast Guard Reserves, he was part of the Coast Guard security team for former President Nixon's residence at the Western Whitehouse at San Mateo Point in California.

During his life, he has designed numerous defense and commercial systems and products in both the hardware and software disciplines as well as managed many product development projects. His last 10 years before retiring were dedicated to training, mentoring and aiding technical leaders in managing projects and people.

He also spent time as a technical investigator, investigating patent infringement claims and acting as an expert witness in court cases involving development processes in both hardware and software development projects. Along with Warren Yates, he developed the 'Control-Feedback-Abort Loop' concept for problem solution analysis being used in a number of high-tech companies to aid in determining how people will use products to solve problems.

He and his wife presently live in Colorado Springs, Colorado writing books, doing research on high-tech development and historical events, analyzing present international events and providing consulting assistance to up and coming design engineers in managing their teams.

He is author of several books on business management and historical subjects such as 'The Barbarians Guide to Management' (2012), 'The First Real Christmas' (2012), 'Amateurs With Egos' (2013), and 'Trouble on the Grand Canal' (2013).

www.ingramcontent.com/pod-product-compliance
Lightning Source LLC
Chambersburg PA
CBHW051412170626
46809CB00006B/2128